The Ancient's Game

 For information, address HarperCollins Children's Books, a division of HarperCollins Publishers, 195 Broadway, New York, NY 10007.

www.epicreads.com

Library of Congress Control Number: 2023944823

ISBN 978-0-06-329643-5

Typography by Catherine Lee

24 25 26 27 28 LBC 5 4 3 2 1

First Edition

THE ANCIENT'S GAME

LONI CRITTENDEN

HARPER
An Imprint of HarperCollins*Publishers*

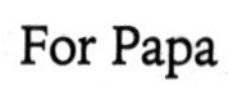
For Papa

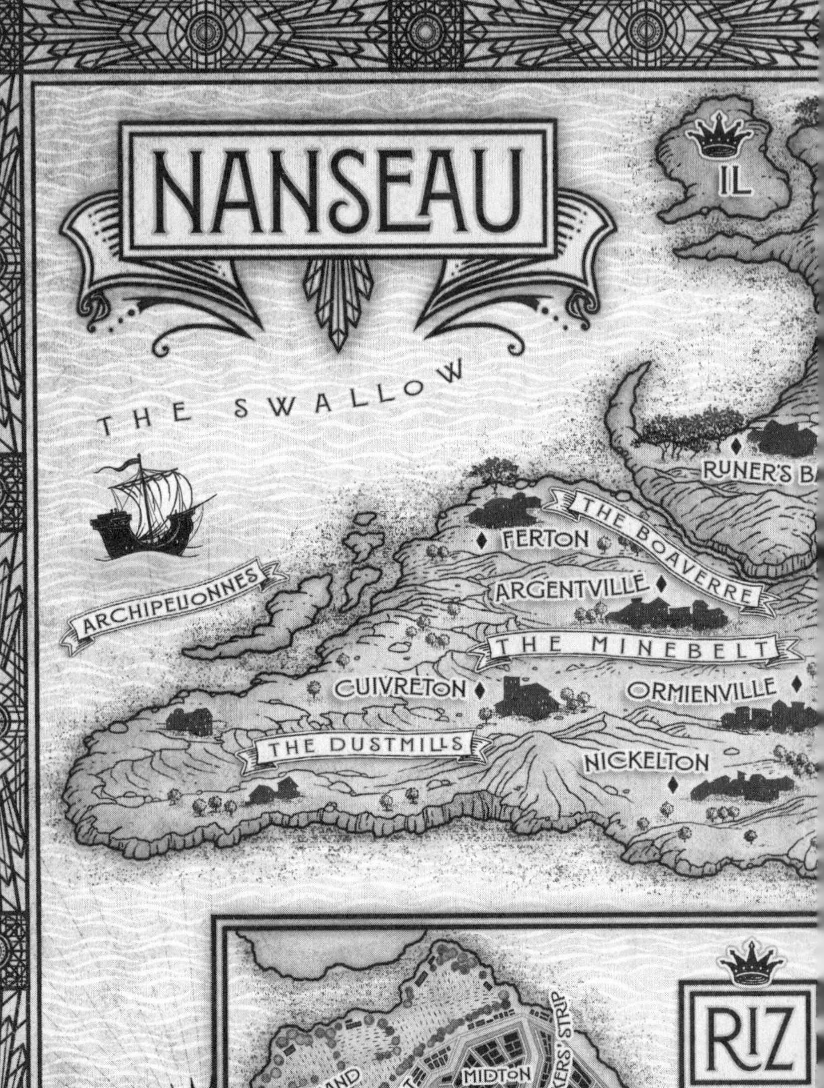
NANSEAU
IL
THE SWALLOW
RUNER'S B
THE BOAVERRE
FERTON
ARGENTVILLE
ARCHIPELLONNES
THE MINEBELT
CUIVRETON
ORMIENVILLE
THE DUSTMILLS
NICKELTON

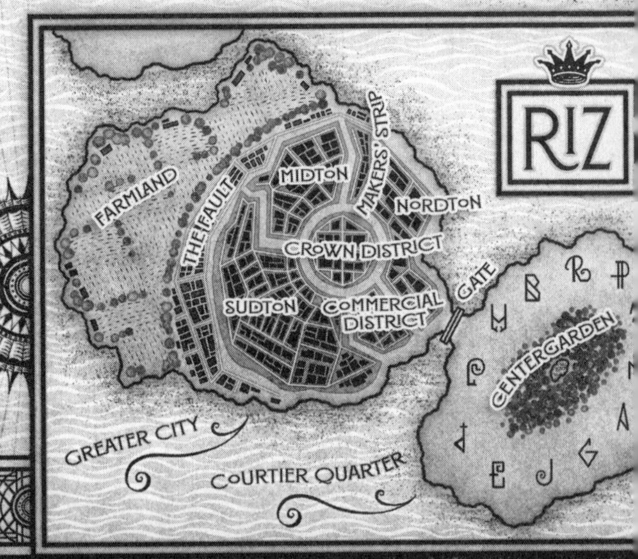
RIZ
MIDTON
MAKERS' STRIP
FARMLAND
THE FAULT
NORDTON
CROWN DISTRICT
GATE
SUDTON
COMMERCIAL DISTRICT
CENTERGARDEN
GREATER CITY
COURTIER QUARTER

THE WAILWOOD
ALCHEMPORTE
N
W
E
S
ZARISBURG
UN
NEW MONTAGUE
FORT GRANIT
RIZ
ROCHERIE
THE EYES
CRYSTALSPORTE
METALSPORTE
~COURTIERS~
MESNY
LAGARDE
GERARD
ROSSIGNOL
DELMORE
ABREO
BONNE
EDOUARD
PROULX
HEROUX
JOLIF
VOLAND

Long ago, spiders glowed.
They lurked behind their webs
and lit the night to lure their prey.
The flies mistook the spiders for the moon.

—Translation. Date unknown. Author unknown. Untitled.

How rich the land. How kind the people.
They glitter in the heat and dance in the setting sun.
Soleil, the Old, dances too.
Obsid, the New, says they will do.

—Missives to the Lidonch empire's Pillar First.
Approx. 2nd of Basaltre. 1 Swallowed.

ONE

When Kellan lived in the namehouse, she took things apart. She started small: picture books by the thread, puzzle toys by the screws. Used her teeth as scissors and flatheads, which proved more effective after her adult incisors came in. When she grew older, bigger, so did the things she destroyed. Telephones. Telegraphs. Once, the first and only automi her namehouse could afford. She always put them back together, though. Never in the way they were before, but always back together.

But curious people didn't belong in Cuivreton, especially loudmouthed little girls without family names. It was a place of routine, a predictable ville of mostly predictable people. Considering that, Ruban, the village train station's ticket agent, should have been delighted to see the now sixteen-year-old Kellan on her way out. *No problem!* he should have said after she'd told him she and Edgar had misplaced their tickets. *We're just glad to get rid of you!*

She should have known better. On that cloudy afternoon, while Ruban sat dry and warm behind his cabin desk, pretending not to acknowledge the one rare break in Cuivreton's routine, rain pounded against the station's crooked iron roof and leaked onto Kellan's head. Each drip was like the tick of a broken clock's longest hand and a bitter reminder of reality.

"This is ridiculous." Kellan banged against the window, her palm rattling the glass in its wooden frame. She kept her other hand in her pocket, tight around a folded flyer, but not so tight she'd ruin it. Just tight enough to remind her of everything at stake. "We bought them last month. The train will be here in, what, two minutes?"

"I guess you should have brought them, huh?" Ruban took a quick bite of stale vending-machine cake. It crunched in a way cakes should never crunch, a crumb of icing landing on the still-damp patch of toddler vomit on his shirt. "Sorry. We don't keep receipts."

"I'm not asking for a receipt. I'm asking for you to be slightly less of a hammerhead than usual."

"A month is a long while, sweetheart—"

"Don't call me that."

"—and I ain't gonna remember one man out of the hundreds—"

"Hardly a hundred folk live here."

"—that pass through. Now, you get me my ten curones, or you head on." Entirely too satisfied, he cracked his back and waved away the crates in the cart near the tracks. "And take that garbage with you."

Ruban used to be one of the village kids who pushed small Dus into the grass and stole their monthly allowance. Kellan hadn't liked Ruban when he was just another miner's musty child, and she didn't like him as a man who stank as badly at twenty as he had at twelve.

Kellan wasn't so little anymore. She was still chubby and still didn't take proper care of her hair, but the namehouse was three years behind her. Before anger got the better of her, Kellan pulled out her flyer and hurried toward the tracks.

Since it first arrived at their doorstep less than a month ago, she'd folded and refolded the flyer in her pocket so many times that the faces of the world's finest makers had cracked and faded, coffee-stain halos topping their heads. Gasper Vandeles, Master Technician from across the Swallow in the Crescent Isles, who showed the world how to meld human nerves with runed metal. Djala, Italish Master Alchemist, whose work in the west ended plagues before they began. And in the center, illustrated in near-perfect profile, stood Master Engineer Madame Mesny: one of Nanseau's twelve courtiers, inventor of the automi, known as much for her peculiarity as she was for her brilliance. The slip of paper Kellan clutched between her pruned fingers might have been reduced to a dull page of torn creases and frayed corners, but to her, it was a symbol of hope.

Madame Mesny was the headliner for Riz's Eighty-Fourth Annual Makers' Exposition. She was a train ride away, and all that stood between Kellan and the solution to Edgar's problems was a waste of a man who reeked of garlic and ghoulpepper.

A breeze bit through her soggy jacket. The clouds had nearly swallowed the sun, casting everything in a thick gray. Even the reddish mountains jagging the horizon smeared a dull streak of russet through the rainfall. Because she'd let Edgar use her umbrella, rainwater had soaked through her socks and made every step sound like cutting through an overripe banana. She could handle it now, heavy rain, if she kept moving. Besides. No umbrella in the world could have protected her from the mud, which coated her shins and had started to harden.

The bench on which Edgar sat had a roof that didn't leak. "I know I brought them, now," he mumbled, searching through his luggage for the fifth time since they arrived. "I know I did."

What little hair Edgar had left was gray from age and thin from too many years of comb pressing. He patted the jacket pockets of his second-best tweed suit, then his pants, then his socks, until he fumbled through the clothes in his suitcase again.

Kellan paced beside him, one arm wound around her middle. She counted her steps, willed the wind and the rain to fall softer, blow warmer, so she could finally think. "It's all right if you didn't, you know," she managed. "We'll get on that train someway."

"You think so?"

"I think so."

“Might want to stop biting your nails, then, if you’re trying to be convincing. Can’t be much left to nibble—”

The namehouse clock clanged, and the clouds overhead crashed in a thunderous boom. She missed the lightning, but not the way Edgar flinched in pain, bit his cheek to stifle his groan.

“What’s wrong?” she asked. Storms had never hurt him before.

Edgar pulled off his hat and schooled his wince into a smile. “Just an ache. Keep waking up in the morning, you’ll find out soon enough.”

The little sunlight peeking through the clouds caught the copper of his prosthesis. He’d lost his right hand to a miscarve a few years back. She’d just turned fourteen when she made its replacement, so it wasn’t her finest work, but design came second to function when an old man’s hand had disintegrated to the wrist.

The change in Edgar since his accident had been gradual, a creeping slope, as the ghost of his loss grew larger every day. If Kellan had thought Edgar was anything less than invincible back then, perhaps she would have noticed it sooner. It, too, started small—forgetting where he set his pen with it still in his fingers—until the problems grew. Leaving the stove on after he went to bed. Remembering too late that he’d let one too many people exit the shop without paying. Before either of them knew it, they were struggling to break even, let alone turn a profit.

Making in secret was one thing, but running a makeshop was another. Legally, she couldn't, and even if she could, she didn't know enough to do it on her own. If she wanted Pape's Peculiars to survive, then they couldn't miss this train. Setting up in Edgar's brother's house, attending lectures, pushing wares at trade shows . . . everything else would be easy.

Well. Almost everything.

It wasn't a heist. Kellan didn't intend to *steal* anything. She only wanted to take a good, long look at the prototype for Mesny's newest prosthesis—state of the art, designed in collaboration with an augmentier from Ital whose name she could never pronounce. Long enough to take notes. To recreate—no, inspire—no, *inform* Kellan's next project. Edgar's new right hand. The hand that would reignite the flame in him that his accident had nearly extinguished. The hand that would help him make again.

But first, she had to get those tickets.

Edgar patted his jacket pockets again, his silver brows knitted in frustration. "I brought them. Double-checked and everything. Don't let this gray fool you, now. I'm still sharp as a—"

Their train's engine roared in the distance, the light at its head faint through the mist. Before Edgar finished his sentence, she ran toward their cart and unlatched the topmost crate's lid. A few slates of gold-plated nickel should do the trick.

"You—hey!" Edgar called from behind. "What are you doing, girl?"

"No time to explain," she shouted over the train's whistle, tucking the slabs under her arm. She plucked the final tool she'd need from Edgar's back pocket and tore for the ticket stand. "Close the crates!"

She caught herself from slipping on the rain-slick ground before she hit the counter. Ruban—first smug, then baffled—went slack in confusion.

"That's not bill."

"Good eye."

"And *that*! You're not supposed to have that! What do you think you're doing?"

"I wish y'all would stop asking me. You know you're gonna see it anyway."

It wasn't the sheets of plated nickel that threw Ruban into a confused panic, nor was it the way she spoke to him, very much unlike how someone with sense would speak to the one who held her fate in their hands. Instead, it was the tool she worked along the skin of the metal, slightly larger than a fountain pen.

Edgar's carver.

Oaken handle, yellow jasper inlay, alchemist's bronze carvepoint well overdue for replacing.

The feel of it in her hand was all too familiar.

She'd stolen a carver from his toy shop when she was six. And after the namehouse matron caught and scolded her, Kellan hadn't missed an opportunity to sneak off and visit. Back then, a day spent polishing stairwells and washing stone walls was well worth the chance to spend a minute behind his workbench.

Once they aged out, most Dus from the Belt worked for their village mine. On Kellan's thirteenth, she'd bought a clean shirt and a decent pair of slacks and started work as Edgar's assistant. He was the only guilded maker in a village of miners and smiths, the only person who always let her take things apart, and the first to teach her how to make things of her own.

If anyone asked, though, Edgar *never* let her use a carver. The Crown didn't allow those without family names to be makers, and *no one* wanted trouble from the Crown. At least the village, for the most part, didn't care what she did, so long as whatever she did do kept her busy enough not to break anything else.

She'd worked around its size since, and she'd work around it now. Ruban kept on. Words like "ordergarde" and "dustmills" tickled her ears, but the rest was a low hum as she focused on the task at hand. She cut metal into sheets thin as wax paper, sparks dancing in the air like the coming storm was an esténun breeze; carved runes through and around and along to harden, shape, and float this piece and the other; filled her lungs with the scent of morning grass and fallen leaves that swallowed the stink of sulfur from the distant mines. All this, made in minutes. All this, from a—

"Box." Ruban, who'd long since gone quiet, stared at Kellan's make in disbelief and disappointment. "What am I supposed to do with a box?"

She wouldn't waste time explaining. Instead, she'd show him.

Kellan unlatched the lid and stepped back. The walls of the "box" dithered away to reveal a golden dwarf rabbit. It sniffed the counter, the glass, the air, then hopped off the ledge and shifted into a tiny glittering mockingbird. Its tail caught the sunlight, and when it did, the bird dissolved into butterflies, filling their rusted train station with the whisper of fluttering wings. Then the butterflies returned, finding nectar in the place where Kellan had first set the box, and melded into a box once more.

"For your sister." She nudged the box closer to the glass and gestured to the spit-up stain on his chest as if the train hadn't screeched to a stop behind her, as if the rain dripping onto her head once again didn't mimic the anxious thrum of her heart. "One of a kind. You might not care about what me and Edgar do at Peculiars, but she will."

The train's engine hissed behind her, and after the sound dissipated in the breeze, a flicker of something overhead stole her attention.

She'd almost mistaken it for a lingering spark. Under the cabin's rusted awning, fainter than the sun behind the clouds, floated a single lightning bug. Or something like it. She'd only ever seen them once before, by the stream in the woods behind Cuivreton's namehouse, where she caught them in empty jars of stolen pickled eggs. It was bigger than she remembered, about the size of the tip of her thumb. But that could have been a trick of the light.

"Okay. I'll take it."

The lightning bug floated away, and Kellan's shoulders caved in relief. "Good! Great."

"And sixteen cogs."

It was better than nothing. Biting her cheeks to keep from chewing him out, she dug into her pockets for spare coins. "This is all I got." A few bronze cog pieces clattered beside the toy. "Now, can I have the tickets? Please?"

He pulled them from the printing machine, signed at the bottom, and set them beside the little box. "Don't let that city spoil you none, you hear? We don't need you coming back thinking you something you ain't."

Kellan snatched them, hoping more than anything she gave him a paper cut. She couldn't stick around to find out, though. She had a train to catch. "Edgar!" she called as she hurried for the tracks. "I got them. You can close your suitcase."

Edgar had already closed it, having watched the whole exchange in silence. "Nice work, girl," he said, patting her shoulder.

One of the train's doors slid open, and out unfolded a tiny pair of steps. The conductor straightened the front of his jacket and blew his whistle.

"Thank you for choosing Greenline," he said in a monotone. "This is the eastbound train to Riz, number 156, by way of Argentville, Cuivreton, Rocherie, and New Montague. Tickets and identification, please."

She left the half shelter of the cabin with their cart handles in hand. The rain slowed as the porter stored their luggage beneath the train. When he returned his attention to them, she handed him their tickets with still-sopping fingers.

"Step in, miss," said the conductor after a long, impatient sigh. "We're on a tight schedule."

"I will, I just. I." Kellan stared at their new tickets, ink still shining from Ruban's pen. The falling rain should have darkened the paper, or bled the black into the Greenline's logo. It should have rolled off her skin, leaving her cold and uncomfortable. The rain should have done *something.*

And it did. Just not what it was supposed to do.

She held out her cupped hand. It didn't touch her fingers, or her tickets, or the conductor, or the platform beneath her feet. But it fell, in too-fat drops of glittering crystal, through and around the paper like bent light. Like something that meant to mimic rain but had fallen short.

The passengers looking through the window didn't notice it. Neither did Edgar or the conductor. With no one left, she turned to Ruban in the off chance he, too, sensed something strange in the air.

But when she spotted him behind the counter, digging wax from his ears with the same pen he'd signed her tickets with, she knew everyone must have found this all to be perfectly normal.

Except, perhaps, Kellan and the golden rabbit on the shelf.

The rain around her slowed, a curtain of water pouring from the train station's crooked roof and warping the rabbit like a wind-strewn tapestry. It stared at her, through her, with eyes like black pearls. Black and, somehow, every color at once.

"You forget something, girl?"

Kellan jumped at the warmth of Edgar's hand on her shoulder, a violent chill ripping from her crown to her soles. Suddenly, the rain fell like rain again, and her world became gray and russet once more. But the rabbit . . .

"Where'd it go?"

"Where'd what—" Kellan bounded up the train car steps. "Would you *hold on*, girl? All the time, racing off like something's chasing you."

She'd seen advertisements for the Greenline in magazines: chandeliers, sparkling decanters, high-polished mahogany, wide windows with spectacular views of rolling hills and powder-blue skies. Whoever photographed them hadn't taken pictures of the rear cars. There was neither a chandelier nor a decanter in sight, the floorboards were dull and scuffed, the wallpaper had yellowed at the seams, and every car she walked through reeked of pretzels and feet. But at least there were windows.

She searched from behind the glass for crystalline rain. Waited for the station to ripple like silk in a storm. Watched for gold and color and black pearls and a gaze that reached through her flesh and shook her core until a flash of gold darted past the open window two cars ahead.

With Edgar and the conductor blocking the exit, Kellan wove her way around idling passengers, ducked under tipping luggage, leaped over stretched legs and stray bags, and always, the rabbit glittered just out of sight. She hadn't carved it to do any of that. She'd carved a toy, an illusion, not an animal so fast it was more streak of light than solid metal.

But then, her runework didn't slow the rain. Didn't still the breeze. Didn't bend the world or make it so that only she could see its change.

No, Kellan hadn't carved it to do any of that, either. Even makecraft had its limits.

Outside, the rabbit paused in the parched grass. Lungs burning, she yanked open yet another train car door, and the rabbit turned its golden head. It stared through the window and spotted her watching from inside the train, its pearl eyes dancing in a light the clouds had long since snuffed. It spotted her, and on all creation, she could have *sworn* it—

Smack!

Kellan collided with something tall and reasonably solid. A flurry of thin yellowed paper drifted from above, blocking the next car door's view.

"Please don't step on . . . Oh no, that one's already—" Someone's voice sounded from behind her, vague and, for now, unimportant. When the last of the pages settled, the rabbit was gone again.

"You're—" the voice said, nearer now. "Could you—"

"Could I what?"

"Your foot."

"What *about* my foot?"

"Could you move it? Pits, you're stepping on—"

She climbed onto what she hoped was a bench for a closer look around the window's edge. Behind her, the voice grumbled as it plucked its paper from the ground. "Did you see it?" she asked.

"See what? See you?" The grumbling stopped, but the hush of palm brushing parchment did not. "If I had, I'd have run in the opposite direction. . . . Or at least dodged in time."

"No, not me. The rabbit."

"Or hid somewhere? Yes, probably hid— Hmm? What rabbit?"

"The rabbit! Gold, fast, dark eyes."

"Most rabbits have dark eyes."

"That's not the . . ." Annoyed, Kellan faced the voice for the first time and frowned at the sight. "Point."

The voice belonged to a boy who knelt at the spot of their collision, tucking his gathered pages between the cracked leather covers of a book. A smattering of freckles dusted his cheeks, and a pencil sat perched behind one of his oversized ears. He handled his papers like tiny baby birds, worried they'd broken a bone in the fall.

"Then what *is* the point?" he asked in frustration, pushing his glasses farther up the bridge of his nose. He hadn't spotted her yet, too focused on repairing his ruined tome. "I hope it's an important one, considering . . . well . . . this."

Was it important? It was certainly bizarre, but important . . .

Probably not? Hopefully not. She'd made the toy and earned their tickets. If the make went rogue, it was no longer her responsibility.

Still, the rain. The breeze. The silk in a storm. Perhaps she needed some sleep. Too many nights spent planning this trip had finally taken their toll. After all, it wouldn't have been the first time she'd imagined something that felt so real.

"Are you lost?"

Kellan jumped, startled by his sudden nearness. Now that he'd straightened, he stood at least half a foot taller than her. His cool eyes had widened in . . . horror? Horror. It didn't take her long to realize why. She stank of mildew from the rain, she still hadn't wrung out her hair, and the mud on her pant legs flaked like dry skin onto the floor.

"No." She straightened her back to stand at her full height. It didn't help. "I'm—"

"Looking for a rabbit."

". . . Yes."

"In the middle of a train."

"Are you *laughing at me*?"

"I'm not in much of a position to laugh, if you hadn't noticed. You see, *someone* destroyed my book—"

"How may I be of service?"

The interruption had come from a machine: an automi. It stood still against the opposite wall, so obscured that Kellan had almost missed it. Only then did she realize where she was.

She'd torn through two train cars and found her way into first class. The sign above the entrance read Refreshments in swooping gold, and the bench she'd climbed on swelled with so much featherdown it could hardly be called a bench anymore. The daylight now pooling through the windows bounced off crystal decanters and gold accents in very-much-not-yellowing wallpaper. And above them, clinking like tiny bells, hung a chandelier.

"How may I be of service?"

"It'll stop once you buy something." The boy tucked the ruined book into the inner pocket of his coat. "There's no gold rabbit, but there are shiny cakes."

The train. The Exposition. She'd almost let herself forget about the reason she was here. And that reason didn't include gold rabbits and shiny cakes. Kellan chewed the inside of her cheek, glanced at the mud stain on the car's velvet cushion, and made for the exit.

"But what about your—"

"It's nothing," she said before sliding the door shut behind her. "Probably a trick of the light."

Kellan found her way back to Edgar in the rear cars. The station would soon creep out of view, and Cuivreton's rust-red mountains would grow smaller and fainter until they disappeared into the fog. Ruban had drawn the broken blinds on Cuivreton Station's only ticket counter. It was a place of routine, after all, and he knew not to expect anything else.

Except, there was something else. The box sat on the shelf

as though it never left, just as she'd made it. Just as it was meant to be. And before the train turned the corner, before the mists swallowed her village whole, she'd spotted the lightning bug hovering by the station's single bench—too big, too bright, and not quite where it belonged.

TWO

Hours after the sun set, their train took a sudden dip, and tunnel lights sped by Kellan in streaks of yellow and gold. She abandoned the braid she'd tried to fashion her hair into and stared out the window, determined to memorize every last detail of the marvel waiting on the other side of the glass. They'd entered the tunnel to Sougare, the City Below.

They called it an unnatural wonder, like the cloud-parting walls in the Vastian Mountains at the globe's northern pole, or the temple on an Outer Crescent isle that only appeared on foggy froigus nights. Sougare was one of the oldest parts of Nanseau, an ancient make discovered during the Liberation. What began as a series of tunnels in the ruins beneath the ground to connect Riz, Il, and Un had evolved into something comparable to them, a second cousin to the nation's three Great Cities. Its burnished steel ceiling sparkled with such intricate runework, it'd take centuries to study. Glittering banners rippled in the half city's artificial wind, and more people wove between its pillars and flashing signs than she'd ever seen in one place.

A mechanical voice from overhead announced that they'd reached their destination, and the train pulled to a stop. Their car erupted in a buzz in seconds.

"Well, ain't this nice," said Edgar from behind her. "Place is even busier come Expo time, looks like."

"Did you bring a map?"

"I don't need a map. Could walk this place blind in my prime. What's a few more shops? The bones are the same, I bet."

"Right. I bet."

When they reached the elevator, Kellan wedged herself into a corner in the back. Iron bars shut with a click, and the elevator groaned as it rose. She couldn't tell if it was the sudden movement or the anticipation that stole the breath from her lungs, but she didn't get the chance to contemplate it for long. Moonlight crept through the gaps in the metal to pool at their feet, and the city lights winked like stars that had somehow found their way out of the sky. This was the nation's crowning jewel. The pride of Nanseau. The City of Progress.

Riz.

The humidity was a welcome change compared to what she'd left behind on the train. Magnolia blossoms the color of amethysts dangled from baskets at the tops of streetlamps. Trumpets and saxophones blared from the sidewalks while car horns and bike bells honked on the roads. Some Rizians wore heels so high that Kellan wondered how they stayed upright, and the sparkle of their dresses and suits rivaled even that of the gold and bronze filigrees that accented nearly all the city's buildings. If she'd thought Sougare was a marvel, then Riz was a miracle, a glittering hub of movement and life.

The others in the elevator didn't stop to appreciate it. They pushed and shoved their way out the moment the gates opened. All that kept Kellan from toppling over was the elevator wall and her cart's handle. "Taxi," she said, suddenly self-conscious over the state of her hair. She tried her best to smooth it down. "We need—"

"You're holding up traffic, girl!"

"—a taxi," finished Kellan under her breath. Edgar waved Kellan over through the window of someone's passenger seat.

"Lemme help, lemme help." The driver, a skinny girl with a frayed cap and crooked tie, beckoned for Kellan to give her the cart. "Won't take but a minute. Get on in."

After Edgar gave the okay, Kellan let the driver handle the cart and settled inside. The back seats smelled too much like hair grease and tobacco. She reached to roll down a window, only to find the crank snapped at the hinge. Outside, the driver closed the trunk.

"Good thing y'all caught me when you did." The driver took her seat and turned the key in the ignition. It didn't start. "Could've been stuck with one of those automiruns. Don't know where they're going half the time, between you and me. Anyhow, where y'all headed?"

“The Fault, they call it now, I think,” said Edgar. “Should be west of here.”

“The Fault? Y’all sure?”

“Very,” said Kellan. “Why?”

“No reason! Just curious, is all.”

“Right.” Kellan glanced once more at the night sky, hoping for another glimpse of color. “Curious.”

They’d crossed three districts to reach the Fault. Kellan counted each gate. First platinum. Then bronze. Then brass.

“Sudton’s the only way through past sundown,” the driver explained, cruising down side streets like they were old friends. “Doesn’t bother us much, though. It’s not like people are fighting to get through.”

The glitter and music of Riz’s Crown District had long since faded, leaving only the faint chitter of laughter and conversation from families on their stoops. The air here, warm and iris-sweet, nearly made up for the unease prickling up Kellan’s spine.

Was it the sudden chill in the air? The silence, creeping like a plague the nearer they grew to the Fault’s gate? Part of her wanted to hide. When the taxi stopped at a line of traffic, that part of her quieted but didn’t disappear. A new sight pinned her to its leather seat.

“What’s going on?” Edgar.

“Not sure.” The driver. “Looks like the gate’s clogged. Let me just . . .”

Cuivreton’s namehouse was tall, as most namehouses

were, a tower erected from corpsestone sometime after the Lidonch first conquered whatever Nanseau was before. Cuivreton was also small, and its Dus were few, so there was little need for anything larger than five or six stories. After the Liberation, as a war-battered island scrambled to piece together a nation from the ruin before the rest of the world could pick at its shreds, the first courtiers saw every column of Lidonch rule fall to rubble. Everything but its cathedrals, which then became prisons for Nanseau's traitors, which then became namehouses for those traitors' children. She'd been told Cuivreton's wasn't as much of an eyesore as the ones in the larger villes and lesser cities. Like she should be grateful for its smallness. Like there were worse places and worse fates.

Kellan couldn't see the Fault's wall. She couldn't see its gate or its cottages, its shops or its streetlights. But she could see its namehouse.

This tower pierced the night sky. It could have swallowed its cousin in Cuivreton. Could have swallowed it twice. She supposed there were many Dus in Riz, considering its size, and its namehouse should be big enough to keep all of them. But to see a namehouse other than her own for the first time chilled the breath in her lungs. Its jagged shadow darkened half the district on the other side of its wall, a haunting reminder that for Dus, there weren't worse fates. Only more children doomed to the same.

"All right, folks. Looks like a blackout."

Edgar fiddled with the brim of his hat. "Bassy didn't tell me nothing about those."

"They've been going on for months. The other districts get flickers sometimes, but when the Fault goes, it really goes. Sometimes, nothing works for days."

For a moment, all was still. The light on the other side of the Fault's wall was a haze of yellow against a bed of navy, less than a thought on the horizon. But when it left, it took the warmth with it. It snatched the comforting whisper of working runework from the air, staining the skyline black in its wake.

Then the dark moved.

The driver tried and failed to maneuver out of the lane, her voice cracking in thinly veiled panic. "I heard it reaches outside the wall sometimes, but I never seen it in person."

"What happens when it does?" asked Kellan, voice too small.

"Don't know. Don't wanna find out, neither."

Porchlights. Streetlights. Headlights. First they flickered, then they vanished like candles under heavy rain. This didn't feel like a blackout. It felt like a coming storm. A tide of dark come to swallow them whole.

Run, little thing.

The dark crept closer. Closer. Closer, still. Kellan pressed herself flush against the back seat, curled into a ball, one arm out to shield—

A scream curdled her blood. Shattered the night. Held her still as stone. A scream, and she forgot the cold and the tower and the dark. A scream, and all she knew was *protect. Save. Fix.*

The scream was Edgar's, who gripped his right wrist.

"It's all right, Ed," Kellan lied. She'd only heard him this distraught once, when his hand first came apart. "It's okay. Everything's okay— *Weneedadoctor, gethimtoadoctor—*"

"Working on that," the driver called over the hiss of rubber on granite. Cars surrounded them from every angle, horns screeching in panic and fear. "It'll be tight, but—"

"No hospital." Edgar spoke through gritted teeth, his wrist pressed to his chest. "I'll be fine. Just a little ache."

"Edgar! No, Miss Driver, don't listen to him, just—"

"There's a small hotel in Midton. The Palace. Take us—" He groaned, and Kellan's heart fell into her stomach. "Take us there."

The driver maneuvered her car through the sliver of space between traffic and alley wall, leaving the starving dark behind them.

A few blocks, and the groaning stopped. It took the journey to another district for the sweat on his forehead to dry to a faint sheen. By the time they reached Midton, his breathing had fallen into an easy rhythm. Kellan counted each breath in the silence and chased it with her own to dull the prickle of her ebbing panic. In and out. In and out.

"He's more stubborn than an oil stain. Reminds me of my pa. Is he your grand?"

"Boss."

"Oh." The driver glanced once at the Palace's entrance and shrugged. "Well, all the same."

Kellan stretched her arms to ease the ache in them, trembling palms to the starless sky. It was all she could do not to storm the tiny hotel and . . . what, she didn't know. She should wipe the room down, for one. Recarve a few of the runes in his prosthetic, on the off chance its malfunction was an unfortunate coincidence. Set out tomorrow's suit and tonight's medicine, or bring some extra pillows, or ask if he was okay.

"Get some air," he'd said after he'd settled into his room. He'd dug into his pocket for his wallet. Kellan had tried to pretend he didn't wince. *"See the city. There's a lot to love, if you know where to look."*

"I'll stay. There's enough dust in here to spin a coat. If I start now—"

"No, no. No. You had a long enough day as it is, and we won't be here long enough for you to enjoy yourself proper. Go on, now. Nothing wrong with a bit of wandering."

"But—"

"No buts, now. I don't pay you to but."

"You don't pay me to wander, either."

"He'll be fine," said the driver, smile bright and reassuring. Edgar's fit, a first it seemed in her young career, had left her rattled enough to make sure he and Kellan made it into the hotel alive. She leaned against the streetlamp pole closest to her car, practicing a coin trick. The cog clattered to the ground. "Rizians are tough, you know. Gotta be, to survive in this city."

Tough or not, everything about that malfunction felt wrong. Aches in the bones when it rained, she understood. But there was no logic in a pain that intense, in a dark that strange and hungry.

Tomorrow couldn't come soon enough. One more night, and she'd have what she needed to build Edgar's new prosthesis. Riz, its runework, and its namehouse would be a speck on the horizon, and Kellan and Edgar would be on their way home, far away from whatever storm brewed behind the Fault's wall.

"So, what's your name?" The driver had since retrieved her coin and, undeterred, flicked it into the air again. "Mine's Roussel. Louise Roussel. Most of us are from Sudton, city-south. Folks call me Lou, though. Everybody calls me Lou."

"Kellan."

"Kellan . . . Is that Outer Crescent? Sounds Outer Crescent, but I hear it's a cultural smorgasbord over there, so maybe not. What's your first?"

"Kellan *is* my first."

"Then what's your . . . your . . . Oh."

Kellan toed a pebble on the sidewalk. It rolled into a crack.

"I just thought. Or didn't think. With the Expo tomorrow and the ports opened, I . . ." Lou took off her cap. A mess of fluffy auburn coils spilled down to her shoulders, which she mussed further with a quick rake of her fingers. "Sorry."

Kellan's smile wasn't a smile. It was an echo of one, a shadow of something short of polite. She'd braced herself for questions like these, knew someone would ask before the weekend was over.

Was it a cousin? Parent? In-law?

Murder or kidnapping? Capital theft? Spy?

Are you old enough to remember? What do they do with the kids that can?

Do traitors' kin bleed red or stone gray?

She never knew how to answer them, partially because most of them were ridiculous, but also because she couldn't. Whatever relative of hers betrayed Nanseau did it long before she could remember. Unfortunately for her, it didn't matter that the only crime against the nation she'd committed was the misfortune of being born.

"Y'know, not to brag or anything," said Lou, clearly bragging, "but I'm pretty close with the best chef this side of the bridge. Could get you a discount if you're hungry! Your grand—your boss, I mean—wants you to eat something. A hot meal will do you good."

Lou stood against the pole, twisting her hat in her hands, lone coin brushing against its satin lining. No phony smile. No pity, no fear. She was kind, Kellan realized. A little odd and a little too persistent, but not extraordinarily so.

And after what she'd seen at the Fault's gate, Kellan certainly did have somewhere to be.

THREE

This time, Kellan sat in the front seat instead of the back, and she and Lou talked for the whole ten minutes it took to get from the hotel to the Crown District. She learned, for instance, that this was Lou's second day as a driver, that she'd saved for three seasons for her car, and that her mother *despised* her choice of employment. "She'd have me busing tables instead," Lou'd explained as they rounded a corner. "Says driving is too dangerous, 'specially downtown, but this brings in more bill. Nicer people, too. Mostly tourists, like you, and ain't but a few of them drunk in a day."

She dropped Kellan off at Crown Hall, where the Exposition would take place. Outside, Nanseau's crown-and-cog insignia loomed over the city: the crown with twelve arches, one for each of the nation's Houses; the cog with three teeth, one for each of its major cities. Foreign cars lined the road, flags from places as far as the Crescent Isles and near as West Ital billowing in the breeze. Inside, Exposition organizers hurried in its marble halls, balancing tables and posters up stairwells and around corners. People from all sides of the Swallow were behind those glass doors. There were too many of them. More than she'd accounted for in all her months of planning, and definitely more than she'd ever evaded before.

Still, she pressed on. A young secretary sat behind the front desk, her hair in a high bun and her chin in her hand. She drummed the tips of her lace-gloved fingers against her cheek, miserably bored amid the hustle around her.

Kellan cleared her throat. The secretary jumped and smoothed the front of her blouse.

"Sorry about that." Her name tag read Ginnel in plain black text. "You look new. Are you here to work? I can point you to the break room, if you'd like, and you can punch in there."

"I want to look around for a little. Here for the Expo, so only the first few floors."

"Of course. Do you have your pin?"

". . . Do I *need* my pin?"

"Unfortunately, yes. Only makers and their apprentices are allowed up today."

Kellan didn't have her pin. Even if she did, the empty copper circle would make her rank clear as day. "But what about—"

"Assistants?" Ginnel's smile softened at the slight desperation in Kellan's voice. "No one but makers and those immediately under them, I'm afraid. You can come back tomorrow, though, when the event starts."

Tomorrow? She needed to see it today. To study Mesny's prototype thoroughly enough to recreate something a *fraction* as effective, she'd need time. Time she wouldn't have tomorrow, with a full schedule and a building full of watching eyes. Time Edgar was quickly, too quickly, running out of.

"I'm sorry," said Ginnel. For what it was worth, she looked like she meant it.

This would be all right. Kellan could find a work-around. All she needed was another plan. A side entrance, a window left unlatched. She'd even brave a fire escape, if they had one—

"Mind the shoulders, préci."

"Coming through, coming through!"

A worker bumped into her, then another, carrying a table across the hall and around the corner Kellan was forbidden to explore. She rubbed her shoulder and moved farther away from the desk, allowing the workers to pass. As she watched them, an idea came to her.

No. Not an idea. Another plan.

Kellan risked a glance at Ginnel and froze under her knowing gaze. But instead of ratting her out, Ginnel looked from the workers to Kellan once, then twice, her coffee cup still pressed to her lips. Then, with all the drama of a daytime talkie, she set her coffee cup down, straightened her back, poised her fingertips over her typewriter, and turned away.

A lone worker shuffled her way over, this time with a gold-framed poster of an engineer whose face she couldn't put a name to. "I'll take this off your hands," Kellan said with what she hoped was a cheerful grin. "You look like you deserve a hot cup of coffee."

It didn't take much more to convince her. "Fifth floor, end of the hall," she said as Kellan struggled under the frame's weight. Sweat beaded her temple by the time she reached the elevator, but she found it empty, and collapsed against the back wall to catch her breath. Soon she found the energy to press the button. *All About Alloys,* room 502. *Budgeting for the Small Makeshop,* room 514.

Kellan hugged the poster close to her chest, elevator groaning as it rose. Workers, she could handle. If she kept her head down and her excuses brief, she could be out of sight in five minutes. Maybe ten.

But then the elevator stopped. Its doors opened. And the three people darkening the other end were very much not workers.

"This city is a circus." An older man in a dark velvet suit stepped in first, followed closely by a boy and girl around Kellan's age. "Your time would be better spent in Il."

"I like it a lot, actually," said the girl, her bobbed hair falling in soft, silky black waves. "It *sings,* you know? The glitz, the glamour, the *music* . . . I bet Elo would like it, too, if he pulled the stick out of his ass."

"Pits, would you *stop talking.*" Elo, a spitting image of the girl, pinched the bridge of his nose. His hair, that same shimmering black, reached well past his shoulders. She'd never seen hair like theirs in Cuivreton, the kind that straightened and shone without heat or salve. "You're like a shih tzu. Find a window and yap at that instead."

Perhaps they were siblings. The moment those words left Elo's lips, they started bickering in a language Kellan didn't understand. They would've carried on forever had the velvet man not slammed the ferrule of his cane against the elevator floor, the clap of metal on metal speckling Kellan's sight and stinging her ears. At once, the siblings stopped, chins dipped and backs straight.

Velvet Man pressed the button for the third floor, *Something from Nothing: Tips and Tricks on Running a Makeshop with Minimal Overhead,* third-floor ballroom—Mesny's panel—and the doors closed again. The pentagonal gold pin glinting on his lapel marked him as an engineer. A theorist, by the two glittering amethysts. His center prong was empty. He was an expert, but not a master.

She'd never seen a theorist's pin in person before and only rarely saw them in photographs. Of all the schools of makecraft within the Guild of Engineers—perhaps within the entire science—theorists were the most protective of their work. She used to think it was because of how vital the school was to makecraft's advancement. Its makers, after all, had discovered the laws and knots that served as the craft's foundation, and without them, the craft wouldn't exist. But now that she'd seen how this man treated his charges, she wasn't so sure.

That would make the siblings his apprentices, then. But when she searched their lapels for gemless crests, she found only two plain gold pentagons. The pins of an engineer's assistants.

"Has your mother not taught you that it is impolite to stare?"

Kellan went cold. Velvet Man looked down at her from the top of his hooked nose, his eyes milky from cataracts.

She shouldn't say anything. She knew how the world worked. Everything from their posture to the cut of their suits told her Velvet Man and his assistants came from bill, and with enough of that, rules were merely polite suggestions.

"Do you speak, child?" he said, firmer this time.

"Yes."

"Then apologize."

"I would, if I'd done something wrong."

The elevator door opened, and the older man froze. His head turned like a slow swivel until his steel-gray eyes met hers. For a moment, they lit with outrage. But only for a moment. The next, they cooled, and Kellan may as well have been a scuff on his leather shoe.

"Remember, children," he said with venom, watching her, but speaking to the twins. "Mind the floors, lest you step in something filthy."

Then they were gone. The boy flicked a speck of lint from his shoulder. The girl shrugged in apology and hurried after him. The door closed behind them, and Kellan was alone again.

◆ ◆ ◆

Kellan stepped back to inspect the poster she'd set up, her core burning from hauling it down the fifth floor's endless hallways. At last, she could read it. Olivier Odil, maker of the runepowered coffee drip, was apparently releasing a book.

With that done, Kellan did her best to look busy and walked the hall, noting each label and room number as she searched for even the smallest sign of Mesny's display. Best to wait until the crowd thinned for the real work to begin. At least, it would be had she not already wasted too much time.

She couldn't take the elevator again. It was too risky, especially if she was the only one with empty hands. She'd passed a door to a staircase a few corners ago, if she remembered correctly. With a quick breath, she hurried for it, careful not to look in too much of a rush. She'd search all night if she had to, scour the hall from the deepest cellar to the comte's office on the top floor. She had no other choice.

In a few steps, she found the entrance to the stairwell. Kellan checked behind her, careful to make sure she hadn't been seen before pressing onward, and opened the door with a creaky push. But she'd been so preoccupied with who may have been at her back that she hadn't considered what may lurk ahead.

At the landing below, his face half obscured by the railing, stood the boy from the train.

FOUR

"What was that?"

Kellan shut the door with a thud and ducked to keep out of view. She needed to find someplace to hide.

It was one thing for her to have somehow run into the boy from the train, but another to find him with Riz's comte. Not only were they Nanseau's highest-ranking officials, second to the Crown, but the comtes of major cities were known to be uncommonly close with the courtiers above them. She didn't know much about Riz's comte aside from the photograph of him in the corner of her flyer, but she knew she couldn't risk him catching her.

She slipped inside the nearest room, closed the door as softly as she could, pressed her back against the wall, and held her breath.

A voice. Proud and clipped, likely the comte's, from what

little she'd heard of him by the stairs. He asked—no, insisted—that the workers report to the topmost floor.

But where was she now? Her vision adjusted to the dark. She sank to the ground and inched to a nearby table, her knees slipping against newly waxed hardwood, and plucked the card from the top. *Advanced Tinkering: Ingenious Applications of C-Level Runes*.

She and Edgar had a place here. It should be an easy lecture. Simple. Practical. Useful but wholly unextraordinary.

Which was precisely why she fumbled at the sight to her left.

Glass caught a sliver of moonlight beneath a shuttered window. Glass, and cherrywood, and alchemized platinum, and makes so beautiful she'd gladly have given her first finger to see them in the sun.

Because one of those makes was Mesny's prototype.

More footsteps. Clicking doors as they opened and shut, growing clearer each time.

". . . *must* go perfectly," came the clipped voice of the comte, muffled through the door but closer than it was seconds ago. "The Exposition begins in mere hours, and those useless goats are still setting up chairs."

"Considering these last-minute adjustments to the lineup," said the boy from the train, "I'd say they're doing the best with what they have."

"Well, it isn't enough."

Their footsteps slowed. Kellan crawled behind a pillar to

hide and wrapped her arms around her shins, her palms so damp with sweat that they slipped against her sleeves.

The door opened and clanged against the wall, sending her heart into her throat.

"Embarrassing. The janitorial staff *must* clean this room again before tomorrow morning," The comte stepped farther in. "It's filthy. Just filthy."

"And I'm sure they will. They've been in and out all day. Someone was bound to leave tracks."

After another look around, the comte's shadow smoothed the front of its jacket, its shoulders too straight. Its chin too high. "Tell Ginnel to remind them as much in the morning. This year's success is crucial. *Critical*."

"Of course."

"I need more than that." The comte's footsteps were gunshots in the silence as he neared the boy from the train. His shoulders, once straight, caved under the stress of something Kellan couldn't see. And his chin, once high, lowered with the weight of a secret. "I need a guarantee. This event *will* succeed. *Must* succeed. Do you understand?"

"I think you're confused again."

"Confused? About what?"

"About why I'm here."

The boy's footsteps echoed off the walls, two easy strides toward the comte. He didn't raise his voice. He didn't have to. He spoke with cool confidence and an almost friendly lilt. Almost. His words carried a dangerous edge, and had she not seen him on the stairwell herself, she wouldn't have recognized him at all in the dark.

"I'm here first on behalf of the House," he said. "The Exposition falls second, and I'm afraid your reinstatement hasn't made the list. I've been patient so far, but even tungsten has its melting point. Do *you* understand, Comte Cesaire?"

Silence. The comte loosened his tie. "Next floor," he mumbled. "I've a meeting with Tremblay in ten."

The comte and the boy from the train closed the door behind them, and Kellan slumped against the pillar in relief. The part of her that wondered what could make the comte so afraid died when she remembered how close she sat to the very thing that would save her and Edgar's livelihood: close enough for her breath to fog the glass protecting it. In a perfect world, she could've sketched it from the other side, leaving the prototype safe in its cage. But the room was too dark, the make was too sleek, and Kellan was too quickly running out of time.

"All right, little box," she whispered to herself, slipping Edgar's carver out of her pocket. "Where do we start?"

Breaking the glass would be foolish. It was likely alchemized, for one, but even if she could, the runes carved along its platinum-leafed edges would, at best, trigger an alarm that would send every ordergarde within a ten-block radius her way. At worst . . . Well, the less she thought about that, the better. She couldn't read the runes either way, as the display's wooden base covered all but a thin line of decorative shimmer.

She pulled her backpack off her shoulder and took what she needed. Gloves. Copper. Bronze. A thumb's length of silver and, although Edgar would have her head for it once he found out, a pinch of powdered platinum.

When she'd carved Ruban's gift, she'd worked big. Simple and grand. Now she worked small and complex. Micro cuts here. The tiniest fold there. Runes carved in script so small she had to press her nose to the metal, the warmth of her work rosing her cheeks. Soon the room's stale air filled with the sweet, earthy scent of wet sand and salt and seagrass until, at last, her make was complete.

An octopus smaller than a cog piece swam through the air. In the silence, she could almost hear the ocean. What she imagined it'd sound like, at least. It was only a toy. But toys, Kellan had learned, could do incredible things.

She guided it toward the dome. It slipped through the seam between the glass and its base, hovered around the prosthesis, wrapped its tiny tentacles around the thumb—

"I don't get paid enough for this."

The ding of an elevator. Shuffling footsteps, and the growing din of conversation. The workers had returned to the fifth floor.

Kellan waved the last of her make's sparks away and sank to the ground, her heart hammering in her chest. Had she run out of time already? The octopus's massive mouth had only swallowed the prosthesis to the base of its thumb. It hadn't even begun to shrink yet. If someone caught her in the act, she was finished.

The elevator dinged again, the hall quiet once more. No footsteps or shadows striping the ground through the window. When the tiny octopus returned, it spat Mesny's prototype at its full size into Kellan's waiting hands.

All the time in the world couldn't have prepared her for how beautiful Mesny's model would be. Intricate runework, more art than script, patterned its platinum casing in what the layperson's eye would see as fashionable décor. To study those alone, Kellan would need at least half a day. Between that and its inner workings, its materials, the runes and sigils she didn't know, and how dangerously close she'd come to getting caught, it didn't take her long to reach an equally dangerous conclusion.

She had no choice. She had to take it.

It wasn't theft if she gave it back. That's what she told herself as she carved its replica from what materials she had left, illusioned copper to a high platinum sheen, mimicked its pattern as accurately as she could. The dupe would fool most passersby, so long as they didn't remove it from its dome and find it hollow.

Once the tiny octopus finished its swap and tucked itself into her bag, Kellan pressed her ear to the exit. No footsteps. No whispers. After a quick peek through the window, she opened the door and crept through—

"You were in there for a while."

Kellan jumped, and the door slammed behind her.

The boy from the train stood with his hands in his pockets at the corner of the hall, the quirk of his lips just slight enough to betray his amusement. "Should I ask who you work for?"

"Depends," she said, shifting her bag behind her back. Inside, her octopus flittered impatiently against the lining. "Do you make a habit of pestering strangers?"

"We're hardly strangers. You ruined my book."

"I don't know what you're talking about. And I work here. Obviously."

"No, you don't."

"Sure I do."

"These workers have been setting up all week. You just got here."

"I'm filling in. Needed the extra bill."

"Where's your name tag?"

"Lost it on one of the elevators."

"Then why were you hiding? Eavesdropping?"

"If you'd said something worth listening to, believe me, I'd have excused myself."

Too quick. Too sharp. She should have bitten her tongue, but it wasn't a crime to look around. Trespassing, vandalism, illegal makecraft, and capital theft, on the other hand . . .

Fear gripped her by the neck. The prize hidden in her backpack would cost her everything. She could lose her life to the dustmills, quarrying stone until her bones brittled to nothing. It was a fate worse than death, and she was one wrong word away from discovery.

"Funny." The boy from the train pushed his glasses further up the bridge of his nose and cocked his chin somewhere over her shoulder. "Comte Cesaire should be in his office on the top floor, so the stairs are clear by now."

He must not have known what she'd done, so easily handing her a path of escape. While she wouldn't stay long enough to find out, her feet slowed once she reached the corner. "Who are you?"

The question must have caught him off guard. He went rigid for a moment, his lips pressed into a thin line. "Axel," he answered, and left it at that.

Axel. She waited only a moment for a second name. It didn't come. "And how did you know it was me?"

He hesitated, then glanced down. She did, too, and found the answer staining her pantlegs the color of rust.

The mud. Of course it was the mud. Cuivreton followed her like a bad smell, more stubborn than she ever could have anticipated. More stubborn than she wanted to accept.

"I should get back to work." Kellan wouldn't spare a thank-you. She left him in the hall like she had in the snack car, looming threat of arrest and all, and ignored the distinct feeling that he'd started to say something else before she disappeared.

It was Exposition morning—rather, Exposition afternoon. Because Edgar slept in, spent one hour deciding which suit to wear, then spent another hour hot combing his hair, they'd missed most of the early lectures. Luckily, his delay gave Lou enough time to pick up breakfast, which Kellan and Edgar ate on the drive over.

His wrist had improved overnight. At least, that's what he told her.

Kellan didn't press, partially because she was too tired from studying the prosthesis all night, but mostly because she had almost everything she needed to build the solution to all their problems. The materials, she'd worry about later. Today, she just had to do something with the priceless artifact tucked in the hidden pocket of her backpack. She'd return it. Somehow. She already had a few ideas, and if she was lucky, maybe one of them would work.

At least, that's what she told herself.

"Man." Lou stuck her head out of the window, whistling low. "I try to avoid downtown this time of year. Never seen it this busy in the flesh."

If Kellan hadn't known better, she'd have thought it was a parade. Wealthier makers brought their automi, who carried the bags their apprentices couldn't. The others lugged their own cargo: crates of blueprints and slabs of metal, suitcases twitching with unfinished makes. One even carried a bucket—*bucket!*—of gears and kept their carver tucked in the ropes of their loc'd hair.

Lou promised to return by seven, and after giving her their thanks and her pay, Kellan and Edgar fell into step with the crowd. They eventually reached the Hall's front door, where they picked up their name tags and stuck them under their pins.

In the crowded lobby, merchants lined the walls with samples of their wares on pop-up stands and engineers debated runetheory in the far corners. It'd only been a few hours, but she'd already come to miss the smell of fresh-cut metal, the sweet tang that lingered in the air after a newly carved rune. That alone was almost enough for her to forgive the heat that came with having so many bodies in one place, particularly when not all of them were very well washed.

"We need the elevator," she told Edgar, minding her pace so he wouldn't lose her. As much as she wanted to tear through it, he wouldn't be able to keep up. "The panels are on the third floor."

"I thought we had a workshop first." Edgar took something from one of the pushier merchants—a smith who handed a sample pack of foil and his business card to anyone with a free pair of hands. He'd set one on top of their crates, too, for good measure.

"No time. Mesny's panel is in the ballroom."

Mesny's panel. One plan of a decent two dozen. The room would be packed enough for her to go unnoticed while she left the box by the stage, illusioned until the crowd cleared and an attendant happened across it.

Yes, it was crude. Yes, it was risky. And, yes, it was more harebrained than she'd ever admit. But at least it was something.

On they went until they turned the same corner Kellan had lied her way around the day before, but they took too long to get there. Worse, there was a line, and it snaked in so many turns that she couldn't see the elevator from their place in it.

"What's the time?" she asked when the waiting had become too much. They'd only taken about three steps forward, and still, the line didn't look any shorter.

"Hmm? Oh." Edgar checked his watch. "Ten."

". . . What?"

"Well, maybe three minutes to, but it may as well be—"

"No!" Kellan startled someone ahead of her, but their glare was the least of her worries.

Edgar, who must have finally understood, canted his head. "Does Mesny's—"

"Yes."

"And we're—"

"Yes!"

"Because of—"

"Yes!"

"Oh, creation. Oh, I didn't mean—I'm sorry, girl."

"It's not your fault. It's not."

"It is." There was a finality to Edgar's tone, but it was guilt-laden all the same. "This place still got stairs?"

"Yeah, but—"

"Take them."

"No." And leave Edgar to be potentially trampled? Or robbed? "We'll make another one."

"You know we won't. Now get." He turned her away by the shoulders. "I'll take the crates up. Save me a seat."

"But—"

Edgar frowned. He didn't pay her to but.

Kellan pushed her way through the crowd until she found the entrance to the stairwell. One flight, two flights. Her lungs burned by the third, but at least she beat the line. She jogged on, squeezing through makers and apprentices alike, until she saw them. The ballroom doors.

And an attendant closing them.

"Wait!" She ran, ignoring her aching thighs, and waved the attendant down. "Waitwaitwait."

The attendant paused. He chewed his gum like a cow chewed its cud. "Here for the panel?"

She nodded with her hands on her knees and tried to catch her breath.

"Who're you with?"

"Edgar. Pape. Tinker."

He flipped through his notepad, running through the list of names with the tip of his pen. "Good. I think there's two seats left."

"Great."

"Gotta wait for him, though. Is he somewhere behind you?"

"He's in line for the elevator. Can't make the stairs. So if I could maybe—"

The attendant popped his gum. "Can't. Only makers and

apprentices can attend on their own. No assistants. Not unaccompanied."

"No. No, no, nonono." She stood on her toes to peek into the ballroom. A few familiar faces on the stage, but no Mesny. Not yet. She still had time. "There's room in the aisles, just let me stand there."

"Can't. Only—"

"Makers. Right. But it's *right* there."

"Listen. My supervisor will have my thumbs if I don't close up, so I'm sorry."

"But no! Wait!"

He didn't. He backed into the ballroom, shut the doors, and was gone with a click of the lock. They shut softly for their size, but he might as well have slammed them in her face.

Muffled applause boomed loud enough for Kellan to guess who'd just walked on stage. Before her heartbreak got the better of her, before she did something she would surely regret. Kellan made for the stairwell to rejoin Edgar in the lobby.

Had she not spent most of the Exposition in a nauseating panic, Kellan probably would have enjoyed the rest of the day. There was much to learn, and Edgar had made more than a few friends in the workshops and panels they got to in time. It also wasn't likely she'd ever be surrounded by so many talented makers at once again. But instead of learning, or chatting, or appreciating the brilliance around her, Kellan spent the last wisps of her energy holding down her breakfast.

She and Edgar sat on a windowsill on the second floor. Dusk replaced day, and with it went most of the attendees, leaving the halls uncomfortably empty as Mesny's stolen—*borrowed*—make grew heavier with each passing moment. Every second Kellan spent with it brought her head that much closer to splitting in two. She shielded her bag and tried to focus on the trees outside instead, but in the streets below, three ordergarde chased someone in a tattered coat clutching a wooden box to their chest.

Kellan struggled to breathe. It seemed she hadn't been the only one to "borrow" something from the exhibition. So far, Kellan's swap had gone unnoticed, but that could change in an instant if anyone looked hard enough, which would definitely happen if the figure in the tattered coat led the ordergarde back to Crown Hall. But Kellan hadn't seen ordergarde in the halls, and she'd heard no whispers of missing makes. Kellan buried her fear and drew closer to study the commotion. She had to be sure first. On the first sign of trouble, she'd run.

Then the figure looked up at Kellan through the window from several stories below. For the briefest moment, the world stopped again, their tatters blowing in a wind that spared the trees.

For the briefest moment, Kellan recalled the rabbit at the station.

"The letter I'm gonna write that boy, I'm telling you."

Kellan jumped, the sound of Edgar's voice pulling her back. "A boy? What boy?"

"Bastien! Won't be a boy to you, but he'll always be knee-high to me. The fool couldn't write one letter. Not one." Edgar fiddled with his sandwich wrapper. "I thought I'd find him at the Expo, what with his trade, but there's something about little brothers when they get older. Catching them is like catching smoke."

Edgar didn't speak much about his brother, Bastien, but she knew he was a maker once. Unfortunately, Kellan was a terrible comfort. In the namehouse, she'd avoided the younger Dus as much as she could. Too much crying. Still, she patted Edgar's shoulder and hoped he could feel her sympathy in the weight of her touch.

When she glanced out the window again, the tattered person had disappeared, leaving the ordergarde to pester passersby for word on where they'd gone. They kept their business to the streets, leaving Crown Hall untouched and Kellan's secret safe.

"There's always next year, if we can swing it." Edgar had been trying his best to make up for his morning tardiness. Kellan had insisted throughout the day that missing the panel wasn't his fault, but he hadn't believed her once, and compensated for her grumpiness by being twice as optimistic. "What's next?"

"A workshop," she said. "Forgot which . . ."

But she hadn't forgotten. At least, not entirely. In that moment, she remembered the last workshop on their schedule. A practical workshop.

Advanced Tinkering: Ingenious Applications of C-Level Runes.

The nausea churning in her belly softened to a fragile, hopeful flutter.

"We've got one more workshop." Kellan crumpled Edgar's sandwich wrapper into a ball and tossed it into the nearest wastebasket. She missed. "Fifth floor. Let's go."

She led the way with their cart, the line to the elevator not nearly as long that time around. They reached the door in seconds and presented their badges and pins to the attendant. This one, who didn't have any gum, let them in without an issue.

"This is nice." Edgar set his bag on their table almost as carefully as he set down his hat. "Can see the stage right proper. We might even get to see what he's doing with his hands for once."

This could be simple. She'd leave the box on an empty seat, or by the stage, or—even better—near the replica. She and Edgar would reach the trades fair before anyone was the wiser. The Exposition would have their treasure back, and everything would be perfectly fine.

That is, if no one—or nothing—got in her way.

Two hushed and faintly familiar voices murmured from the hall. The dull thud of approaching footsteps fell in a crooked rhythm. And then came the sharp click of a cane against the tile.

"Pape?" asked an attendant, whose face was a mountain range of pimples and cysts.

"Edgar Pape, yes," he said. "Tinker."

"You don't have a place here."

"We don't?"

"You don't."

If she'd looked a second later, she'd have missed them. The Velvet Man from yesterday strode out of sight. The girl didn't meet Kellan's eyes. And the boy didn't seem to care either way.

"You're wrong." Kellan quivered in budding rage. "But you know that, don't you."

It wasn't Velvet Man's smirk, or the boy's apathy, or even the attendant's weak will that infuriated her. It was the pointlessness of it all. Why them? Why now? Because she'd stood up for herself? Or because, even when she stood, they still found her small enough to kick.

The attendant read Kellan's badge and pin. Just her first name. Just a tinker's assistant.

"I have a chart." If his smile had been any terser, the pimples around his mouth would have burst. "It says you don't have a place."

"Then the 'chart' is wrong."

"Maybe, but it's the chart, and according to that, you don't belong in this room."

Maybe he didn't deserve it. Maybe he needed the bill, needed this job, and Velvet Man held a rank with the power to take that all away. Kellan didn't care. It'd been a long and exhausting day, and she was a breath away from taking out that exhaustion on him. His salvation came in the form of the workshop doors, which opened with a flourish, dusk's warm light casting the room in soft yellow. And a voice that Kellan could have recognized in her sleep, a voice that sounded from Edgar's shop radio at every possible opportunity, a voice that demanded all the room's attention and then some.

"Charts? Oh, how I *hate* charts. Someone burn them."

The voice of Madame Minora Mesny, Master Engineer.

FIVE

"There's only one chart, though, Madame. This one."

"Then burn *it*."

Madame Mesny was surprisingly willowy in person: all arms and legs and sharp angles. The knife-point tips of her heels thunderclapped against the floor, and between the severe cut of her jewel-green suit and the gold that glinted from its buttons and the chains on her shoulders, she reminded Kellan more of a general than an engineer.

"And these rows!" she said as she took in the setup, placing her briefcase on the instructor's desk. "This won't do. This won't do at all. Young man?"

"Yes? Madame?"

She patted the pimply attendant on his shoulder, and he reddened from collar to hairline. "The fire will have to wait. For now, help these good people rearrange the tables. I want a circle."

"Madame?"

"The desks. I want them arranged in a circle."

"But, Madame, the chart—"

"Should be burned first, yes. Smart boy. Do that. Your scheduled instructor," she said, facing the class, "is nowhere to be found. I, good friend that I am, have agreed to instruct on his behalf. However, I like rows almost as much as I like charts, which is to say not in the least, so I would be forever grateful if you all were to help me rearrange this horrible room. . . . Well. Perhaps not forever, but I would be grateful all the same."

After a long moment of stunned silence, the room was overcome with hushed conversation and table legs squeaking against the flooring. Makers, assistants, and apprentices alike pushed and pulled their places into something that resembled a circle, judging from what little she could see through the haze of her shock.

"Kellan." Edgar snapped the fingers of his natural hand by her ear. "Close your mouth, girl. You'll swallow a fly."

Kellan stood still the entire time. Mesny was *here*. Here, feet away, and helping her automi pull the drawing board into the center of a still-forming circle. Feet away from a counterfeit of her own design. Feet away from the real treasure, hidden in Kellan's secret backpack pocket.

She couldn't decide whether this was a dream or a nightmare.

"C'mon, now. I can't move this on my own."

"Table. Right. Sorry." She pulled herself together enough to help Edgar push their table until it joined the others.

"Better." Mesny plucked a piece of chalk from the tray beneath the board and drew. The squeak of chalk on slate stone drowned out the class's swelling whispers. "You all have metal? Gears? Carvers? Good. I propose a little contest. Five runes, all level C and below, and a quarter of an hour to make me something nice."

Flex. Fall. Mend. Pulse. Spark. Simple runes, easy to carve. Mesny drew them with a quick and practiced hand, each line, angle, and curve expertly executed. It was something out of a textbook. No, more than a textbook. From the Greenline's spokes or Sougare's ancient steel.

"You will learn as much from those around you as you would from me. Possibly more, as I've an unfortunately short attention span and a tendency to withdraw when I'm bored. So don't bore me. Questions?"

Silence. Only the faint hum of Mesny's automi's runes, and the not-so-faint thump of Kellan's frantic heart.

"Good. You've fourteen minutes. Begin."

The room erupted in a flurry of clinks and clangs. Assistants and apprentices pulled slabs and strips of metal from their bags. High grades, too. Natural and alchemized gold and silver. Some even had a sheet or two of platinum. Sparks of amber and palest gray danced and flew and ricocheted, chased by scents of maple wood and sunlight, fresh cotton and a fleurnus breeze.

The fear, she could set aside. This lesson could teach her what she needed to take Edgar's new prosthesis from passable to phenomenal. Years of dreaming, of stolen hours of practice and study, led up to this moment. To the chance to learn from the best, if only for the better part of an hour. And for even the slimmest chance to save Edgar's shop, Kellan would have taken the better part of a minute.

"Any ideas?" Kellan opened Edgar's bag and, after she set out the metal, shifted through his sandwiches in search of his carver.

"A little cuckoo clock could be fun," he said. "Haven't made one of those in a while."

"She said not to bore her." Kellan had reached the bottom of his bag. Nothing but lint, a few cog pieces, and stale pumpernickel crumbs.

"Ain't nothing boring about a cuckoo clock. It's a classic."

"Do you have the carver?" She checked the pockets. Crumpled sheets of sketchbook paper. A fraying handkerchief. Three spare tortoiseshell buttons.

"Carver? It should be in there somewhere. I packed it this morning."

"It's not here." She checked again. When nothing turned up, she turned the bag upside down. Sandwich after sandwich fell in a pile onto the table, but no carver. *No carver.*

"That's not it right—oh."

"What?"

Edgar pointed to one of the smaller copper rods. It was pen-like in shape and admittedly carver-sized, but unfortunately for them both, not a carver. Her fault. She should have made sure. Instead, she'd overslept her alarm, exhausted from studying the work of something that didn't belong to her.

That feeling, she'd set aside too.

"Foil." Kellan plucked the smith's sample from the top of their cart. "Do you still have yours?"

Edgar set his foil pack in her waiting hand. "Don't be reckless, girl. Ask the instructor for help."

Kellan opened the packs and splayed the sheets across her part of the table. Four sheets each of iron, copper, and agold. She could work with this. She could even work with half.

She took an iron sheet and rolled it into a thin tube, slighter than a cheap carver's smallest setting, took the tip between her teeth, and pinched and rolled until it came to a rounded point. It wasn't perfect, but she knew she could pull it off.

She knew it would be great.

"Time."

Mesny shut her pocket watch. Their fourteen minutes had come and gone. She ambled around the circle clockwise, her hands folded behind her back. "Acceptable. We will discuss the inspirations behind each choice, and hopefully, we will all have learned something before our hour is up."

She stopped at each table and inspected each make in turn. Most were common things with flashy additions—floating clockfaces, animated bookends. The mechnitian beside Edgar and Kellan presented a heavily geared flashlight.

"Effective." Mesny cast its glaring light on the ceiling and the floor. "Functional. You would certainly turn a profit. C-level rune licenses are famously affordable, and most consider the flashlight a modern household necessity. But why alchemist's gold?"

"Took to the Spark rune better," he said, barrel chest puffed in pride. "The light is nice and bright."

"Hmm." Mesny handed it to his apprentice. A step or two later, she stood before Kellan and Edgar. Naturally, she spoke to the latter. Kellan was only an assistant, after all. "And what have we here?"

"Well." Edgar nervously adjusted his bow tie. "Ma'am—er, Madame—we, em. Well, I'll just."

He unfolded his hand and revealed a model lightning bug a quarter the size of his palm. The proportions weren't exact; she'd only ever seen a few, and rarely up close. Still, considering her limited time and tools, she couldn't have made anything better. Its light winked in and out from behind the bug's caged bodice, its wings a golden blur akin to a hummingbird's.

Mesny took the little thing into her hands, careful not to crush it between her fingers. "Delightful. Truly. Its construction?"

"Foil," he said. "Copper body, agold wings."

"And how did you get the wings to move as they do?"

"Um." He glanced at Kellan, who nudged him in his side with her elbow. "Carved Flex along the peripheral and Pulse at the joints."

"Wonderful, wonderful." By then, Mesny held it so close to

her face that the light made her eyes water. She didn't squint. "And the glow?"

Edgar cleared his throat. "I, em."

"A copper disk."

Mesny, who had been busy inspecting the little bug, finally noticed Kellan. "What did you say?"

Kellan wiped her sweaty palms against her pants. "A copper disk. Foil. Fall laced along the circumference, Pulse and Spark knotted in the center."

". . . Knotted. Enormously tricky work, knotting runes. Delicate, too. Risky." She pinched one wing to take a closer look. "And how certain were you that the copper wouldn't catch fire? Tinker Pape?"

"Practice, I guess! You don't get as old as I am on dumb luck."

"I suppose you don't." Mesny handed him back the floating model, but not without a glance at Kellan's badge and Edgar's trembling wrist. "Marvelous work, Mr. Pape, quite so, but I've one more question. If you would indulge me."

"Of course, Madame."

"Why not alchemized gold? For the body and the disk? I see you've a few sheets left, and a precious metal could have only helped its execution. A delicate bounce to the float, if you spaced the Fall runes appropriately. And, if expertly done, with less risk of it catching aflame."

Why not agold? Kellan picked at a thread along the outside edge of her suspenders. She'd needed to get the knot just right, else the foil would burn, and the body would have been too heavy to hover. Copper was safe and familiar. And far less valuable.

"Copper got the job done just fine," said Edgar kindly. "And the agold foil is nice. Wanted to take some home, see if it's worth buying in bulk."

"That is as good a reason as any. Again—good work, Mr. Pape. Very good work." She nodded to him again, but to Kellan as well, and glanced to her badge once more before moving on to the next table.

In the end, a Journeymin Tinker from South Vast won Mesny's contest with a glittering self-tipping top hat. He earned the prize of a "job well done."

Edgar yawned, leaning back in his seat. "I'd say that was the best of the day."

"Yep." When Mesny announced the end of the hour, all the makers and their company packed and left. Kellan stuffed her notebook in her bag, her lightning bug floating at the corner of the desk. Its wings still hummed, but it hovered a little closer to the tabletop, and the glow had begun to flicker.

Once she finished with her bag, she moved on to Edgar's and piled his sandwiches on top of their leftover copper. With the lesson concluded and the cleaning crew likely on their way, all Kellan had to do was leave the box somewhere safe but findable. Behind the door? On a windowsill, between the glass and the curtains? The stage could work if she placed it near the chalkboard—

The clink of metal against the floor interrupted her thoughts. Strange. Most of the attendees had cleared out by then, Mesny included. That left Edgar, Kellan . . .

And Mesny's automi.

Kellan dropped Edgar's bag. It landed with a squishy thud on the table, a wayward copper rod smushing one of his sandwiches to an unrecognizable lump. Mesny's automi was even more immaculately constructed up close. Dozens—no, hundreds—of gears connected even more panels of beautifully runed rose gold on the planes of her delicate face alone.

"I am Xo," she said. Even the pitch of her voice, the rhythm of her speech, was almost human. "The Madame has instructed me to leave this with you." She pulled a neatly folded piece of paper from her pocket and handed it to Kellan.

Kellan took the note in trembling fingers, the paper velvet to the touch:

For Kellan.

The Parlour, Makers' Strip. 8:17 p.m.

I have a proposition.

SIX

"She what?!"

The exposition ended with the trades fair, and they left with slightly less merchandise than they'd come with. Kellan had set the prototype beside her counterfeit the moment Mesny's automi had cleared the floor. Lou made it in perfect time, parked right in front of Crown Hall with three coffees and a half-finished po'boy sandwich.

"You heard right!" Edgar said. "Mesny was gone by that time, you know. Busy woman, busy woman. But her automi came right up to her, handed her this thing—we didn't know it from a gum wrapper at the time, and—"

Lou made crab-claw hands again, reaching for Kellan in vain and sprinkling bread crumbs onto the floor. "Lemme see, lemme see!"

The letter in question, if she could call it a letter, remained clutched in Kellan's fist. By then it was wrinkled and sweaty, and she'd have considered herself lucky if the ink didn't run. She gripped it tight enough for her knuckles to burn. If she let it go, it'd disappear, and she still wasn't sure whether or not she wanted it to.

Lou must have picked up on it. She sat back, understanding, and hugged her headrest. "Well, what're y'all gonna do? Ain't never been to the Strip before, specially not no automi parlor. Most everything there costs more than me and Mama make in a year. I mean, I'd be happy to get y'all that far, but I mean, it'd only be polite to drive y'all to the door. And I mean, maybe walk y'all inside, cause what kind of driver would I be if I let y'all wander by your lonesome? Eastern hospitality and all that."

Someone honked behind them. Lou flipped them the bird with the hand that still held her sandwich, which must have taken an enormous amount of dexterity, and pulled off. She and Edgar were too excited. It was a note. Just a note.

"Our train leaves at ten tonight." Edgar stuffed his empty coffee cup into one of their bags. "I think we've got time. It's not something you can say no to, girl."

"We've got to pack," said Kellan. "And we probably shouldn't push our luck with the train. Sougare's bound to be crowded, since it's the last day—"

"Then I'll pack," said Edgar. "You go on by yourself."

"What? No."

"Yes." He folded his hands in his lap. "I'll be done by the time you're through, and Lou can take us both after with plenty of time. I packed light anyhow."

The word was on her tongue, but she swallowed it. He didn't pay her to but.

"You're a big girl, Kellan," he said, and patted her shoulder. "You can do this on your own."

"I wanna see, too, anyway," said Lou. "I hear it's real nice in there. Tiny part of the city, but it's where all the taxes go, if you know what I mean. So, yeah. If you're scared, I'll be the one driving you. And if anyone asks, I'm your chauffeur. Or bodyguard. Or whatever."

It was decided. Lou pulled up in front of their Midton hotel, where Edgar waved goodbye to them both and went to pack. He gave Lou the last of the sandwiches, which she kept in her passenger seat. Kellan couldn't think about putting anything else in her stomach. Even breathing made her nauseous.

Lou drove with one hand and ate with the other. "You ready?"

The surrounding city didn't care about her nervousness. Somewhere, a clock chimed. Somehow, the sound was heavier than that of her little Cuivreton station. Midton was in full swing, its bars and restaurants awash in navy as the eighth hour rounded. She'd reduced the letter in her hand to a crumpled mess of paper and ink, and Lou's back seat was suddenly too empty, the colors and lights of the city too much. Too loud. Too big. Too bright.

"Yeah," she said. "Yeah, I am."

"Good, good. You've arrived early." Mesny herself opened the door to the study above her makeshop. She hadn't changed since the workshop, but she seemed several inches shorter. Looking down, Kellan learned why. She'd taken off her shoes. "Come. We've much to discuss."

Kellan snuck past, a suspender wound so tightly around her finger that she couldn't feel it anymore. A phonograph sat in the corner, nestled between two marble pots of silkstem grass. And they were small, so small that Kellan nearly missed them, but little metallic bugs hovered above them like bees. No, they *were* bees, gold ones, likely the work of a well-learned sculptor. Most makers disregarded tinkers as a school of makecraft, but even the most elitist scholar couldn't deny the skill required to carve something like this. The bugs flitted around the phonograph as if the horn were a flower, and the music, nectar.

Mesny lowered the volume until the saxophone settled into the background, then motioned for Kellan to sit opposite her desk. This was fine. Her hands were officially clean. She had nothing to worry about. Hopefully, her heart would soon settle with the music so she could breathe without fear of vomiting all over Mesny's rug.

"You've brought the bug, I hope."

In answer, Kellan pulled it out from the bag's side pocket. By then, its glow was more akin to an ember, and the bug itself hardly hovered an inch above her palm.

Mesny took it and pulled a pair of many-layered magnifying spectacles from her desk drawer. Edgar owned a set, too, but his were dated and clunky. Mesny's were wire-rimmed and full-mooned, and each lens slid easily into place as she inspected the make. "By now, you're aware I don't believe for a second that your mentor made this."

Kellan's heart dropped into her stomach. Perhaps there would be no saving Mesny's rug after all. "I—"

"And that assistants, by law, are not allowed to make, never mind your familial status."

"Technically, but—"

"It was a foolish and reckless thing you did, making in plain sight."

"They don't really enforce that where I'm from."

"This is not 'where you're from.' This is Riz." By then, Mesny had pulled apart the entire make. Its wings flapped helplessly beside its body, which curled like a cracked cocoon. She'd taken the disk at the center with a tiny pair of tongs. Kellan had been generous to call its half-hearted flicker an ember. One flit of a bumblebee's wing would snuff it out completely. "Tell me about your carver."

"I didn't have one. Just curled a sheet of iron foil."

Mesny looked up at that, her eyes three times larger behind the glass. "You did all this *without* a carver."

"Yeah?"

"And how old are you?"

"Sixteen?"

"Sixteen." Mesny sat back, pulled off her spectacles, and practically tossed them onto the table. "Knotting is not a teachable skill. To carve runes is a matter of practice, memory, and a steady hand. To knot them requires all those things, but also a depth of knowledge in metallurgy and runetheory that takes decades to cultivate. Decades to hone until they are intrinsic enough to practice, let alone properly execute. And you're sixteen."

Kellan didn't like this. She didn't like it one bit. If Mesny wanted Kellan arrested, better to be blunt about it. She could still run. She knew where the doors were, could even give the guard at the entrance the slip . . . if she could get her legs to cooperate.

Mesny opened another drawer. This time, she pulled out a brick of natural gold no bigger than her pointer finger, and the nicest carver Kellan had ever seen: a bubinga handle with a platinum point and fluorite inlays the color of sea foam. "Make me something. Use any runes you know. I'd like to see another knot, if you're capable."

This was a trap. It had to be a trap. . . . but she'd never felt bubinga before. And fluorite? The best Edgar could afford was petrified wood.

"What about the whole 'this is Riz' thing?" She took both despite her hesitation, turned one of the carver's dials, set it to its slightest setting, then tested it on the tiniest corner of the bar. The gold may as well have been a stick of warm butter.

Mesny sat back, grin so subtle it was hardly there at all. "The only laws I follow in my house are my own."

And that, for now, was enough.

It took Kellan about thirty minutes and half a dozen different runes—three of which she'd knotted—before she considered her make complete. She'd borrowed Mesny's spectacles without permission since the make was so small, but Mesny didn't seem to mind. When she finished, the scent of honeycomb and esténun lilacs filled Mesny's office, and a bee like those that still hovered by the phonograph buzzed to the tune of the horn that played softly from the corner.

"Incredible." Mesny watched it land on one of her piled books. "You're familiar with Tinker Gallo's work, then?"

"Who?"

Mesny opened her palm for the clumsy little bee. It crawled between her fingers and along the backs of her rings. With her other hand, she put on her spectacles once more and inspected the creature in a silence long enough for two songs to play. Kellan nearly asked for permission to leave before Mesny spoke again. "I would like to make you my apprentice."

A different quiet settled in Mesny's study. A quiet that gave for the music and the buzz of Kellan's golden bee, but not the rhythm of her breath. Not the pulse of her heart. Those may as well have stopped.

"I . . . me?"

"Well, certainly not the bee. You'll have to earn your seat in the Guild first, of course."

"Earn? But I don't—I don't have a—"

"Name, yes, I know. Not to worry, that should be the least of our problems."

"The *least*?"

"This year's Gauntlet is *uncommonly* fierce. I'd expected as much, considering the circumstances, but I do find myself wishing the Guild would shelve its pony show in light of it. . . . Although I'm shamed to admit that part of me has taken a liking to the drama."

Mesny went on, but she was as much a drone as the music behind them had become. The Guild of Engineers was the most elusive of the four guilds of craft, all its collective knowledge and traditions shrouded in secret except one—the Gauntlet, their annual apprentice games. To win an engineer's sponsorship and compete for a spot in their ranks was a privilege reserved for the rich and brilliant, and even then, only one of a handful of hopefuls would succeed. One who had proven themselves brighter and fiercer than the greatest young minds in the world.

It was impossible. Impossible. Kellan, fighting for a seat she didn't want that others had killed for. Kellan, the Du from the village of sulfur and chicken dung. All she could think as her fingers dug into her chair's leather armrests, palms slicked anew with nervous sweat, was—

"I can't."

Mesny stopped. Something in her expression hardened, the angle of her brows or the sharp, even gaze of her eyes. Kellan had almost forgotten. Madame Mesny was more than an engineer. Madame Mesny ruled a nation.

"Edgar. The toy shop. His hand. A week." The telephone on Mesny's desk rang, its sound echoing in the quiet. Kellan took a breath and tried again. "It wouldn't last a week without me." He wouldn't last a week without her.

Mesny balanced the bee on the outside edge of her thumb, picked up the receiver, and set it down again. "His prosthesis. That was you as well."

"Yeah."

"It's clunky, but functional enough." The ringing began again. After forever, Mesny ended that call too. "Not your best work, I assume."

"I did what I could with what we had."

"And now you would do what you can't with what you don't."

The music stopped. So did the bee.

Mesny opened the largest drawer in her desk. She pulled out her prototype, set it on her stack of papers as one would an extra pen or a worn paperback.

And then she pulled out Kellan's counterfeit.

Was it shame? Guilt? Terror? Kellan couldn't tell what iced the blood in her veins, shallowed her breaths, sent Mesny's office tilting left and right, over and under. But she knew she was caught, and that the place they'd send Kellan for her crime would make her beg for the namehouse's cold walls. She opened her mouth to protest, but her words refused to leave her parched throat.

The telephone rang. This time, louder. This time, Mesny let it. "This is not a threat," she said. "This is a proposition."

The telephone, blaring now.

"Compete for your spot in the Guild."

Kellan's heartbeat, blaring now.

"Join me. Work with me. Do this, and I will teach you things beyond your imagination. Do this, and I promise you, your life will change forever—"

"Why are you doing this?"

She'd said it in a gasp, her voice smaller than she ever liked it to be. She wanted to shout. To scream. To throw something, anything, through Mesny's stained glass window and onto the streets of a city that didn't welcome her. But all she could manage was a fragile, shaking breath.

The ringing stopped. The silence in Mesny's study softened to a gentle quiet. Mesny eyed the bee that sat on the tip of her pointer finger.

"Because I believe you to be uncommonly brilliant, Kellan DuCuivre." The bee floated away, joining the others by the phonograph. "And brilliance mustn't go to waste."

With her finger free, Mesny picked up her phone. She only listened, her expression unreadable. Yet Kellan sensed a change. A pull in the air like the moment before a sandstorm, slight, and small, and terrifying.

SEVEN

Kellan DuCuivre had seen death in her namehouse. She'd tasted it on her tongue, sweet, cold, heavy. She carried the burden of it in her bones and her flesh, and always she imagined death looked like water, or Lidonch stone.

There was no stone here, a private suite in a private practice, blocks from the Parlour. Here, windows opened wide, welcomed the smell of cut grass and night air. Here was warm, and clean, and soft, and not at all like her namehouse tower. Here, she learned that death could shift shape. But the weight of it never changed.

The call in Mesny's study had come from Xo. Lou'd found Edgar twitching on the hotel lobby floor.

Thorned vines choking a maple tree. That's what she saw when the physician rolled up Edgar's sleeve. Not *his* blood, dark with disease and throbbing purple under the suite's stale white light. Not *his* skin, hard and cracked and greenish gray.

"It's not as bad as it looks, girl." Edgar's jaw tightened when the physician tried to roll his sleeve down. He waved him away to finish it himself.

"He's right," said the physician, tone frank. "It's worse."

"Now, hold on."

"He's lucky we caught it when we did. A week longer, even a few days, and he'd be—"

"I said *hold on*, now. You're scaring her."

"It's Crépin's syndrome. Miner's rot."

Miner's rot. Kellan counted the vines, the thorns, the cracks in the bark. The time it would take for the rot to swallow his shoulder. His chest. His brain. His heart. Had she miscarved all those years ago? Used the wrong metals, or sigils, or salves?

"Think sepsis, but slow, stealthy, and four times as fatal—"

"She's a child!" Edgar was shouting now. She'd never heard him shout. "She's barely sixteen. You talk business with me, you hear? Talk with me, and leave her out."

Did she do enough? Did she ever do enough? No. Never. Not for him. Now the arm that had saved her rotted from within. Thorned vines. Tree bark. Water. Stone.

Cool metal pressed against her shoulder as Xo stepped forward, a small gesture of comfort. But Kellan would find no comfort tonight.

Because this was all her fault.

"Ser Physician," said Xo, her voice the lone calm in the chaos. "May I speak with you in the hall? It will be in everyone's best interest."

Silence, as the physician considered. Silence that set her lungs aflame. Her fault. This was her fault. The voices around her warbled. The suite, once a soft green, darkened to the muddied gray of rust and rock, and she was sinking, kicking, shouting, *screaming*, but the water swallowed it all—

"So!" Edgar sat up, his back against the headboard. "How'd it go?"

Something buzzed behind her ear. Landed on her shoulder, her cheek, her nose, a tiny make of gold. The bee from Mesny's Parlour office left her for the suite's windowed entrance, where Xo and the dark-eyed physician looked at her with . . . She couldn't place it. Pity, maybe. Pity, but not for Edgar. Pity, because they knew who held the cards, and knew that Kellan had none to play.

This is not a threat, said Mesny. *This is a proposition.*

Kellan may have believed her in another world, but Mesny's intentions didn't matter anymore. She was caught, and Edgar was dying. Although she didn't know what would await her on the other side of this contest, she knew she had a better chance at saving him outside the dustmills than in.

"She wants me to be her apprentice." Her gaze never left the window. The moment the words left her lips, Xo and the physician spoke with each other again as if nothing had happened. As if Kellan's decision was an inevitability.

Edgar would stay in Zarisburg, Kellan had been told. For treatment. He'd take the fastest, most comfortable train with the latest, most accommodating automi. He'd have Nanseau's best physicians, its most talented augmentiers. They even gave her names and addresses, photographs and reports, but she couldn't remember any of it. Only that there, he'd have the best chance.

"You'll be okay?" she'd whispered amid the flurry of paperwork and seals.

"If I wasn't sure of it, girl, I'd have told you straight." He'd ruffled her tangled hair, and she was three feet tall again. "You always been bigger than Cuivreton, Kellan. It's about time someone other than me saw it, too."

Something had flown in her eye. A speck of dust, or gold, or pollen. Kellan tried to dig it out with the back of her hand. She'd tried as they walked out the door of the dark-eyed physician's private practice and even as they left the Makers' Strip. Yet there it remained, its weight heavy against her lashes, its warmth burning against her skin and blurring her vision. Kellan tried to hide it. On their way back to the Crown District, she kept her gaze low, and as they left Lou parked above to take the elevator back to Sougare, she brushed remnants of it away. But the closer to their—to his—train they'd walked, the harder it was to pretend she was okay. Still, she'd tried anyway.

The northbound train's whistle blew. It was Edgar's time to leave. Because her hands were too busy helping his bags and crates into the undercarriage, guiding her arms into a too-brief hug, fluffing the feather in his hat, whatever was in her eye won out. By the time the train disappeared into the distance, became no more than another tunneled light leaving Kellan alone in the rush, she'd run out of excuses. Her hands were free. The tears she'd been holding back fell, and her heart felt a little less whole.

The gate to Courtier Quarter was wrought in gold. There were no lines. No traffic. It stood so tall she couldn't imagine how anyone had managed to stand it up, and its metal curved in patterns and shapes she'd never seen before. On any other night, she'd have admired its beauty. She'd have noted how its whorls stirred something in her the way music sometimes did, prickling her nose and hollowing her chest. She'd have questioned what such a strange make was doing in a place it didn't appear to belong. But that night wasn't any other night.

"Hello?" Lou rolled down her window and called out into the night. No one answered, so she drove closer to the entrance. The gate didn't budge.

"What's wrong with it?" asked Kellan, throat dry. It was the first time she'd spoken since the train. "Is this normal?"

"No clue. Never been here before." Lou sat back and pulled off her cap. "I guess they can't let just anyone in whenever they want. It'd be a mess, wouldn't it? Courtiers wouldn't get a minute of privacy."

"That doesn't help us any."

"Well, I know that." She tossed her hat onto the passenger's seat. "Did she tell you anything about how to get through in that meeting of yours? A password or a secret way . . . Wait."

"What?"

"That." Lou pointed straight ahead. "Someone's coming."

Kellan peered through the window again. Through the ancient patterns on the Quarter gate, she spotted an automi strolling toward them, and as the shining shape of metal grew closer, the gate groaned, and its doors parted. Only when they opened fully could she and Lou see what awaited them beyond.

Most of Riz was paved roads and huddled buildings. The entrance to Courtier Quarter was a paradise of green. Sure, flowers hung in the baskets from the Crown District's streetlamps, and she'd spotted a few baby palms on the Makers' Strip. But in the Quarter, live oak trees with mossy branches and great, curling boughs canopied a single road of cobbled claybrick. The earth rose and fell in gently rolling hills, and with the breeze came the faintest smell of the sea. Riz ended at this golden gate, behind which Mesny's automi Xo stood aside to let the car through.

Xo wouldn't join them on their journey. She was off on an errand she wouldn't explain. But she made her introduction and pointed Lou in the right direction. "To reach the manor," she'd said, "keep left on the road until the sixth fork. Then turn right."

There was only one main road in all of Courtier Quarter, and above it, lanterns glowed softly in the settling night. Lou turned down the sixth fork, where the trees weren't as thick and the lanterns not as many, until the trees cleared and their journey ended. Or had just begun.

Mesny's manor sat on a cliff. Nothing but a single man-dug pond stood in the center of its roundabout, which made the manor itself seem even more surreal. There were so many wings and towers that Kellan could hardly make out the building's original frame. Some of them even defied gravity, dangling over the open sea like a fisherman's lure.

"Well," said Lou, "at least now we know why that Quarter gate is so tall. Can't imagine a regular old city gate hiding a place like this. I'm surprised I never saw this house on the skyline. It's *huge*."

She parked, and they climbed out of the car. They walked up the steps, each footfall heavier than the last, until they faced a pair of mahogany doors twice their height. In the last few days, Kellan had seen skyscrapers and noblemin, touched platinum and spoken with machines, but despite all those things, standing at the mouth of Mesny's home made lead weights out of her feet. "You want the honors?"

"Nah," said Lou, voice cracked. "She invited you, right? I'm just here to see you past the door. Go ahead."

"You're the native. You should knock."

"I'd be a right-awful host if I did, though, so—"

"But you're not a host, you're a—"

Neither of them got the chance. Slowly, one door opened with a low creak. Unlike the fence or the gate, it didn't act on its own.

Behind it, not but five feet from the ground, stood another automi. She peeked out from the crack, the room beyond cast in shadow. This automi had cobalt chrome plating, porcelain glamours fashioned into a modest and unassuming dress, mother-of-pearl inlays, and a round and soft-featured face. She was beautiful. Adorable, almost. At least on the surface. There was a sharpness behind her large eyes, which may have been doe-like any other day. She glared at Kellan and Lou with intense suspicion. "Who are you." It was a demand, not a question.

"Kellan. Ms. Mesny—"

"Madame Master Maker Mesny."

"*Madame* Mesny." Luckily for both of them, Kellan's leaden feet kept her from kicking the little automi in the shin. "She's expecting me."

Lou leaned forward before Kellan could stop her. "This one's nice, too," she said, admiring the runework on the metal and at the gears. "But why is its face like that?"

The little automi turned its nose up. "There is nothing wrong with my face."

"I ain't say nothing was wrong with it."

"What if I questioned the structure of *your* face? Hmm? You would assume that something was wrong with it, for why else would anyone question a face?"

"I was just wondering why you was frowning so, that's all—"

"Cyn!" Mesny interrupted from somewhere inside, far

enough away that her call echoed off the walls. "Be a dear and let them in, please?"

The automi named Cyn grumbled something unintelligible and pulled open the door.

Kellan had never seen anything like it. Massive portraits of Mesnys past framed in gold hung from every wall. The ceiling was so high that Kellan couldn't make out the pattern on its tiles, the chandelier so large it'd shake the manor's foundation if it came crashing down. It was all so big, all so open, and all made her feel incredibly small.

"Madame Master Maker Mesny said to expect a bushy-haired girl with an unfriendly face and 'horrendous dress sense,'" said Cyn from behind. "Madame Master Maker Mesny spoke nothing of a lanky second."

"Well," said Lou, "I'm sure Maker Madame—"

"Madame Master Maker."

"Master Making—"

"Either Madame or Maker Mesny will do just as well. My full title is very much a mouthful."

Footsteps clicked from above. Mesny had changed into a jewel-green robe with matching kitten-heeled slippers. Kellan briefly wondered if she coordinated her day- and nightwear on purpose. "And who might you be?" she said to Lou. "You haven't a badge, so I will assume you weren't a part of the Exposition."

Kellan's face went hot. Did she still have hers on? She unpinned it as subtly as she could and stuffed it into her pocket.

"No, ma'am. Uh, Madame," said Lou with surprising ease. "I'm Louise Roussel, Sudton Roussels. You can call me Lou, though. Kellan's friend and driver. Mostly friend, though, and a driver when she needs one. Didn't want her wandering on her lonesome, see. She's a little nervous."

Kellan stiffened, the prick of her pin digging into her palm. "I'm not nervous."

"All right, well, she might not be nervous, but she's about as used to the city as a stone to the sky, so I figured I'd come as moral support."

After too long, Mesny grinned a small, sharp grin and said to Kellan, "I like her."

Lou gave Kellan two thumbs up.

"But Cyn, however blunt, is right in part. It is rather late, and as we've much to do in the morning, I would prefer to show Kellan to her room swiftly so I can retire to mine. You're welcome to visit, of course."

"I am?"

"She is?" asked Cyn and Kellan together.

"You will find, Kellan, that there are precious few people I like. When I come upon a new one—that is, a person I deem relatively tolerable—I think it only polite to feed them, at least. I will assume, Lou, that you eat breakfast."

"Oh, I love breakfast."

"Only the best of us do. On the morning after the next, as I'm afraid Kellan and I will be far too busy tomorrow, I believe we're scheduled to have blackened redfish. Does nine work for you?"

"Nine works fine!"

"Marvelous."

Lou, after smiling wide, looked to the window and sucked her teeth. "Dammit—Darnit. Sorry, ma'am—I gotta go. Mama might kill me if I'm not home in ten."

"And we don't want that, do we?" Mesny shooed her away. "Off you go."

Lou waved goodbye on her way out the door, but stopped with one foot over the threshold. "How am I supposed to get back in? The Quarter gate was—"

"It will open," said Mesny. "You've been invited."

Invited. For as long as Kellan had worked in Edgar's shop, she'd never once heard of a make that functioned like that.

She and Lou exchanged confused glances. The door clicked shut, leaving Kellan alone with Mesny and her annoying second automi.

"What a lovely girl." Mesny tightened the sash around her waist. "You make friends quickly, I see."

"I barely know her."

"Very well. How often can we say we truly 'know' anyone, after all?" Mesny let the silence sit for a moment before she walked back up the steps. "Thank you, Cyn, for answering the door. Kellan, with me. I will show you to your room."

Cyn bowed and left without so much as a glance back. By the time Kellan registered that she'd been given an order, Mesny had already cleared the first staircase. Kellan took her suitcase in one hand, hitched her backpack higher on her shoulder with the other, and rushed after her.

"I hope you don't mind that I've chosen one of the north-wing rooms." Mesny climbed the steps with ease, heels clinking against the marble. Kellan didn't fare nearly as well. She'd lost her breath somewhere on the third flight of stairs. "It's reasonably close to the second workshop, but unfortunately far from the nearest kitchen and dining room, so the walk to mealtimes will be a bore."

"Right."

"But you wouldn't know the way to the kitchen yet, would you? No matter. I'll send Cyn for you. She'll show you the way in the morning."

Kellan wheezed. "Okay."

"Or Xo, of course, but I'm sure they'll settle the matter of who between themselves. Your suite includes a restroom and a study, but if you find either uncomfortable, you're free to use whichever others you prefer. There are quite a few of each in the wing, so if you—"

"How does the Quarter gate work?"

Mesny stopped, and her heels' last click lingered in the quiet. The painted eyes of her ancestors stared down from high-hung portraits on darkened walls. Their expressions were hard, their chins high and mouths drawn taut, the cut of their clothes sharpening from hand-dyed bond rags to gold-threaded finery as the bloodline went on. Kellan found the resemblance in a painting of a man in a fashionable hat, who shared Mesny's aquiline nose, and whose tired smile was faraway. "Pardon?"

"The Quarter gate." Kellan took the pause to catch her breath. "I can't figure out how it can open and close like that based on—"

"A spoken invitation." Mesny pulled her robe further around her. "The same question has baffled many a maker. The short answer is that we don't quite know."

"And the long answer?"

"That gate is the oldest part of the city, and one of the few parts left standing after the Liberation. Old, old make, predating the Conquering, but not quite ancient."

Kellan looked out the window, where the Quarter's strange golden gate stood defiantly against the city's modern skyline. The Conquering and the Liberation were the two wars that defined Nanseau's history—the first, when the Lidonch invaded the island and Nanseau's motherland mysteriously fell to the sea, creating the Swallow at the center of their world map and marking the beginning of a thousand-year reign; the second, just over three hundred years ago, when Lidon fell and Nanseau sent them sailing north once more. Most Nansis didn't talk much about either, and sometimes Kellan wondered if historians named the wars so plainly because they didn't want to think about it any longer than they had to. It was a history that the nation couldn't afford to dwell on, despite how much they'd lost. Lidon left its mark in their language, their music, their art like ash from the fallout, but the world left them no time to search for what they were before. Not if Nanseau wanted to survive.

Mesny looked at Kellan like a puzzle she couldn't solve. "Do you know what I find nearly as curious?"

"No?"

"Of all the questions to ask on your first night in a strange woman's home, you choose to ask about a gate miles away."

Kellan had more, of course. If her room was closest to the second workshop, how many were there? What time did the postofficer arrive on weekdays, and at which door? But the gate. Not one law of makecraft justified such a peculiar function. None, at least, that she could figure on her own.

"It was bugging me," she said with a shrug. "That's all."

". . . I see." Mesny's expression softened. After another moment, she continued down the hall without another word.

Eventually they arrived in the north wing, and soon after, the entrance to Kellan's new room. Mesny opened the door for Kellan to slip through first. The study alone was two—no, three—times larger than her attic bedroom, its walls lined with cherrywood bookshelves and gold-handled cabinets. A writing desk stood by the window, with a workbench just beside it. In the center sat a sofa with velvet throw pillows threaded in gold. The lamps on either side of it cast the room in a warm glow.

"There are metals and gears in the workbench drawers," said Mesny from the entrance. "We'll have to get you a carver of your own, but until then, you're free to borrow one of my spares. Your bedroom is just beyond that archway."

Kellan stepped farther inside. The bed was larger than any bed should be. It could easily fit five of her. Six, if she skipped breakfast. And the view that awaited her beyond its window seat . . . all night sky and open sea.

"Lou, I suspect, will bring the rest of your things come morning?"

Kellan set her suitcase down and pulled her pathetic little bag from her shoulder. If she held it a certain way, Mesny wouldn't see the holes. "This is all I brought."

"That won't do at all. I'll send for someone to purchase suitable clothes as well."

"Oh, you don't have t—"

"What is your dress size?"

"Really, that's—"

"It may be best to have you properly fitted? Yes, yes, that sounds much better. I'll send for my tailor by the week's end. In the meantime, rest. We've quite a day tomorrow."

Before Kellan could protest again, Mesny was gone in a whoosh of chiffon. She closed the door behind her, and the quiet of the Quarter set in. Rustling oak leaves from the center-garden. Katydids chirping from the branches. A lone mourning dove, its call unanswered in the open air.

She sat on the sofa, patted the velvet cushions on either side of her. Soft. Softer than anything she'd ever touched. It was too much at once. Too much. No number of deep breaths could ease the weight of all the change, of all she suddenly didn't know. Of all she'd left behind.

The moon, the stars, the lanterns in the trees weren't enough to light the night. She followed the call of the dove, of the rustling leaves, and curled on top of the window seat. With her back against the glass, she made a pillow out of her bag. It smelled like mayonnaise, shoeshine, and corroded iron, but that night she didn't mind. That night, at least something smelled like home.

"The Snake and the Isle"

"The Lion and the Hare"

"The Spider and the Shadow"

"The Sky and the Sea"

—*Lost Tales from the Swallow.* Table of Contents.
Translation by Bron-Priame Boivin, 297 Guilded.
Author unknown.

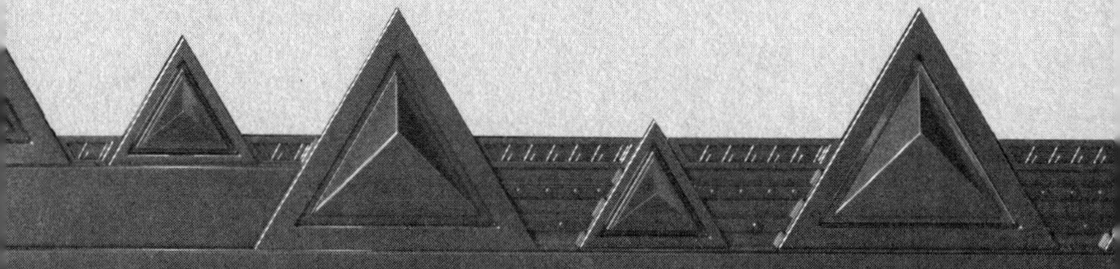

EIGHT

"Second stairwell . . . two lefts . . . one right . . . the door next to the top hat . . ."

Kellan leaned against the banister, tangled hair hanging over her face. She didn't know how long she'd been searching. The first three of Xo's instructions were easy enough to follow. Without them, Kellan would have been lost in the manor's many halls for days. But as she ran up and down the hall those directions led her to, past framed golden sculptures and tiny automi hard at work, she couldn't find a single thing that so much as hinted at a top hat. It was vital that she find that door as quickly as she could.

Because Kellan DuCuivre was late.

Had she known Madame Mesny planned her first lesson so early in the morning, she would have set the alarm clock. Instead, she'd spent too long fussing with expensive clothes that didn't suit her frame, trusted Cyn when she led Kellan to breakfast, filled up with babyhead biscuits and mushroom pol, and learned too late that Mesny liked to start her days with the morning birds.

"You did not tell her?" asked Xo when she'd found Kellan in Mesny's smallest kitchen forty-five minutes after schedule.

Cyn had shrugged a glittering shoulder, tone dripping with spite. "She did not ask."

Now sweat darkened Kellan's new cotton dress in unsightly patches, and she had no idea where she was. At least Cyn hadn't followed her. A moment longer with that self-important mechanical brat, and Kellan would have tossed her over the railing.

"Second stairwell. Two lefts. One right. The door next to the top ha—"

Something bumped against her boot. One of the cleaning automi, built to reach the corners of things the larger ones couldn't, tried to polish her dirty shoes. In the silence, traces of music trickled in through the walls. There was something familiar in the jazz. She followed that instead.

The sound was loudest behind an oaken door a few yards down the hall. Beside it hung a little bronze top hat with the words "Maudelaire Mesny, Master Engineer" inscribed beneath its brim. She must have run past it five or six times.

The tiny automi hadn't relented. It tried again to climb on top of her toes, so she shook it off as she knocked. The music softened, and seconds later, Mesny opened the door.

She'd decided to wear orange that day. It would have made

anyone else look like a pumpkin, but somehow Mesny found a way to make it look intimidating. "I see you've eaten breakfast." She said, and moved aside for Kellan to step in. "Do you intend to save those grains of pol for later?"

Kellan wiped her cheeks with the back of her hand. "I didn't mean to be late, I didn't know—"

"I don't care about your intentions." Mesny closed the door on the tiny automi, who bumped into the oak a few more times before scurrying off. "I care about what you do."

This study must have once belonged to Maudelaire, House Mesny's courtier of two generations ago, whom Kellan knew little about. Kellan hadn't known Mesny for long, but it looked nothing like her. She kept her office above the Parlour clean and open, decorated it with paintings and figurines. This one was cramped, with no windows and one other door, half a dozen typewriters, too many cabinets, and not a single piece of art. Yet bright patches checkered the wallpaper where frames used to be. Kellan wondered if Mesny had torn them down, forgotten to put up pieces of her own. The only thing in the study that looked remotely *her* was the small phonograph atop one of the desks. That, and the engineering tools on the middlemost table.

"Has Cyn been helpful?" She'd splayed out sheets upon sheets of gold and platinum, a dozen kinds of gears in twice as many sizes, foil, spectacles, a delicate weight, and two basic carvers. "I crafted her to organize the books in the north-wing library. She's strong for her size, but unfortunatcly for us both, she has the social grace of a lead weight."

"Hadn't noticed."

"Good. Then we can begin." Mesny turned the music down. "You've impressed me. That is a feat in itself. Your technique, however, is flawed. You lack control at the wrists. You take longer routes than you should. And worst of all, you hesitate."

Kellan's mouth went dry. She may as well have swallowed sand. "Oh."

"Lucky for you, these are all things that can be remedied with time, practice, training, and a few tricks." She handed Kellan one of the carvers and a sheet of gold foil. "How many of these did you use for the bug's bodice?"

"Um—"

"Don't hesitate."

"One. One. Just one."

"Good. Now." She returned to the workbench and moved aside some of the tools she had so carefully arranged. "What would you have done if the make required two sheets?"

"Um—"

Mesny glared. This woman wasn't intimidating. She was terrifying.

"I'd use another metal," Kellan managed. "Platinum, maybe."

"Say this is all you have. Say you *must* use gold."

"Then I guess I'll borrow somebody else's."

The clatter of Mesny's tongs against the tabletop echoed off Maudelaire's barren walls. She clicked her nails against the wood, the hinge of her jaw so tight Kellan worried she'd crack a tooth. When Mesny stood taller, rolled her shoulder, and cracked her neck, the air in Maudelaire's study chilled as if in anticipation.

"What did you think of the Exposition?" she asked calmly. "Did you learn much? Did you make any friends?"

"Learn?" Kellan wiped her palms on her thighs. "Yes? Friends, no. It was our first Expo, too, so with nothing to compare it to, I guess it was pretty nice."

"Pretty nice." Mesny chuckled humorlessly, crossing to the workbench's other side. Nothing stood between them now but space and silence. "Is that how you imagine the trials? A place to learn? To make friends? That you'll get away with a few clever quips and toymaking parlor tricks?"

"Toymaking is *not* 'parlor tricks'—"

"You will face the brightest young minds in the world. Students of the Inner Crescent. Savants from South Ital. One boy from the Bones patented his first knot before his eighth nameday."

By then, Mesny had cleared the distance between them, the click of her heel's last step lingering like smoke after fire.

"Every one of them knows what it takes to earn their pin. They will steal. They will lie. They will scheme and sabotage, and when they sense the *slightest* whiff of weakness, they will crush its source with their bare, talented hands."

Kellan lifted her chin, face hot and fists trembling. "So you pick a thief and a liar. Is that what I'm learning today? The highborn art of crushing what you think's lower than you?"

Challenging the most powerful woman in the nation was a dangerous bluff, especially when Edgar's fate depended on their success. She didn't know exactly when her anger swallowed her fear. She also didn't know which she hated more: the chance that she was right or the part of her that almost understood.

She'd never know either way. Mesny left Kellan without an answer, taking her place behind the workbench as though nothing had ever happened. "Sit." Traces of iron hardened her tone. "Perhaps you'll finish your first trial with your bones intact."

Their lesson began with what Mesny called the basics: the three core principles of runetheory that made up makecraft's foundation. Francom's Theorem of True Matter, Kellan knew, explained why makecraft demanded metal. She hadn't, however, known the gruesome history of malchemy behind it, which Mesny described in vivid detail in case she ever felt compelled toward the taboo of carving into skin or bone. Heroux's Equation, she'd learned from watching Edgar, who preferred low-grade alloys over high-grade gold and silver, as they forgave his mistakes and didn't mind his simple runework. Mesny reviewed the third as a formality. The Balance Paradox stated that makecraft could neither create nor destroy. It only altered what already was.

Kellan spent hours carving to Mesny's increasingly bizarre conditions:

"One metal, no cuts."

"Carve this bird to fly with two runes that don't include Flight."

"One word: 'lackadaisical.' Twenty-two minutes. Begin."

After that, she judged Kellan's makes just as she said the forum would, assessing them for ingenuity, usefulness, and demonstration of potential. Kellan only passed once, and only because Xo pulled Mesny aside to take an emergency telephone call and repeating all the ways Kellan failed would have taken too long. Only when Kellan's fingers twitched with stifled frustration did Mesny slow down. "Come to the table," she'd said, "and I'll show you a trick."

Mesny set her carver to its dullest setting and handed Kellan another pair of magnifying spectacles. Good, because she wouldn't have been able to see what Mesny then carved into the center of the foil without them. She'd never seen a mark so small or a move so slight and practiced. Kellan put on the glasses and fumbled with the knobs until Mesny's carve shone clear and focused.

The rune for Pull. She recognized it immediately, as it was one of the simplest runes to carve. Then Mesny took out a second sheet of foil. Copper.

"I thought you said only gold?"

"I did." Mesny tore a piece off the corner and carved another rune in its center. This one was equally simple. This one was for Push.

There was little use for the Push rune in engineering, unless something required a levitating bit for show, but tinkers used it all the time. Tailors for hats and shoes with floating gemstones, sculptors for pieces that would normally tip over from excess weight, knackiers for . . . she wasn't sure what knackiers used the Push rune for, actually, but she was sure they did. It was odd, watching one of the most famous engineers carve a rune so many labeled as useless.

"Do you know what happens when you knot opposite runes?" Mesny held the sheet of copper to the light and adjusted her spectacles, checking her work.

Of course she did. It was that miscarve that had cost Edgar his hand all those years ago. In the early days, theorists leveled entire regions experimenting with complex runes and elaborate knots in the name of scientific advancement. One wrong curve in the wrong metal . . . Edgar had been lucky to walk away with the rest of his arm. "The results are—"

"Varied, yes, but most end in catastrophe. What use, then, would I have for these two opposites?"

Kellan must have looked like a fool as she racked her brain for an answer. She couldn't think of anything, and even when she came upon a theory that—

"Don't . . . hesitate."

"Idon'tknow," she blurted in one word. She slowed down. "I don't know."

Mesny nodded like she expected as much. For some reason, that made Kellan feel worse. "Observe," she said, and took the little sheet of copper into a pair of tongs.

It happened so fast that Kellan almost missed it. Mesny

hovered the copper corner an inch above the gold sheet, the Pull rune perfectly aligned with the Push, and turned the copper until the gold below hummed like a working make. When the humming rose to a window-cracking pitch, the sheet vibrated until it split from the center into a dozen parts.

Kellan didn't have a compass, but if she had, she'd have bet a month's profit that the foil split at equal angles. Mesny set the tongs and copper aside and spread apart the triangles. The cuts were so clean that Kellan worried Mesny would slice the pads of her fingers. "How?"

"It's a clever little trick, isn't it?" said Mesny with an amused smirk. "Well guarded among the engineers, where quickness is a necessity. As for how, we don't quite know. It's the culmination of decades of guesswork and experimentation, answering one question only to raise another. I liken making to a language. Nuanced. Alive. We're simply linguists deciphering the tongue."

Kellan pulled one of the triangles closer to her, peered at the pointed tip to make out what remained of the Pull rune. There was hardly any evidence of an indentation. And the edges, as she'd suspected, were sharp enough to cut.

"My hypothesis," Mesny said, gathering more supplies from the pile of tools she'd pushed aside, "is that it has something to do with tension and proximity. Because they are two separate sheets, the runes can't possibly knot, you see. Now, before I show you . . ." Mesny pulled off her spectacles. "What in the name of destruction is that noise?"

A slammed door. Shouting down the hall. One of the voices was familiar in the way of a faint, hard-to-reach itch.

"—truly the most incompetent piece of machinery," said the voice. Once Kellan recognized its haughtiness and uniquely clipped drawl, she put a face to the sound. "Minora! Minora, call off your machine, please."

Mesny raised a finger, excusing herself to open the door. Cyn, her snow-white hair out of place in her hurry, stood beside none other than Comte Cesaire. "Madame," she said, hands behind her back in a sloppy imitation of Xo, "he did not have an appointment, so I—"

"I don't need an appointment, you defunct—"

"Pierpont." Mesny smiled tightly and smoothed the front of her blouse. "A pleasure, as always. But I must ask that you keep your insults to yourself."

Kellan had only seen his silhouette before. The comte was an unremarkable-looking man with ruddy cheeks and manicured eyebrows. His suit was pinstriped and navy, and an obvious attempt to minimize his impressive belly. At least he was polite enough to remove his hat. "Ever so sorry, Minora. I'd have arrived sooner had the swamp rabble not decided to dance in the streets from dawn's break," he said with a hurried bow. "You know me and my temper."

"Too well, my friend. Too well."

"Right!" With a brisk laugh, he invited himself in and set his hat on the worktable. "You're a busy woman, so I'll get straight to . . . Oh. I see you have a guest."

"I do, indeed," said Mesny. "Meet my bid for the Guild of Engineers. Kellan DuCuivre."

"It's a pleasure to make—" The comte's eyes had glazed over, but once Mesny's words sank in, he stood at alert. His ruddy cheeks caught color when he took her in: the carver in her hand, the unruly mess of woolly hair at the top of her head, how her dress bit into her stomach in a way that made her look like an unfortunate sack of flour. Kellan didn't know much about style, but even she could see how this pastel green made her complexion look less like burnt umber and more like bloated driftwood.

"What was it you wanted?" Mesny returned to her spot at the worktable and straightened the bits of metal that the comte had disturbed with his hat. "If it was breakfast, I could always have a plate fixed for you to go."

The comte recovered with disturbing quickness. He smiled wide with too-white teeth and adjusted the collar of his waistcoat. "If I may speak with you privately, Minora," he said evenly. "I would hate to cause your 'company' any undue concern."

Mesny sighed and set her carver on the worktable. "Very well," she said, on her way to the mysterious other door. "Be quick about it. Today is a busy day."

"I'm sure." Comte Cesaire followed her out. "Machine," he called, not bothering to look back, "send them in once they've found their way."

Kellan hadn't noticed Cyn waiting by the threshold. She

didn't give time for Kellan to look very long, anyhow, before she turned on her heel and left to wherever "they" were.

The walls weren't thin enough to keep Mesny and the comte's conversation private, but he sure did try. His voice was a hiss that seeped through the crack beneath the door: ". . . social suicide. You've lost your mind."

"I misplaced that poor thing years ago." Compared to the comte, Mesny sounded especially calm. "Creation, I hate this room."

"Have you thought of the precedent this would set? How livid this would make—"

"Mind your tone in my house, Pierpont, and try harder not to interrupt me. Now, if you'll just . . ."

Kellan knocked once against the workbench to keep from slamming her fist in frustration. Working with Madame Mesny . . . She could get used to it. Eventually. She had to, for Edgar's sake and her own. But the look on the comte's face, equal parts dismissal and disgust, left her head pounding.

". . . is a mistake? If enough of the other courtiers find this at all inappropriate, it's your name they'll have. It's your wrists in the cutter."

"The Court has neither the nerve nor a sharp enough blade."

"Then what of mine, Minora? People are *missing*!"

Kellan loosened her fist. Mesny and the comte lowered their voices further, making it impossible for Kellan to hear them from her place at the workbench. Riz was a massive city.

People must go missing every day, but that was a problem for the ordergarde. Not a bureaucrat. Not unless the people missing were many and the reason behind it posed a threat to the city at large. Something like that would rule the airwaves. There'd be no way Kellan could have spent three days in Riz and never heard of a situation so dire.

And even then, what did that have to do with the Guild of Engineers?

Kellan approached the second door with careful steps. Even when she pressed her ear against the wood, she couldn't catch more than whispers. Whispers and the soft creak of cabinet hinges on her side of the wall.

Light from overhead caught a scuttling flash of gold on its way out of Maudelaire's study. The tiny automi from earlier, most likely, come to finish its work. Kellan left Mesny and the comte to their secrets and peeked inside, where she found several empty, dust-coated jars and an old oak box.

It belonged to another time. The lacquer had worn, and the clasp had rusted, but the engravings on the lid were still deep enough to trace with her thumbnail. It may have been chipped, and the linework uneven. But something about the symbol felt . . . grand. Powerful. Familiar, almost, but strange all the same. Before she could think better of it, Kellan undid the latch and opened the box.

It was full of shattered glass.

Kellan slumped against the counter. What had she expected, tiny copies of schematics to new automi models? A chunk of unrefined rhodium? It wasn't well hidden. It wasn't even locked. She took one of the larger shards and held it to the light, and nearly yelped when she spotted two people by the door in its dusty reflection.

Axel stood with a biscuit in his left hand. To his right, Kellan recognized the Crown Hall secretary from her first night in the city. Now that she wasn't behind the reception desk, she stood shorter than Kellan had thought she would, but the way her voile dress hung on her wispy frame made Kellan tug at the bow at her hip. Both looked as surprised as Kellan felt, but at least the secretary had the decency to try masking it. Axel stumbled to catch the biscuit he'd dropped before it hit the ground. "You?"

"Me."

"What are you— How did you—"

"Same as you. Two legs through the front door."

"Cyn sent us up," said the secretary. She'd pulled her hair into a higher bun but left two long curls loose by her ears. "Are they behind that door? What are they talking about?"

"And why are they screaming?"

"Come in," called Mesny from inside. "All three of you. I've had enough of this."

Mesny opened the door with such force that it scattered the foil on the workbench. No wonder Mesny hated the spare room. It was one broom shy of a broom closet, dank and windowless and entirely too small to fit five people.

Mesny smoothed her top on her way into the study. "Why

don't you all take a seat? You make me nervous, standing as you are."

"No need," said the comte. "We're on our way out."

"Already?" Axel looked between Mesny and the comte. Kellan couldn't tell if he was grateful or confused. "I didn't hear a decision. I'd barely call that a conversation."

"It seems the Madame has plans of her own." The comte gestured with a flick of his wrist for Axel and the secretary to follow him, but neither of them did, still recovering from the sight of Kellan in the middle of Mesny's workshop.

"Oh! Goodness. All this chaos, and we've forgone propriety. The lady here"—Mesny gestured toward the secretary, who waved—"is Ginnel DuRiz, Comte Cesaire's assistant. This young man is Axel Bonne, Monsieur Bonne's eldest."

The box of broken glass slipped through her suddenly cold fingers.

Axel caught that, too. There were few names that carried the kind of power the Bonne name did. Mesny's was one of them. Monsieur Bedoier Bonne, whose grandfather invented the runic engine that earned Nanseau its place on the world stage, was supposed to be devastating for his age. The heirs to his house—Axel's siblings, she realized too late—were the epitome of highborn class and beauty, brilliant and graceful, but ruthless and calculating, and Monsieur Bonne's presence was said to be so intense that it sent any room he entered into a chill. Perhaps Axel was still growing into his father's exactingness, because when she looked at him, she felt no such coldness.

"We should go." He handed Kellan the box, lid closed and clasp shut. "Before he starts screaming again."

"And we wouldn't want that." Mesny patted his shoulder and led the way. "I'll walk you down. Kellan, feel free to make yourself comfortable. I shouldn't be long."

Axel hesitated, but eventually followed along. Before leaving, he looked to Kellan once again, and that time, she saw the apology in his eyes. That and a trace of something else. He was gone before she could place it.

Kellan and Ginnel were only left alone for a few moments. With the shouting ended, jazz filled the study once more, gentle and clear.

"Another tower rat?" Ginnel folded her arms and laughed. "I wouldn't have guessed."

Neither would Kellan, but the moment Mesny had made the introduction, Ginnel's surname made it clear—DuRiz, of Riz, just as Kellan was DuCuivre, of Cuivreton. She could usually tell from the given name, but like her, Ginnel must have been enormously lucky the day she arrived on her namehouse's steps—the two syllables their namehouse matrons plucked from the bowl at least sounded vaguely Nansi—but Ginnel carried herself like a woman of stature and poise, like the weight of her stone tower somehow hadn't left her as broken as the rest of them. She hid her scars well. "How long?"

"Five years now," Ginnel said, picking at her blouse's cuff. "You?"

"Three."

"I imagine the Mesny manor is a nice trade-up."

Kellan chortled humorlessly. If only Ginnel knew the cost. "Yeah. Pretty nice."

Ginnel smiled as softly as the music. It was a rare sort of smile, more in the eyes than the mouth, the kind Kellan shared with the rare DuCuivre who chose to stay in the village. The kind that read *I see you, and I know.*

Ginnel shared more in that single smile than she could have in an hour-long conversation. "Good luck," she said, and turned to leave.

Kellan should have said something else. Ginnel might not have been a DuCuivre, but she was a Du, and one of the few people Kellan knew now who would understand how out of place it felt to be surrounded by so much wealth and power. They were dirty boots on porcelain tiles, sweaty fingers on stained glass. If they didn't tread lightly, the Court would wipe them out. Them, and any trace they'd have left behind.

But she didn't. The click of Ginnel's heels faded as she hurried to catch up with the other three, and Kellan spoke too late. "You too," she said into the silence. "You too."

NINE

Mesny filled almost every second of the next week with tests, lectures, and drills. When Kellan slept, she dreamed of theorems. When Kellan ate, she tasted metal. When she found rare moments of quiet, where she could sit and be and catch up to the circumstances that had changed so suddenly around her, the contest's first trial cast its shadow from over her shoulder. Eight would go in. Two would be left behind.

She'd mistakenly thought she'd have enough time to write Edgar a letter on a day in between. And technically, she did. She had two free hands and a few minutes to spend outside before the sun set. It was a beautiful evening, the sky slate-blue with new dusk and the grass beaded with dew. Unfortunately, because Kellan stood spread-eagled by a hiccupping, out-of-date automi armed with cold metal fingers and measuring tape, she could hardly enjoy it.

Mesny's tailor, an old man set in his ways, had sent his

bolt-kabob in preparation for Kellan's new wardrobe. "The forum will judge everything you do from the moment you step onto the stage," Mesny had said in warning. "Dress like you're worthy, and they'll believe it, too." While the automi measured the inside seam of her leg, Kellan tried to draft a few more sentences. Apparently, putting her arms together was too much movement for this bolt-kabob, so it gripped her biceps in its squeaky metal claws and straightened her arms for her. Again.

Lou, who had stayed for dinner, threw stones down the cliff and into the sea. They sank with soft plops over radio commercials for trainlines and Chromerollers, news of the Fault's curfew changed from seven to six, and in stretches of quiet in the broadcast, the background song of the Quarter's humming runes. It was harder to tell in the busier districts, but in the Quarter, the hum was a constant drone, faint as a kitten's purr—a reminder that despite Kellan's circumstances, Riz was still a city of wonder, rebuilt from the ruins of war into a place teeming with more makecraft than she could explore in two lifetimes.

The automi soon finished its work. Lou let the last of her pebbles fall to the sea. Kellan watched her drive away until she became a dot in the distance, taking with her the last moments closest to what Kellan could call peace.

When trial day finally arrived, Mesny and Xo had traveled east to Ital. Kellan had gathered that there was some sort of political emergency from what little she'd caught of their whispers the night before. "You're as ready as we could've made you," Mesny had insisted on her way out. "Lou will be your escort, and Cyn will make your introduction." Now Kellan, Lou, and Cyn stood in front of Lou's death trap, and Kellan had never felt less ready in her entire life.

"It is even more hideous up close," said Cyn.

"Hey!" Lou pointed at Cyn in warning with the hand that wasn't busy unlocking the door. "I worked my ass off to afford this thing."

"I do not understand that turn of phrase." Cyn climbed into the front seat after Kellan opened the door for herself. Slamming it on Cyn's metal behind would have meant denting a make worth more bill than she could earn in three lifetimes, so she settled for a glare and sat in the back. "No amount of work could possibly result in the loss of your gluteal region."

It took a few tries for Lou to turn the engine. On the drive, Kellan wrote, Lou and Cyn argued over semantics in the front, dusk gave way to night, and Riz's streetlights lit the dark in a single flicker. Once they reached Sudton, Lou wove through side streets and backstreets, turning up the radio when Cyn picked at her technique or insisted on a more "optimal route." Kellan was counting the bulbs when a frayed sawdust-colored coattail dashed across the road. It was gone before she could get a second look.

"You sure this is the right place?" asked Lou when they left Sudton's neighborhoods behind. Here the road cracked, and warped wood shielded broken windows of shops long abandoned. "I know this place. The guy who runs it, too. It can hardly fit the three of us, let alone half a guild."

"The Madame does not make mistakes," said Cyn.

"Everybody makes mistakes."

"So says one who has doubtlessly made countless of them."

Lou pulled into a run-down car shop. Models rusted from wear and rain peppered its tiny lot. Kellan could see neither price marks nor signposts, but she did find an old man at a workbench under a crooked awning carving into steel, ash gray sparks drifting along the breeze.

"See? It's just Mr. Matthieu. We call him Ol' Matty since he's been here forever. He even sold me this—"

"You talk too much," said Cyn, who had already stepped out of the car.

"Wait, what are you— Get back here!" Lou called. "He's busy! And I'm still two payments behind!"

Kellan followed Cyn out of Lou's car, tension easing at the quiet and fresh air. Theirs was the only running car in the lot, and were it not for the glint of metal on Ol' Matty's collar, Kellan would have thought Mesny'd made a mistake, too.

"Got a stinger in your neck," said Ol' Matty. He never looked up from his work.

Mesny taught her the passwords only days ago. She'd whispered them before bed, on her way to breakfast, as she stretched her fingers between lessons. Still, fear iced her spine in the waiting silence.

"I've been watched for too long."

Something clicked behind him. A lock, by the sound? But the only door to Ol' Matty's shop was already cracked open. She couldn't see what lay beyond it.

"Go on." He handed her a carver. Firwood. Quartzite inlay. Alchemized steel carvepoint. "Or you'll miss the show."

Lou stood dumbfounded by the car. After a long, lung-aching breath, Kellan walked in step with Cyn. When she gripped the doorknob, it was loose and cold. She pulled the door open, forcing her eyes not to close. And the moment she stepped over the threshold, she was engulfed in total darkness.

Then the door shut behind them. There was no breeze; only the smell of earth and metal lingered. But from where? Light from nowhere lit seats atop a pillar so tall Kellan had to crane her neck to see it fully. The forum, Kellan suspected, but something was off. She counted seven engineers and one empty seat.

"There she is! Our eighth."

Kellan jumped back from the sudden voice, arms raised in defense.

"Whoa! That's a delicate instrument, not a prison shank. Did I scare you?" A boy held up his palms in mock surrender, his wide lips still curved in a mischievous grin. "I'd apologize, but everyone's tense, given the ambience. So really, it's not my fault, is it?"

Kellan took him in when her eyes adjusted to the dark, lowering the fist she'd curled around her carver. Lanky. Short, bushy hair. Clean face. Long nose. Eyes almost like hers, so dark a brown they were almost black. He moved with a swagger that suited him as well as his obnoxious bow tie, which wasn't very well at all.

"Why does everyone talk so much?" grumbled Cyn.

"This one *talks*! You should see the other automi, Eighth. Might as well be statues. Right creepy in the dark."

"You have a number, too?" Kellan asked dryly. "Six? Seven?"

"Number one, preferably, but no. Everyone else knows everyone else's name, but yours is a mystery. Exciting—"

"There's one seat open."

"—stuff. Seat? Where? I've been standing for hours."

"The forum." Kellan pointed to the huddled shapes atop the pillar. "If you're down here, then they're the ones judging us. There's supposed to be eight of them."

The boy hmm'd in thought. "Maybe they took the scenic route?"

"Funny."

"Was it really?" came another voice. "I didn't think so."

This voice came from a young girl. She looked to be around ten, perhaps eleven, and entirely too close to Kellan's side for comfort. She hadn't even heard the child approach. Long saddle-brown hair hung uncombed down her back, the kind of straight that was as uncommon to Nansis as snowfall. It bent weakly with the ghosts of undone braids. Through its curtain, the brass downward arrow pin of an alchemist caught the distant light. Two garnets: expert physician. The savant from Ital.

"The game's rigged." This voice, she recognized. The

girl from Crown Hall's elevator approached with a playful smile. "I'd put my bill on the alchemist, if Nansis weren't so gamble-shy."

Kellan followed the girl's gaze to the alchemist. Before Riz, she'd never met one beside her village physician. They rarely settled west of the river, as the minebelt's villages offered little to further their craft. Of all the schools of makecraft, those under the Guild of Alchemy were the only ones who regularly practiced on materials other than metal, requiring a level of discipline that put them in league with the finest engineers. The girl from the elevator was right. If Edgar's life hadn't been at stake, Kellan knew exactly where she would have put her money.

Behind the girl, the boy she'd called Elo stood among the other half of the bids—all who, excluding a particularly nervous one no one let speak for too long, looked like the first trial was more an inconvenience than a requisite. She remembered the language Elo spoke all those weeks ago, the old theorist in velvet who kept them near. If anyone was the boy from the Bones who'd patented a knot at eight years, it was him.

"Don't mind my brother," said the girl. "Today and . . . you know. Back then. What happened at the Exposition, it wasn't his fault, you know? It was—"

A bell chimed from overhead. Two automi left the other bids to collect the child and the girl from the elevator. Kellan wasn't particularly interested, anyway. At least, not in what

Elo had to do with Mesny's workshop. She didn't have the time to be. Right now, she had to focus on how to beat him.

"We're the odd ones out, it looks like," said the lanky boy. "Alliance?"

"I'm all right."

"I hope so. You won't last long if you aren't."

The bell chimed again, and the lanky boy stepped back into the darkness with a wink and a lazy salute. "Good luck," he sang, voice softened from distance.

A mechanical voice introduced the forum foremin—a theorist whose work Kellan didn't know much about.

"Welcome, bids, to your first trial," she called, her voice booming from every corner. She and the forum watched from so high a platform Kellan still couldn't make out any of their faces, even when the dark lifted over a small section of stage, where the bids would make their introductions.

"First bid?"

An automi and the skittish boy from earlier stepped onto the lit stage. Well dressed. Nervous. He reminded Kellan too much of a mouse tossed into a snake den.

"Expert Maker Avenelle Avis," announced his automi, "School of Architecture, nominates Assistant Engineer Harmon Barbier of Nanseau, New Montague."

"His reason?"

"T-to build Nanseau's future," said Harmon, his voice cracking near the end.

"Does the panel accept this bid?"

"The panel accepts," said five voices in answer.

"They can reject us?" Kellan whispered to Cyn as quietly as she could.

"The Madame mentioned nothing of rejection," she answered with unconvincing confidence. "But she shared very little of the process."

The bids went on forever. Izod Thoreau, a muscled boy from Runer's Bay, nominated without even an assistant's pin. Faustin Quain, the grinning boy from earlier, bid as an alchemist's assistant. Navud Tinzraut, from one of the Crescent Isles, was somehow on a first-name basis with half the panel. And Orana, the child from the Itaisian Coast, had reached expert in every other guild of makecraft. Their reasons ranged from money to honor, power to plain curiosity. Some, Kellan even believed.

"Expert Maker René Villiers, School of Theology, nominates Assistant Engineers Maricar and Marielo Bitao of Gumbat'kanao, the Bones."

The twins from the elevator stepped onto the stage. Kellan had guessed right.

"Two? The reason?"

"Asylum," said Maricar.

It was slight, but she stiffened right after, as if ready for the forum's blow of refusal. Kellan didn't know much about the Bones. It was a cluster of tiny islands farther east, just below Old Lidon, that won their liberation a few hundred years after Nanseau's. By the look on Maricar's face, though, Kellan worried the fight hadn't entirely left its shores.

". . . I see. Does the panel accept these bids?"

"The panel accepts."

"And so it is written. Eighth bid?"

Her turn. Kellan took her place under the light, willing her heart to steady. It was just a formality, after all. Cyn lifted her slightly trembling chin and spoke. "Madame Master Maker Minora Mesny, School of Invention, nominates Assistant Tinker Kellan DuCuivre . . ."

Whispers. Voices, fabric, footsteps. Eyes bore into her from above and beside her, itchy on her skin.

". . . o-of Cuivreton, Nanseau."

Kellan wanted nothing more than to sink into the dark, the light above her head so bright she swore it burned her scalp. She stretched her fingers to the side to keep from picking at her pants and breathed, breathed, *breathed* through the quiet. Six sets of eyes bore down at her. Some, wide with horror. Others, cool with intrigue. One pair, however, she couldn't read at all, the light shining above whiting the glass of his spectacles.

That pair of eyes belonged to Axel Bonne.

"A Du and a tinker." An engineer with thinning cornsilk-dyed hair laughed, bending forward for a better look. "And I thought I'd seen it all."

"We're still in session, Maker Jourdain," the foremin said tensely.

"I'm well aware. Is this not the point of the reasons? To discern whether our bids are worthy to participate?"

"Do you know who he is?" Kellan asked Cyn while the

forum broke out into debate. The only thing Kellan found familiar in Maker Jourdain was the anger that simmered at the dismissal in his voice.

"I do not," said Cyn. "The Madame may have spoken his name in passing once or twice, but rarely for long, and rarely in fondness."

"Dus cannot make! They are legally forbidden," Maker Jourdain exclaimed, tone light as though this were a conversation at a country club bar. "If she's law-abiding, she's wasted space. If she's practiced, then we let a criminal into the games?"

"It wouldn't be the first time," said another engineer.

"You'd turn our guild into a farce. Look around you—the forum is one body short, we've already accepted a Vastian pirate, of all things—"

"A hunter from Runer's Bay," the theorist said, venom in her tone.

"—and now, traitors' kin? On the whim of a—"

"I'd tread carefully, Jourdain," said Axel coolly, "unless you think you've climbed high enough to survive a fall from House Mesny. I hear it's a long drop."

The forum fell silent. Even the bids stopped gossiping, leaving the darkened stage in an uncomfortable hush. Kellan was prepared to face many things on her first competitor's stage, but a defense from Axel Bonne wasn't one of them. Perhaps it wasn't a defense at all—he'd only mentioned Mesny, and he'd only spoken the truth. Whatever it was, it bought Kellan a moment to think through how to get past this step. Unfortunately, a moment wasn't enough.

"Oho! What's this?" Maker Jourdain spoke with what Kellan knew he hoped was collected confidence. But Kellan had lived with fear long enough to see his haughty slouch for the bluff it was. Despite the flicker of hesitation in his voice, he leaned forward with a leering sneer and spat his next words, aiming each like a bullet to Axel's chest. "The Bonne Bastard speaks."

Someone dropped their pen, and it boomed like thunder. No one spoke. No one breathed. And Axel sat perfectly still.

Unlike Mesny, who only stepped into the spotlight on Crown and company business, House Bonne was worshipped around the world as celebrities. When Madame Mesny first introduced them, Kellan had thought it was strange that she hadn't recognized the name and face of House Bonne's heir. Now she knew why. Axel wasn't an heir. He was illegitimate. To House Bonne, Axel was more blight than blood.

But he was here. She wouldn't pretend to know whether he'd won his seat through his father's influence. What did it matter to Kellan? She was here for a reason too. Edgar. Kellan held on to that thought, that purpose. She let it ground her as she straightened her back to speak.

"A cure," Kellan said, cutting Jourdain off with her reason.

They looked at her again, a mix of confusion and offense. But at least they stopped arguing.

"For miner's rot," she continued. "Physicians and prosthesiologists only know how to slow it down. I want to reverse it."

"Why engineering?" asked Axel. "Why not alchemy or mechnitics?"

"Because this contest gives me a chance."

After the forum deliberated, the foremin cleared her throat. Smoothed the lapels of her jacket. Did her best to appear unaffected, as if she weren't about to speak history into the stage's pregnant silence. As if, in the next few seconds, everything wouldn't change.

"Does the panel accept this bid?"

". . . The panel accepts."

"And so it is written."

Kellan held her hands together to keep them from trembling in relief. Mesny could never have prepared her for that. She should've seen it coming, but after working in the Quarter for so long, she'd almost forgotten what the world beyond its gates looked like. Almost. Cyn guided her out of the light, the forum's last message a jumbled mass of faraway noise until the foremin announced the trial's task.

"Your first trial is to create something from nothing. There are three rules: You will not exceed the time. Your makes will be original to the best of your ability. And you will *not* engage in physical violence."

The dark dissipated, revealing an expanse of wild earth. Rolling hills curved the horizon in lush greens, and mountains red and winter gray pierced a bright morning sky. Rivers sparkled under the light of an illusioned sun, winding through valleys to find home in crystal blue lakes. It was more than

Kellan had ever seen in all of her days, let alone more than what could reasonably fit inside Ol' Matty's shop.

"You've exactly three hours. And it begins . . ."

The theorist carved onto the podium, and from it floated a massive cloud of glittering gold dust so high it almost eclipsed the sun. It whorled and gathered into the shape of a clock, its tick echoing against the stage's invisible walls. Three hours. Three hours to cement her place in the game. Three hours to prove them all wrong.

". . . now."

The other bids and their automi scattered before Kellan could get her bearings. Someone ran into her shoulder, sending her tumbling onto the ground, where she met grass instead of concrete.

"Get moving, tower rat," said Izod with a low snicker, a satisfied smirk twisting the scar along his cheek. Before Kellan could answer, his broad-backed silhouette disappeared into the trees.

Kellan's face heated in rage as she struggled to stand, Izod's laughter fading as he chased his head start. Mesny'd warned her days ago that her competition crushed the weak the moment they sensed it. But he wasn't the first bully she'd proved wrong, and he wouldn't be the last.

"Quick."

From behind Kellan, a faintly familiar voice and shadow towered. Marielo Bitao offered a hand to help her up, his expression just as distant as she'd come to expect. When she took it, Kellan's palm stung. A scrape from the rock.

"Here."

He pressed a carver into her palm. Hers had likely fallen out of her pocket in the tumble. Then he took off as quickly as he'd come.

Kellan gripped the carver tight despite the pain. As she searched for a direction to take, the glittering clock ticked once over rust-red mountains, its face like a compass. A guide.

Three minutes down. But now she knew exactly where to go.

Kellan led Cyn down hills and through valleys, over streams and behind waterfalls. The pillar at the center of the ring split into seven pieces, the watching engineers observing from above.

By the time they reached the reddish mountains, Kellan had lost an hour and couldn't feel the soles of her feet. Everything south of her hips ached, her palm still stung, and she was only half sure she'd made the right decision anyway. Still, she kept going. She had to keep going.

"Why have you chosen the land furthest from the starting point?" asked Cyn, her even voice grating Kellan's ears more than usual. A benefit of not needing to breathe, no doubt. "You have wasted valuable time."

"Copper." Kellan fell to her knees and palmed the rock at the mountain's base. "Because it's copper."

She laughed a breathy laugh, equal parts exhausted and relieved her bet had paid off. After sixteen years living in a village known for these mountains and this ore, Kellan could recognize it anywhere. The others may have seen the world, studied more than Kellan could ever make up for, but she knew copper like the planes of her skin.

She'd never carved into raw copper. Between its dips and its curves, it'd be far from easy, but not impossible. She'd soften it to a putty, extract it with her bare hands, and work from there.

One rune. Another, to knot. The air around her reeked of sulfur, but tonight, she'd stomach it. "It's working."

"I would hope so," said Cyn. "I will not imagine the Madame's disappointment if it had not."

She continued the pattern over the ore's peaks and planes, minding the spots that'd already softened. She'd ignore the clock ticking overhead. She'd ignore the looming pillar, far enough away to keep out of sight but close enough to cast a shadow. She'd ignore the stench of chicken dung, the memory of her namehouse tower, of the stone and the water and the ache and the *burn*—

"Your hand! Mind your hand!"

Cyn's voice rang over her hurried thoughts. The pain in her palms sharpened from a slight sting to something feral, climbing its way up her fingers and wrist, so sharp and strange that she couldn't have screamed if she'd wanted to. Shock held her still. The runes in the ore burned bright, and the smell of sulfur shifted to brimstone, the sparks to smoke.

Her carver. The nib had cracked. And Kellan had miscarved.

"Stay still! Do *not* move that point."

Another voice, faintly familiar, joined her from the right.

Maricar met Kellan's carvepoint with her own. A glance was all she needed to finish Kellan's work. By the time Maricar pulled out the ore, the blinding pain in Kellan's arm had ebbed, and the stink of sulfur had faded.

Maricar fell back into the grass, catching her breath with a relieved grin. "That was a close one, huh?"

Kellan curled and uncurled her fingers. No discoloration, no missing patches of flesh. Besides the scrape on her palm, everything felt perfectly normal. Then the trembling began. A moment longer, and she could've died.

Maricar laughed. "I'll take that as a yes."

"Thanks," she said, and meant it, trying to steady her quaking voice.

"Don't mention it. Can't have you bleeding out on the first day, can we?"

"I'll save the bleeding for the second." Kellan made a workbench out of the dried grass and readied her carver, remembering too late that it'd nearly caused catastrophe once already. But what else could she do?

"Use mine." Maricar, her shining hair strewn from her hike and her forehead gleaming with sweat, handed Kellan her carver. It was an exact replica of the one Ol' Matty had given her at the stage's entrance. Each bid must have been given the same, to level the field.

"Won't you need it?"

"I finished a while ago. Came up here to kill some time, add a little something for pizazz, you know? But it can wait."

Kellan risked a glance at the clock. An hour and fifteen minutes left to go. "I'll be quick," she said, and she set to work.

"Relax! I'm happy for the quiet, to be honest. Most of the boys headed straight to the stream, looking for gold. It's like a war down there."

"And you chose copper for 'pizazz'?"

"It's my favorite ore, you know. You should, coming from . . . Cuivreton, is it? The minebelt, south of the river?"

If Kellan had the time, she'd have checked to see if Maricar was teasing her. But she sounded genuine, tone light with curiosity. Kellan didn't answer, hardening her puttied ore into a slab. Then two slabs. With the trick Mesny taught her that first day, she turned two into twelve and expanded them all. Plenty to work with, if only she had plenty of time to go with it.

The least she could do was keep the girl who may have saved her life some company, so Kellan did her best to chat as she worked. Maricar admired the color of Kellan's native copper, how it whorled like marble with its ocean teals and greens. She said it reminded her of the sea and the stars both, which gave Kellan pause.

"Ever seen blue goldstone?" asked Maricar, looking to the sky.

Kellan shook her head, brows knit in concentration.

"It's gorgeous. Deep, deep indigo with the tiniest specks of orangish yellow. They call it goldstone, but it isn't gold. It's copper."

With five minutes to spare, Kellan collected the pieces

of her finished make and returned Maricar's carver. "That enough time for you?"

"I can do it in half. Elo may be the smart twin, but I'm the quick one. And between you and me—the clock."

"What?"

Maricar pointed over Kellan's shoulder, where the second hand of the glittering clock stopped moving. Across the stage sounded the distant murmur of a babbling brook and whispering in the trees. Every sound Kellan would've expected to hear in the middle of nature, if anything about the ring was natural at all. But it was an illusion. Makecraft, powered by runes she couldn't see.

Runes, she noticed at last, that no longer hummed.

It started from the west. The lights flickered first. As did the sky overhead, leaving what was once pink and periwinkle the dark red and green of a bloodied bruise. Then went the trees and the streams, the grass and the blooms. The flickering spread like ripples in the sea, like when Lou dropped a pebble from the cliff, until the ripples grew large and fast, light and color bright, then dead, and always nearer than before. Kellan met Maricar's horrified gaze, relief and terror washing over her. Relief, because this was not Kellan's imagination. Relief, because Maricar saw it too. This wasn't like Cuivreton's train station, where only she could see the rabbit and the crystalline rain. At least this time, she wasn't alone. But her relief was short-lived.

Because soon the dark would drown them all.

TEN

Kellan, Cyn, and Maricar struggled for balance as the fabricated world around them fell to darkness and decay. The ground trembled underfoot, quaking as the runework beneath them flickered and gave. One by one, the towers where the forum watched them carve from above crumbled to the ground in plumes of ash-gray dust, their screams and cries joining the cacophony of metal crashed into metal, their carefully spun illusion unraveling.

"The Madame did not mention this part of the trials," said Cyn, frightened but steady.

"The blackouts." Maricar climbed to her feet, carver gripped like a dagger's handle. "Is that what they call them?"

"Yeah."

"But blackouts don't—"

"I know."

Across the stage, metal illusioned into the morning sky

became metal once more, crashing to the ground in an iron hail. Kellan's hand found Maricar's shoulder on instinct, desperate for something solid to keep her upright. Maricar had done the same. A glance was all it took. In that glance, Kellan found desperation in Maricar's eyes, the brown of warm coal before the spark. Desperation to live.

Run.

Kellan led them down the mountain. She did not look back. Not when the earth roared under the weight of collapsing trees. Not when the air went thick and murky with metallic dust, the only thing the black left behind. Around her, panicked shouts filled the air as the engineers' pillars crumbled, their structures sapped of power by the hungry dark.

"Do you know where we're going?" Maricar called over the wreckage.

"No. But the quicker we can get away from that, the better—"

What was once hilled earth cracked and bubbled under them. They stumbled back as a crevasse formed between them and the other side.

"I cannot jump." Cyn sounded terrified now, her grip on Kellan's forearm tightening. "I have never jumped. I was not built to jump—"

"There's another way around," shouted Kellan. "Has to be."

But the longer Kellan searched, the wider the crevasse became. The dark around them closed like vengeful fingers at the throat, tightening slowly to savor the feel of flesh gone cold.

"Eighth! And look at that, all whole and unsquished."

A small silver light grew bigger and brighter from across the crevasse. Orana held a glowing white sphere in her palm, and beside her stood Axel and Faustin catching their breaths.

"Come on," called Axel, arm outstretched. "Before it gets any wider!"

"I cannot jump," Cyn repeated from behind Kellan's back, the heat from her runes prickling her skin. "I cannot, I cannot—"

"Maricar." Kellan stepped back, taking Cyn with her. Another boom sounded from above. "Go first. I'll talk her down."

Maricar nodded, putting as much distance between herself and the chasm as she could for a running start. She leaped and rolled into a rocky landing. Faustin caught her by the bicep just as the hardened piece of earth under her feet fell into the crevasse.

"I cannot jump," muttered Cyn again, voice tight with fear. "I cannot jump, I cannot jump, I cannot—"

"You have to. Cyn, look at me."

She did, blue eyes so full of life Kellan couldn't believe they were made of metal.

"Just run and leap. You watched Maricar, right? You'll watch me. You'll learn, and you'll make it to the other side, just like the rest of us."

"But I was not built to—"

"You weren't built to be crushed, either!"

"Any time, you two," called Faustin. "It's not like the sky is falling."

Kellan jogged back, careful not to look at the crack in the ground, widening like a toothless smile. The light was too bright to focus on, but it lit the planes of Axel's face, so she focused on him instead. Kellan counted down from three, just as he did, syncing with the subtle shaping of his lips. And on one, she ran. She ran and leaped, and the thunder of crashing steel paled under her booming pulse. She ran, eyes closed, into darkness, and didn't open them until her knees met hard ground.

"There she is!" Faustin's voice sounded behind Kellan as she scrambled to her feet. It was followed by a clap on the back. "Bet you're double-thinking that alliance thing now, aren't you?"

At the force of the contact, Kellan stumbled into something warm, tall, and reasonably solid. Axel kept them both from falling, the weight of him around her sudden, but sure. Then it was gone, Axel holding his palms up as though afraid they'd catch fire, and Kellan quick to put a comfortable distance between them once again.

"Cyn'll be heavy," Kellan warned after clearing her throat. "If her jump's shy, she'll need all four of us."

"Careful of her runes, too," said Maricar, already lowering her stance. "They'll be hot."

The gaping ground widened. Cyn stepped back, closed her eyes, and bounded forward. But her jump was shy of the landing. Kellan moved without thinking, leaping to meet her with an outstretched hand.

"PULL!" Maricar shouted from behind.

Cyn kicked into the crumbling earth in search of a foothold. Kellan ignored the blinding ache in her shoulder and pushed through the sear of runed metal against her flesh. Just a few more feet. A few more, and they'd all make it out.

Axel, Faustin, and Maricar pulled Kellan and Cyn out of the crevasse's mouth just as the earth under them fell into the dark, but there was no time to thank them. Once Cyn found her feet, Orana led the way to the entrance, where the foremin stood with the door ajar.

"I've got four," Axel called.

He ushered Orana out the door first. The densest night Kellan had ever known blanketed their corner of Sudton. Orana's floating light caught plumes of debris, the ghosts of complex runework shimmering in the night like curled fog. When her eyes adjusted to the dark, she tried to count how many people now peppered Ol' Matty's car lot. She'd nearly gotten a solid count before Lou met them at the door in a frantic jog. "What's going on in there?" she asked, voice cracking in panic. "No one's saying anything."

"A blackout has consumed the stage," Cyn explained. "We have just escaped."

While Cyn caught Lou up, Kellan assessed the damage. Izod bandaged a wound in his side, wincing atop a rusting car hood. Harmon sat on the ground, dazed. Maker Jourdain stood in a huddle of three other engineers, flailing his arms in rage. Although Kellan wasn't sure if everyone who went in had made it out, she knew change when she saw it. No one left Ol' Matty's garage the same person they were when they arrived.

"Elo." Maricar stopped just over the threshold, eyes wide with horror. "Where is he? Is he still in there?"

"I'm not sure," the foremin said. "I just made it out myself. Sit. I'll ask the forum, and we'll see—"

"I need to find him." Maricar stumbled back. She gripped the doorframe for balance, her eyes glazed and lost. "I need to find him."

The ground trembled again. Ol' Matty's shack of a shop stood still under the starless night as, inside, the world the Guild had crafted crumbled into dust. One moment, Maricar was on their side of the threshold. The next, she was gone, and the world stopped. The light against the curling dust shimmered in a way that was just shy of right.

Through it, the golden rabbit from Cuivreton Station stared at Kellan. It sat where Maricar had just been before she'd ran into the dark after Elo.

Kellan could think of few things worse than death, and if she stood still, that was the fate Maricar would meet. If it hadn't been for her, Kellan might not have survived the first trial. She couldn't just do nothing.

So Kellan ran.

She ignored the shouts of the others calling for her to come back. As she raced forward, the dust parted to make a path for her, and she followed the rabbit into the dark's waiting hand.

She expected shattered metal. Broken pillars. The embers of failed runework, or Maricar calling into the wreckage. Instead, she found stone. The cold gray of ancient granite, greened with coppery water, tendrils of light dancing on its walls. Kellan's breaths came quickly, but they were breaths. The pain in her arm howled from somewhere far away, dampened by shock and adrenaline. This was not a dream.

"Kellan?"

Maricar's voice came from everywhere and nowhere, close enough to hum in Kellan's chest and far enough to echo against the walls. Then, in the distance, Kellan caught a glimpse of gold glinting off the light piercing the fog. A twitching ear. A cotton tail.

She chased the golden rabbit through the greened gray, and as she did, the world around her changed in ways she didn't understand. An engine roared, warbled by the water she couldn't feel. The stone reeked of burning rubber and motor oil. The rabbit left a trail of flowers blooming in the cracks between slabs. Nothing made sense but the shade of her name against the rock, its echo soft as a whisper. She wanted to cling to that. To follow it like a hope, a light, a breath waiting just above the skin of the sea.

But then, another sound boomed.

Have you wandered, little thing?

A voice she didn't know tickled the shell of her ear, crawled between her ribs. A voice from everywhere and nowhere and all the places between.

Bringing trouble, little thing?

Drip. Splash. A puddle grew at Kellan's feet. Not of water, but of the night sky, starless and deepest blue. The night sky, and Maricar's friendly reflection.

"Protect him," said the Maricar in the puddle at Kellan's feet. "And forgive him."

As the world tilted, lights dotted the water. They blotted the sky and the stone, the blooms and the gray. But even when Kellan slipped into unconsciousness, she knew they weren't stars. They couldn't be. They were too bright and too many.

ELEVEN

"Is she dead?"

"No, Cyn, she's not dead. See that? She's frowning. Dead folk don't frown— Oh, look, she's groaning now. They don't do that, either."

When Kellan opened her eyes, Lou and Cyn eclipsed the lamplight of an unfamiliar room. When she tried to sit up in an unfamiliar bed, every muscle in her body pounded in protest, and her *arms*—

"Easy, now. Easy." Lou helped her sit up, propped a pillow against the headboard. It didn't help.

Kellan rolled her aching shoulders and tried to look around. It was a beautiful bedroom, if not well used. Dust coated the side table and windowsill, but the potted plants stationed along the length of it thrived under the morning light. "Where are we?"

"One of the Madame's friends' place. Tall? Pretty? Big ears."

"Axel Bonne," said Kellan and Cyn together.

"Right, that's . . . Wait, *Bonne*! As in . . . *Bonne?*"

While Cyn used many creative ways to berate Lou for her ignorance, memories of last night came back to Kellan. The trial. The copper. The rabbit. The dark, swallowing everything in its path. The reflection that wasn't hers, and the plea she couldn't make sense of. *Protect him.* "Does anyone know what happened last night?"

"Of course we know," said Cyn. "We were there."

"It's all that's on the radio." Lou leaned forward conspiratorially, voice low. "I'd only just turned it off when you came to."

"So what are they doing about it?"

"Still trying to figure it out, I guess? The capitol's even getting involved now, I hear."

"And Maricar? They got her out, didn't they?"

Lou looked like Kellan had spoken another language. Before Kellan could ask why, the bedroom door swung open, rippling the curtain and casting the room in a brief wash of light. A short, plump woman in physician whites stormed in, mouth twisted in a frown. Kellan didn't have time to ask who she was before she pulled Kellan's blanket out from around her shoulders. "Doing better this morning, préci?"

". . . I—"

"Well, you look better. Fever's gone, color in your cheeks. Let's see those arms, though."

"My arms—"

Kellan hissed as the physician unwound the gauze from around her right arm. Searing pain ripped up her wrists to curl behind her eyes. She blinked, gritted her teeth, and when she opened her eyes again, she couldn't look away from her hands. Blisters and blood marred the familiar umber of her skin in livid reds and sickly pinks. She hardly recognized her palms anymore, peeling gray and swollen.

"I reset your shoulder first thing," said the physician. She replaced Kellan's old gauze with new ones, which immediately yellowed with pus. "It's all second-degree, thank the stone, but you'll need proper care for the pain and a hospital to hurry the healing along."

"Is it infected?"

"Not now, but—"

"Then don't tell Mesny. . . . Please."

Kellan cursed the desperation in her voice. She tucked her hands back under her blankets and ignored the pain. *When they sense the slightest whiff of weakness, they will crush you with their bare, talented hands.* Kellan had almost forgotten. Mesny once fought for her pin, too. If Mesny knew the state of her hands, she'd find another bid to back before Kellan finished packing her bags, and Edgar's rot would spread until it left him an empty husk. No. Her hands would heal on their own, as bodies did. They had to.

The physician went on to order that Kellan rest until at least sundown, so Lou ordered food for them. Cyn, who couldn't eat, pretended not to mind when Lou helped herself to an extra serving.

Kellan did her best to eat. She tried big bites and small ones, her fork in her left hand's fingers. Even built a disaster of a sandwich out of the biscuit, fish, and pol, which made a mess of her already ruined blouse. She should taste something. She should *feel* something. But the conversation around her, the laughter and banter, sounded underwater. Sound and smell and light churned her stomach. Still, she tried. Because when she didn't, pillars crashed around her. When she blinked, red cut the dark of her eyelids like running blood. And in the quiet, the laughter faded away, leaving only vague memories of stone and sea and stars.

Once Lou tired out, Kellan left her and Cyn in the guest room to explore the rest of Axel's place, since she'd seen no sign of him. The sea and the pier sat low on the other side of his massive window, the speckled shapes of fishing boats and bloated sails drifting on sun-dappled water. Bookshelves covered nearly every other wall, sagging under the weight of cramped tomes and safe behind runed glass doors. Axel's place was less of a living space and more of an unkempt library, littered with stray papers and pens.

Then something touched Kellan's shoulder. Kellan knocked it back.

The motion sent pain shooting from her wrist to her skull again, sharpening the never-ending ache she'd accepted as a part of her for now. It would heal on its own. It would heal on its own.

"Kellan?"

She found her balance, blinked through her pain-dotted vision. Axel stood in a doorframe, arm slack and eyes wide.

"Sorry. Sorry, I didn't mean . . ." Axel wore his worry like a second skin. He glanced from Kellan's matted hair to her wrinkled pantlegs, his gaze lingering on her bandaged hands as though he'd find her answer in the weave. When she hid them behind her hips, he looked pointedly away. "It's good you're here, actually. Minora asked for a package. . . . This won't take long, so have a seat, or, um. You know."

He stepped over a pile of books and through a side door, leaving Kellan alone in the study with nothing but silence and fading sunlight.

"You save the gravitas for the highseats?" she asked to fill it, lest her mind fill with darker things.

"I don't know what you're talking about."

"'You've climbed high enough to survive a fall from *House Mesny*. It's *quite* a long drop,'" Kellan said, repeating his words from the trial.

Behind her, papers rustled and boxes thudded against the ground. "That's not what I said, and it definitely isn't how I'd have said it. Is that accent supposed to be highseat or Crescent? It's an awful imitation either way."

"It's supposed to be you. Or half of you, at least."

"Because you know me so well."

"Because I know a liar when I hear one."

"Jourdain," he called from the back room, "is an arrogant, power-hungry bigot in desperate need of humility."

"From the boy who almost cried over a broken book."

"I did *not* 'cry.' I was upset, with reason. I still am."

"Clearly."

"Do you ever intend to replace it?"

"No." Kellan said, ignoring his groan of annoyance in response. She found a desk topped with oddities. Little dolls woven from straw and dyed linen. A curiously shaped spool of fine, shimmering thread. Tubes of wood mesh, filled with pale powder that glowed when she shook them, glittering like something alive. His sketchbooks were inky with scribbled notes and ancient buildings. South Vastian shrines and North Vastian palaces, temples from Ital and the Crescent Isles. Even Lidonch cathedrals, stone roofs pointed like knives to the sky, so like the namehouses Nanseau left standing after the Liberation that Kellan couldn't bear lingering too long. She'd seen enough to guess his school, anyway. Axel was an architect, more scholar than maker. A journeymin, at least, to have earned a seat on the forum.

Beneath his piled sketchbooks poked copies of missing persons flyers, brown from water stains and tire tracks. Fathers. Daughters. Children. People from the Fault and western Sudton, gone with no trace to follow. He'd tucked them between his sketches, dotted the corners with ink. She imagined him tapping the paper with the tip of his pen in thought as though working through a puzzle, making a connection where there might have been none.

Then she saw it again. A symbol, ancient and familiar, doodled in the corner of a sketch of Sougare's runes. She'd seen this twice before: once on the box of glass in Maudelaire's cabinet, and just now on the spine of one of Axel's glass-protected tomes.

He went on about how priceless the book from the train was, how he'd never find another like it, when this and why that and because another thing, all a comfortably distracting drone as she pulled back his bookshelf's glass door in search of that strange symbol. There it was. Cracked, faded leather. Parchment so thin her fingers shone through the pages. The tome's weight in her palm, still raw and burning, set her nerves on fire.

She couldn't read the text. She didn't try to. Instead, she flipped through the illustrations, color and linework faded with age. A spider, burrowed in the dirt. A lion, curled under a tree.

A rabbit, stealing honey from a hive.

Our little thing was always a thief, came the rabbit's familiar voice. *Wasn't she?*

The world tilted. Axel's study washed away in a tide of blue, green, and rust-red water. Kellan fought for air she couldn't find, a dozen daggers in her chest, sharp and shallow.

She takes so much, and so little. So much, and never enough. I wonder what she will steal this time? I wonder if it will make a difference?

Which came first? The cold, a million tiny legs skittering in her skin? The fire, burning wild in her lungs? The book crashed to the ground. She tried to scream as the world around her grayed and greened, stone and sea—

"Look at me."

Something soft warmed the backs of her hands. She felt it through the gauze, the blood and pus, the cold and the flame. It pulled, firm but gentle.

"Kellan, *look* at me."

At some point, she'd plugged her ears. She heard clearly now, the warmth's voice close and unwarbled. When she opened her eyes, the green and gray slowly faded away.

"Five things you can see." Axel's shoulders and chest rose and fell like the tide, voice soft as sea foam. "You don't have to tell me. Just name them for yourself. Anything."

Anything? Kellan mimicked Axel's rise and fall. Maybe then, breath would follow. To her left was the arm of a worn sofa. It was splotched from spilled coffee or tea. At her feet, the book she'd dropped lay spine up on the ground. And the boy in front of her had freckles, ochre against tawny brown skin. Eyes like smoky quartz, wide and clear and glittering.

"Good. Really good." Axel nodded in that same rhythm. "Four things you can feel."

Air. A breeze through the window. Hardwood, cold and unyielding against her bottom. The imprint of wallpaper against her arm through her blouse as she sat huddled in the corner beside his bookshelf. Lean, long-fingered hands around her own, their grip gentle and sure.

They went on like that for a while longer, through what she could hear, and smell, and taste, until her breaths came easily again. Until the daggers fell from her chest, dissipated in the breeze of his lullaby voice. He sat with her in the silence of the pier beyond the window, of the gulls and the waves. She took her hands back, and the ache returned. Dull but manageable.

"That book—" Kellan said in a whisper. She almost didn't

recognize the sound of her voice, small and worn as it was. She gestured to the fallen tome with a cock of her chin. "What is it?"

"This?" Axel lifted it carefully from the ground, checked its spine and its pages. "Hard to say. If I could wager a guess, a book of myths. Coastal East Aigan."

Aigo. The empty heart of the modern world map. The continent swallowed by the sea. The motherland to which the island of Nanseau had once belonged. At least it explained the curiosities she'd found in his desk drawer, one of which lay not far from where she'd dropped the book. The dust within the wooden mesh still swirled like trapped smoke.

"Don't worry too much over this one," he said, handing the book back to her. "It'll be fine. That case is full of them. Poetry and epics about creatures, beasts, spirits. I suspect a few of them are novels, some even biographies. Five East Aigan nations, seventeen written languages . . . Still doesn't put a dent in all there is to know."

"You can read this?"

"Not well enough, but I know a few stories."

She opened the tome and turned a page. Then another. People wandered lush woodlands and frozen wastes. Empty temples and throne rooms buried under mounds of gold and gemstones shone in brilliant detail. A few illustrations had been ruined beyond recognition, their colors bleeding into one blurred mass, but even they stirred something in her that was bigger than curiosity.

She knew little about Aigo as a place. When the Lidonch

invaded, they'd robbed its people—Nanseau's ancestors, she supposed—of their languages, shredded their families, wrecked their bodies in the stone quarries for their gods and towers and trade, and that went on for a thousand years. But that was it. Education in the namehouses wasn't a priority, and history wasn't something Kellan could learn through practice and trial and error. She knew just enough, just what she'd overheard from the older villagers who remembered from their grandparents, and them their grandparents before that.

Should she tell him about the rabbit? Ask him about the world beyond the trial door? The words caught in her throat. Not today. Not when she couldn't tell what she'd seen from a nightmare.

"I grabbed this when I put together Minora's package. For your hands. I had to wait until the physician left. They're not too keen on 'alternative' medicine."

Axel pulled a glass vial of translucent purple liquid from his pocket. An alchemist's work, most likely, but no alchemist Kellan had ever heard of would have bottled their make in something so plain.

"You get that from wherever you found these books?"

". . . No. But it works better than anything you'll find on the market, trust me."

"Even though you won't tell me where it's from?"

"Do you think I'd poison you?"

"Not without a good reason."

"Then what are you scared of?"

"I'm not scared."

"Could've fooled me. You're guarding your hands like they're all you've ever had."

Her breath hitched, and she pulled her hands out from behind her hips. Of course they weren't all she had. She had food in her belly and shelter from the rain. She had a memory tighter than a master duodecknot. She had Edgar. But her hands had helped her climb out of the namehouse and into his toy shop. They were all that separated her from the other DuCuivres. The only way she could save Edgar's life. She wasn't special, but her hands made her useful, and for Kellan, that was all . . . all she needed.

"It's from Orana." Axel uncapped the vial with his teeth. "She's young, but she's good. Her tribe keeps its secrets close, so to share this with you . . . She must've been worried."

Worried. Like Lou, when Kellan moved too fast in a stranger's bed. Like Cyn, who made sure Kellan finished her plate before letting Lou sleep. She'd only known that kind of worry once before. From Edgar, who'd taken in a feral little thief.

Slowly, wordlessly, she set her hands palm up in her lap. Axel smiled slightly and warmly, and pulled one closer, his hold just as gentle. Her hand may as well have been one of his curiosities, or a page in his ancient books, or, if he cared at all, one of the only things she ever had.

TWELVE

The ride from Nordton to Mesny's manor took forty-five minutes. This was unusual, because it should have taken ten.

Their trip took longer after an announcement on the cab's radio told of a strange phenomenon near the Fault's wall. Lou, partly because of traffic and mostly because of her curiosity, drove Kellan and Cyn through west Sudton near Ol' Matty's car shop. At least, what little was left of it.

When they passed Ol' Matty's lot, Kellan didn't find a car shop in ruin. She found flowers. Foxgloves. A wild garden of them, blooming with color and life, swaying in a breeze that didn't exist. Moonlight danced on its petals and stems in watery waves, bent by an invisible sea, lighting the dark and leading the bees to nectar like ships to shore.

They called it another unnatural wonder. No one knew how or why it appeared. Only when: the night of the blackout and the Guild's first trial. The night a rabbit left a trail of blossoms in its wake. She'd expected to feel the same panic that took her when she'd followed Maricar into the shed, but when Lou passed the peculiar field that was once Ol' Matty's shop, her heart ached for a different reason. She'd only felt so hollow once before: in the face of the Quarter's golden gate, a piece of a world she didn't know and never could.

By the time the car pulled into the circle, her hands had already started to heal. The blisters shrank, the redness faded, and her fingers smelled like lavender and peppermint. Still, when she stepped onto the cobbled claybrick, exhaustion made molasses of the air, and Mesny's package under her arm pulled with the weight of an age.

She knocked on the manor's front door with her elbow and leaned against the frame, a weak but icy wind chilling her cheeks. It'd been a long two days, and all she wanted to do was collapse onto her borrowed bed and sleep again. Maybe now she could close her eyes. Forget for a time. But that would be difficult.

Xo welcomed Kellan back and led her to Mesny's quarters in the west wing, facing the centergarden. After an almost endless walk, they slowed in a hall that ended with a massive double door, slightly cracked, a faint sliver of lamplight striping the marble floor. Xo took her leave, and Kellan knocked with her foot before stepping inside.

She'd grown so used to being surrounded by music and gold and skittering automi that the sight of Mesny's quarters was an uncomfortable change. It was a wide, open space with parted sheers on the windows and plants on their sills that made it all smell like linen and fresh cut grass. She'd tucked stacks of sketchbooks in the corners so high they almost reached the ceiling, taped diagrams of her future projects on the walls. And her bed, pits, no one should have a bed so wide. It looked like even Mesny didn't know what to do with so much space. Its dressing was completely undisturbed, except for the farthest edge.

Mesny stood by one of the windows. She stared into the garden, eyes glazed and arms hanging limp as if the days had weighed on her like they had on Kellan. But that moment passed when the floorboards creaked beneath Kellan's feet. "There you are," said Mesny, and her expression brightened anew. "He's sent all of it, then?"

"I think so," said Kellan. "He didn't tell me what's in it."

"Smart boy." Mesny took the package in her arms and set it carefully on the nearby chaise. "Tinker Pape warned me of your tendency toward overexertion, but I didn't believe it until now. Sit, before you collapse."

"You talk to Edgar?"

"We write. Brilliant though you may be, you're still a young woman underage, and Tinker Pape is your guardian in all but title. It'd be cruel of me not to keep in touch, let alone irresponsible."

What Cuivreton's postmin must think, delivering a letter with the Mesny seal to their tiny village toy shop. For how long had they been writing? Kellan didn't even know Mesny had time to write at all, never mind to a lowborn tinker south of the Boaverre.

"He's well," said Mesny after a time. "More, he doesn't want to distract you. If you'd like, I can arrange—"

"No." Kellan didn't know if she could handle hearing Edgar on the other end of a telephone. The last thing he needed was to know how much danger she'd put herself in for him. She'd say everything was fine, of course, but for some reason, he was the only person she'd known who could catch her in a lie.

"Hmm. Very well." Mesny pulled one of Axel's books into her lap, another East Aigan tome. She laced her fingers atop the leather. "We've an early start tomorrow. The Guild has called a meeting at their Midton library. It is there where we'll learn whether or not you've passed your first stage. In the meantime, I've a gift for you."

Kellan didn't want a gift. She didn't want anything, or any of this. She picked at her sleeve as Mesny set Axel's book in a drawer and pulled out a satin box—long, slim, and shallow.

"It's time you have one of these."

Kellan looked from Mesny, to the box, to her own still-healing hands. Her fingers trembled in her lap. "What is it?"

"I suppose you'll have to open it to find out, won't you?"

She took the box despite her shaking, the satin soft against the pads of her fingers. After she willed her hands to keep still, she managed to open its lid.

Edgar's carvers had always been too thick for her, but she made them work. Mesny's were too long—her hands were slim, delicate like a pianist's—but Kellan made do. The carver that sat on a bed of crushed blue velvet looked the perfect size. She ran her finger along the carvepoint's edge, glittering agold sharp enough to draw blood. Its blackwood handle shimmered with inlays of a dark stone that resembled the night sky. She traced the pattern of whorls and angles but couldn't find the end or the start.

"Curious crystal, isn't it? It's man-made, but quite rare, rumored to only be manufactured by a small company of alchemists just south of Il. They call it blue goldstone."

Blue goldstone. Deep, deep indigo with the tiniest specks of orangish yellow. They call it goldstone, but it isn't gold . . .

"It's copper."

Mesny hadn't heard her. She hardly heard herself. She set the carver in its box, nodded her thanks, and trudged to the door.

"Kellan?"

She stopped and glanced over her shoulder, gripping the box at her side tight enough to sting.

"I don't intend to send you out after dark on your own anymore. If you have plans independent of your studies, I ask that you return long before dusk."

"Why?"

"Things are changing, Kellan. Perhaps for the better, but . . . no great change comes without its casualties. I won't have it take you, too."

◆◆◆

Kellan hardly slept at all the night before she and the other competitors would meet at the Guild's hidden library. When Mesny's automirun led them to the alley between Midton Palace and the record shop beside it, she wasn't even aware enough to be surprised. All she knew was the trembling of her still-healing fingers as she braced herself for the Guild's decision.

They left the automi parked across the road. Mesny held her guild pin up to the record shop's keyhole, and as if sensing its nearness, her pin shifted into a key. The first time Mesny opened the door, she'd opened it to an archive. The second, a lounge. She'd stopped after the third to lead the way off Midton's sidewalk and into the low light of their destination.

Inside, Kellan and Mesny stepped into what looked like an academic war room. Color shone through massive stained glass windows, dawn's sunlight dancing atop a round table cluttered with dusty tomes and sketchbooks. Portraits of famous engineers hung high on the walls, and although it was almost certainly Kellan's imagination, even they shrank further into their backdrops in dread.

Izod, the scarred runehunter from the Bay who'd shoved her to the ground, dozed off against a surprisingly sturdy bookshelf. Orana, the young alchemist, sat cross-legged on the ground, reading a book. Faustin snored, sleeping at a desk in a dark corner. Nearby, engineers whispered across the table, tension radiating from them like heat from a forge. She looked around the room a second, then a third time. Elo and Maricar were nowhere to be found.

"Are we running late, gentlemin?" When Mesny spoke, the entire room stood at attention. Even Faustin sat up, wiping his eyes as if to be sure they hadn't betrayed him. "And after all that fuss. Had I known, I would've stopped for coffee."

"Madame Mesny," said Maker Jourdain, who, stone keep his heart, tried his best to hide his disgust when he noticed Kellan beside her. "Of course not. We thought it best to meet as early as possible—get ahead of things before the city . . . talks."

Mesny motioned for Kellan to stay while she joined the other engineers. Most of their pins glittered purple with amethysts. Kellan didn't know if it was normal for so many theorists to gather in one place, but seeing them all together was a staunch reminder of how deadly the trial and its fallout must have been. When one particularly ancient-looking engineer caught her staring, he whispered something to the others, and they spoke in such hushed tones that Kellan wondered if they could even hear each other. After too long, Maker Jourdain took to the front of the room, his expression grave, and with just five words, sapped whatever small amount of energy Madame Mesny's arrival had given them.

"Assistant Maricar Bitao is dead."

The room went cold, and the light stopped dancing.

"Riz's ordergarde confirmed her death late last night. This, of course, comes after the loss of nearly half the forum. Normally, we use this time between trials to provide constructive criticism of your work, but considering the circumstances, we thought it best to get to the meat of it. If you are here, then you have passed the first stage, and it is time to prepare for the next."

The silence was so thick Kellan nearly suffocated. She tried to catch Mesny's eye, but Mesny stared blankly ahead, her expression unreadable.

"Right. Well." Maker Jourdain cleared his throat. "In the spirit of transparency, Harmon Barbier will be joining you in your second trial. We've alerted his sponsor, so he should be back in Riz by the night's end—"

"Harmon? The twiggy one?" Izod stood up, his low voice rumbling. "He barely finished. No way he passed with everyone else."

"Technically speaking, he didn't," said Maker Jourdain. "But Assistant Maricar's loss left a vacancy, and the forum thought it best to see it filled."

"Someone dies," asked Orana from the ground, "so he gets to step over their corpse? Why?"

"Because the number is six," said a voice from the door. "It always has been, so it always will be."

The ferrule of a cane clicked against the ground as Velvet Man strode into the room. Marielo stood at his side, several shades paler than Kellan remembered him.

"Maker Villiers," said Jourdain through a terse smile. "Welcome."

The Guild's first trial hadn't given him so much as a scratch. If he'd really been somewhere inside when Maricar first dove into the shed, he'd have been lucky to walk away at all. But "lucky" was the last word anyone could use to describe Elo Bitao. He trailed his sponsor's shadow in a way that made Kellan wonder if, perhaps, he hadn't gotten out. If he'd died too.

The rest of the meeting was a blur. Jourdain spoke of foreign dignitaries arriving from across the Swallow but wouldn't say who; he stressed that their next stage would be more public than it had been in the Guild's history but wouldn't say why. By the end, Kellan didn't need to talk to her competition to know that they had more questions than answers, if the shock of Jourdain's first announcement hadn't left them dazed beyond comprehension.

"It seems the rat knows how to climb." Maker Villiers stopped in front of her on his way out, cutting the light in two. He didn't wear velvet today, but he wore his distaste for her just as plainly. "I suppose congratulations are in order."

"I'll be okay without them."

"I'm sure." For a moment, Kellan thought his eyes lit with approval. Of what, she didn't know. It was gone a moment later. He clicked his cane against the ground, and Marielo followed him out the door, quiet as a ghost.

THIRTEEN

One month. That was how much time the forum gave its competitors to rest after the catastrophe that was their first trial—just long enough for the Guild to clean its mess and regroup for the second. It was barely long enough to nurse their wounds, let alone grieve the loss of one of their own, but it was more than the Guild usually gave in the wake of a death. At least Mesny took pity, having reduced their drills to once every other day. She even ended their lessons early when Kellan's grip faltered in her still-healing hands, under the impression that she'd been struck by nerves since Kellan still hadn't told her about the burns.

To give her hands a much-needed break, Kellan had offered to run some of Mesny's errands. This one took her to Riz's Southern Commercial District. Truth be told, she'd rather have been anywhere else. The closer to the shore the shop, the more pretentious the merchant. What Kellan had hoped would be a break from Mesny's endless assignments in preparation for the next trial had soured into a showdown with a burly, tattooed shopkeep who looked like he could snap Kellan in two with a twitch of his impressive mustache.

"A rat couldn't get their hands on something like this unless they stole it," he said in his baritone while Kellan squirmed uncomfortably in her new waistcoat. "Doesn't matter how nice you're dressed. It's easier to find a bootlegged suit than it is to forge a courtier's seal."

"Then check it. I hear there's a machine for that."

The burly man glared at her, and Kellan loosened her bow tie, tapping her toe against an ornate rug worth more than three of her lives.

"It's not like I can steal anything." She gestured around the shop, high-ceilinged and glittering with sunlight on metal and glass, gears and ores safe behind runed and bolted cabinets. "If I try, you know what I look like. Toss a pebble in the air around here, and it'll tip a guardsmin's cap. Won't take long to chase me down."

He looked close to hitting her then, but after perhaps thinking better of it, he spat on the ground and slipped through a door behind the counter, off to discover that the seal on Mesny's note was as authentic as it could get. About time, too. If that argument had lasted any longer, she wouldn't have finished by dark.

"Kellan?"

Kellan jumped. Ginnel stood in the doorframe, a paper cup in each hand. She smiled brightly and waved with her elbow, looking again like something from a magazine. She'd cut her hair into a short, bold bob that Kellan imagined took hours to keep straight, but it was slightly frizzed and wind-fussed. The lamp overhead hollowed the dark circles under her eyes.

"Didn't expect to find you here," she said, slightly out of breath. "Does the Madame have you running errands? I figured you'd have more important things to do, considering."

Kellan opened her mouth to answer but couldn't help but glance at the lidded cup Ginnel shoved under her nose. The steam warmed her face, smelling strongly of . . .

"Coffee?"

"Lovely, right? Sort of sweet, sort of—"

"Bitter. Lot of bitter, actually."

"Don't knock! One sip is all I'm asking for."

One sip. It wouldn't kill her. Judging by the look of giddy expectation on Ginnel's face, death by steaming beverage was more likely than Ginnel letting her go without tasting it first.

"Pits, my apologies," came a panicked voice from behind the counter. "I didn't realize. Madame Mesny usually sends her automi for pickups, I just assumed—"

"Bleugh!"

The burly man had returned in the middle of Kellan's disastrous sip. Disastrous, because the drink was both gross and scalding, neither of which she was fully prepared for. Half of what she hadn't swallowed dribbled down her chin and stained her itchy new blouse. The rest browned the shop's luxurious rug.

All three of them stood still, Kellan dripping coffee, holding her cursed cup as far away as possible; Ginnel with her gloved hands covering her shock-opened mouth; and the burly shopkeep, trying his best to maintain his composure.

"I'll wrap these up for you." With one last disgusted glance at the spit-up staining his expensive rug, he retreated to the room behind the counter again.

Kellan looked at Ginnel. Ginnel looked at Kellan. Outside, the district carried on as it had, car and bicycle horns honking and tinkling above the chitter of idle conversation. Inside, the two Dus broke into a fit of absolutely undignified laughter.

Doubled over with one arm wrapped around her middle and the other slapping the countertop, Ginnel tried to speak between her giggle fits. "Stone under soil, did you see— Did you see his—"

"We should probably run before he comes back with a hammer," said Kellan, wiping tears from her cheeks. "Looked like he'd risk the dustmills over this rug."

"No one should care so much about a rug. It's not even—not even—"

"It looks like someone spat up on it already, and the tailor said—"

"'Let's just call it a pattern and sell it for a crestload!'"

The shopkeep handed over Mesny's order, and Kellan and Ginnel left as a pair. The comte was "in a mood," Ginnel said, so to put off returning to Crown Hall, she'd walk with Kellan to Sudton, where Kellan had one last stop to make. It was nice, speaking with someone who knew nothing of what had happened the week before, who didn't ask where Kellan went when she drifted off in silence or why she slowed when they passed the odd lampposts, the black ink of missing persons papers faded brown from their time in the sun.

"I know her," said Ginnel, stopping at a poster of an old woman with kind eyes and a patient smile. "She makes the best gumbo in the city. Date's wrong, though. She stopped coming around the community kitchen late Craich."

"Ginnel the Altruist, huh?"

"Nah. I lived there until a few weeks ago. Just moved out. Curfews got in the way of work."

They stood, watching the paper flutter in the breeze, until a strange voice cut through the district's song of idle chatter and bicycle bells.

Oh, how much we've changed.

Kellan froze, the warmth in her chest cooling with the wind.

"What's wrong?" asked Ginnel in concern.

Are we distracted, little thing? Will we remember, or will we forget?

Laughter, frail as an echo, traveled from the other side of the street. Kellan's pounding pulse dampened the chatter and bells, dulled the touch of Ginnel's hand on Kellan's back as she whirled to face it. Because now it had a face, the voice that'd haunted her since the first trial.

An old woman, small and silver-haired, sat cross-legged on the other side of the road, the wool of her frayed trench coat splayed around her like wilting foxglove petals. Kellan remembered that coat from the alley behind Ol' Matty's shop. From the fifth floor of Crown Hall.

"There she is." The old woman smiled a toothless smile. "Our girl in the dark."

A car horn blared, screeching to a stop at Kellan's hip. She didn't know when she'd stormed into the street, only that desperation had carried her forward. A desperation that fogged the world around her from sound to sight, leaving only the old woman in sharp relief. She had been there, on the sidewalk in front of Crown Hall the first day of the Exposition. She had been there when Maricar ran into the dark and never returned, and when Kellan's mind filled Axel's study with stone and rusty water, the woman's familiar voice had echoed in Kellan's ears. Kellan remembered those eyes, too—two black pits that pierced her through the glass.

The woman knew something. She had to.

"Pricking your eyes will not make you deaf," she cackled. "Cutting your ears will not make you mute. You will feel, and hear, and see, and remember no matter how far you run."

Something held her back, gripped her by the wrist. Her healing shoulder throbbed as she pulled, determined to close the distance between her and those bottomless eyes.

"Will you take this one into the dark with you?" The old woman's smile darkened. The world went red. "Will this one survive?"

"Kellan, stop it!"

Ginnel stepped in front of her, cut through the fog with

the sound of her name. They stood a stone's throw from the other side, a line of roaring cars at their backs. Rain pelted the ground in icy torrents, drenching their hair and soaking their clothes through.

By the time Kellan remembered where she was, the old woman was already gone. A peculiarly lit flower bloomed from the crack in the concrete where she once stood. And when Kellan opened her mouth, she could only manage four small words, trembling in the wake of her disappointment.

"You saw her, too?"

Ginnel nodded. "Let's get you back to the Quarter," she said, guiding Kellan off the street. "I'll take care of the rest."

The answer didn't bring Kellan relief. Instead, it filled her with dread.

It rained for several nights after, a downpour so cold and heavy the weathermin thought froigus had come early.

After nearly a week, Mesny received word of the Guild's second trial: one of wit, where Kellan must not only impress the panel, but also dazzle the most elite names of makecraft and merching in the world.

"The Makers' Ball is not a party. It's a viper's nest," explained Mesny after reading the Guild's sealed letter. "To pass, your talent won't be enough. You'll need charm, poise, a modicum of rhythm, and a great deal of showmanship."

Kellan DuCuivre had none of those things. To make up for the lack, Mesny insisted she only carve half as often as she refined her posture, set aside tracing runes to memorize which fork was meant for salad and which for shrimp. When Kellan asked about the one part of the trial that required talent, Mesny handed her a box of reels of Balls past and sent her on her way. "Don't overthink," she reminded Kellan. "You're strongest on your toes."

With only a few weeks between the letter's arrival and the ball, Kellan spent her free time studying old trials and sketching plans for her own. Better that than lying awake at night, consumed with thoughts of pit-black eyes and trench coats frayed like the petals in Ol' Matty's lot. At least the nightmares stopped waking her in cold sweats. She'd learned to breathe through the gray. When she couldn't, she counted what she could see. It was a small victory, but one she'd take. With the second trial fast approaching, she had little focus to spare.

Soon after realizing she was a terrible example of decorum, Mesny enlisted Axel's help in readying Kellan for the wolves. Every other day, they'd sit across from each other in Mesny's smallest dining room, eating air and practicing polite conversation. Every other day, his fake highborn accent grew more ridiculous, their inside jokes more obscure. If he noticed something off with her, he never mentioned it. She appreciated that most, because every other day, she smiled a little more. And every other night, she found sleep a little easier.

For the last few days, Mesny'd tried teaching Kellan the gris—a tearfully boring dance to tearfully boring music. Kellan and Axel stood in the middle of an underused ballroom, naked windows striping the tiled floor with white. The dust had an easier time dancing than they did, floating gracefully in the sunlight. Again, Axel stepped forward. Kellan stepped back. He usually didn't start grunting in pain from Kellan stepping on his feet until the seventh or eighth measure, and Mesny usually didn't show mercy until measure sixteen. This performance was so abysmal that Mesny couldn't wait the full sixteen, having lifted the phonograph's needle not ten seconds in.

The record's last note rang in the empty room. Axel pretended to polish a smudge off his glasses with his kerchief. Kellan shuffled her unbruised feet, wringing her hands behind her back. And Mesny aged at least five years.

"Better," said Axel after Mesny excused herself for fresh air. "Better! That was . . . better."

"Think if you say it a few more times, it'll come true?"

"No harm in trying, is there?"

Kellan kicked off her shoes and sat cross-legged on the cold tile, right in the middle of the patterned square she and Axel spent hours trapped in, forever stepping and misstepping to a song Kellan never wanted to hear again for the rest of her life. Making, she could do, especially now that her hands and shoulder had healed with Orana's help. The rest felt hopeless and infuriating all at once. What did it matter to the Guild if she had the rhythm of a mudslide?

"They want to know if you'll fit in," said Axel from beside her, long legs splayed in front of him. "It's a 'measure of character.' Or something like that."

"Character or pedigree?"

"For most of them? There's no difference."

They let the quiet be, however tense with the unspoken truth. Unless captains hosted charm schools on their ships, she might have a chance over Izod from the Bay and a halved one over Orana from Ital, a brilliant but strange young girl who wouldn't care for niceties either way. But Faustin had enough charisma to fill a drinking well, and Marielo was impossible to predict.

"I have an idea," Axel said, climbing to his feet. He jogged across the room and flipped through the handful of records that leaned against the ballroom's phonograph, his tongue pressed against his cheek in concentration, before deciding on one whose title she couldn't read from so far away. "This one should do it."

"Do what, exactly?"

He placed the needle on the vinyl and tapped the side of his nose. The song he'd chosen was a touch faster and much more lively, but Kellan couldn't see how a change in accompaniment would make her any less likely to break his toes.

"I noticed you look at your feet a lot," he said, unbuttoning his cuffs to roll up his sleeves. "And your lips move, like you're muttering the steps."

"That's because I'm muttering the steps. There's a lot of them."

"And I've got the bruises to show for it, thanks to you." With a soft smile, he stepped toward her, carefully, as though waiting for her permission to close the last stretch of distance between them. It was only one step, but without Mesny present to fill the massive ballroom space, it felt like . . . more.

But that was ridiculous. A step was a step, and they'd danced just fine minutes ago. If anything, practice would go much easier with Mesny and her rusting ruler out of the way.

"Most people think dancing is about memorizing steps, but it isn't. Well, it kind of is, sometimes, but not— My point is, it's about being present and being aware. You've got to listen to yourself, and your partner, or your troupe, and respond. It's a conversation. You can't have a conversation with your feet."

Then he closed part of the distance, positioned his hands a breath away from where they should be, like something lurked in the sliver of air between his hand and her palm, his fingers and her waist.

"Did Mesny teach you that when I wasn't looking?" Kellan asked.

"My mother did. Later, my father tried to teach it how Mesny's doing now, only not as nicely and not on his own. But it's like trying to unlearn how to read. You can't do it."

Monsieur Bonne. Axel rarely mentioned his father. Then again, Kellan hadn't asked about him. Axel shared so much so easily that, were it not for how he glanced away from her, toward the window and its dusted light, she'd have thought it a passing comment. A boy talking about his family. Their quirks, their faults. But like most things with Axel, it seemed it wasn't so simple.

Kellan closed the tiny bit of distance between them, offering her waist and her hand as she rested hers on his shoulder. Without Mesny looming over them, most of the pressure had all but dissipated. There was still the matter of their closeness, which was all very new and somehow stranger without prying eyes to keep them company.

"Just look at me," he said. "You know the steps. Staring down will only trip you up."

"You say that now, but I don't wanna hear a word if this gets you another bruised toe."

"You won't," he said with a reassuring smile. "I promise."

They started slow, ignored the music echoing in the hall to first learn how the other moved. She listened instead to the gentle pressure of his palm on her hip when it came time for them to turn; the slight squeeze of her hand just before a twirl; the mischievous glint in his eyes before he dipped her, which always left her in a fit of hysterics. Soon they danced like the sunlit dust, cutting the stripes with their silhouettes, filling the silence with laughter and footsteps. Until they sensed another presence close by.

Kellan and Axel jumped apart upon spotting Mesny by the door, a cup of coffee in her hands. She sipped, watching them with idle curiosity, a look that, strangely, warmed Kellan's cheeks. They were practicing. That was all. Yet, when she caught Axel's eye and he smiled again, she couldn't help but feel like they shared another secret now.

Soon autompne made way for froigus, and the Makers'

Ball nipped at their heels. Soon Mesny's lessons on decorum ended, and the real work began.

"Life" was the second trial's theme. Kellan's plan was to fill rooms with metal dancers that moved with the music and made partners out of party guests. Together, she and Mesny honed her performance until they deemed it close to perfect. When one metal dancer sent a visiting repairmin out the door in giggles and spins, Mesny patted Kellan's back, and Kellan basked in the warmth of a job well done.

"Excellent work," said Mesny. "Charming, too. I was beginning to think we'd never get this fitted."

Xo held up a gown that, at first, looked more like still water than silk. "Is that what you're wearing?" asked Kellan, folding the hollow metal dolls into sheets.

"Of course not. It's yours."

Kellan froze. She'd always admired Rizian fashions, but like a fish admired the sky—from afar, as it wasn't meant for them. It was too flashy, too expensive, too . . . much. But this gown was a work of art. The silk wasn't still water. Midnight blue shimmered like a calm and endless sea under the moonlight of the chandelier, and gold sequins glittered like stars on the skin's reflection. She didn't touch it. Instead, she picked at her hair, dry and matted and unfit for something so beautiful.

Mesny's grin softened. "I've a plan for that, too."

FOURTEEN

When the night of the trial finally arrived, Kellan and Cyn rode with Mesny to a place Mesny hadn't yet shared, as those invited never knew the Ball's exact location more than an hour before its start. Kellan had heard whisperings that it'd happen at a hotel on the Makers' Strip, where kings and queens and movie stars vacationed when Nanseau opened its docks. But Mesny's automirun never stopped in front of a hotel. Instead, it slowed at a snack stand, a lone woman closing shop.

"No stars tonight," said the woman behind the stand, wiping down her tiny kitchen. Moonlight caught the gold of her pin and its three glittering pieces of tiger's eye. An architect.

"I see suns in the water," Kellan said in answer.

A square of sidewalk slid away, revealing a narrow set of stairs. Kellan climbed out of the car, drank in as much fresh air as she could, and took one step after another until she was swallowed by darkness.

Kellan felt her way down the narrow stairwell, her hands on either wall. Eventually, she came upon a door at the bottom step. No lock. No knob. She pushed until it gave.

The air shimmered and hummed with jazz and runework, the band's brass section reflecting it all, bouncing the light so that it danced on the room's steel pillars and walls. She recognized their carvings immediately. The walls' ancient arrays of sigils seemed to move with the musicians, the dancers, the crowd. This wasn't a hotel at all. This was Sougare, the City Below.

Even the people were more glitter than flesh, from the bits of metal in their clothes to the wire fashioned into shapes and animals they'd woven in their hair. Her gold-threaded braids felt dull compared to some of what she'd seen in flashes: elaborate clockfaces and flamingos, constellations and magnolia bouquets.

"This is a nasty habit of yours, Eighth," someone chuckled. "Being late."

Kellan jumped and let the curtain fall. The hole in the sidewalk led her to the back of a stage, where the bids waited with their automi assistants. She hadn't looked at them yet, but Faustin stood a safe distance away, grinning stupidly in his showy suit. "Better than being nosy."

"I prefer concerned. We're an alliance, remember?"

"No. I don't."

He tsked, straightening his sequined bow tie in his automi's reflection. "Might want to jog your memory. Tonight's trial looks like it'll be—"

"Ahem."

Someone cleared their throat behind her. Izod, in a suit too small for him, stood beside a distracted Orana, who hummed idly while twirling the ribbon at her waist in the air. He looked like he'd swallowed something hard and refused to cough it up, squirming in place with his cheeks flushed and his shoulders tense.

"Is he going to say something?" asked Faustin.

"I'm not sure if I want him to," muttered Kellan, anger tightening her chest. The last time he spoke, he'd shoved her to the ground and called her a tower rat. A ticking clock had kept her from shooting back, but now she had nothing but time to make stupid decisions.

"Go on," said Orana. "Just like we practiced."

He hesitated. "Sorry for pushing you that day," he said, after a long, awkward pause. "I didn't expect you to be so weak."

"And I didn't expect you to be such a coward, but here we are."

Cyn pulled Kellan back by the collar. "There will be no fighting before the Ball's end. This gown is priceless. I will not have it returned to the Madame torn and bloodstained."

But Izod didn't look like he wanted to fight. He met Kellan's gaze and lifted his chin, the corner of his mouth twitching in . . . Was that a grin? Either way, he walked off without explanation, tossing his too-tight suit jacket on a nearby chair.

"That was *not* what we practiced," mumbled Orana, letting her ribbon hang down her skirt. "Good luck, Kellan."

"You too. And thank you."

For the next hour, the bids kept to themselves.

Izod stretched in the far corner, looking more like he was preparing to fight than he was preparing to make. Orana looked in deep conversation with her automi, a model Kellan was sure was incapable of talking back. Harmon Barbier, the mousy boy from New Montague who took Maricar's vacant place, wore a dent in the ground as he paced back and forth, biting his lips bloody from nerves.

Marielo stared straight ahead. Although they stood too far apart for Kellan to read his face, she knew determination when she saw it. But it was more than that. Hunger. Hunger and something she couldn't place. She looked away in fear of what it could be.

This trial was nothing like the last. Whereas the first trial's panel sat high above them all, its stage shrouded in secrets, now the panel stood in the audience and sipped sparkling wine as a master of ceremony announced each bid with pomp and jazz. Faustin went first, though he left the audience more enamored with his charm than his demonstration—the illusion of a tower more decorative than practical. After him went Orana, who soared over the audience in a glider carved from aluminum. Then Izod, who warped metal into weapons Kellan had never seen before, and Marielo, who carved runes she hadn't known existed. That left her and Harmon, who still hadn't looked her in the eye from their spot behind the curtain. Soon she learned why. Moments after the master of ceremony called his name, after Harmon took the stage and a long, deep breath, he carved into a sheet of brass before a waiting crowd. And then, metal dancers came to life.

Cyn held Kellan back by the waist as weeks of work charmed the audience, taking makers and merchants into dips and spins to music that didn't follow the band. She didn't know what infuriated her more: that he'd somehow managed to copy her entire performance or that he couldn't even get the runework right. Her fingers had just brushed the curtain when Cyn pulled, forcing Kellan to stumble into the wall.

"Think." Cyn held one arm out in case Kellan tried again. "Storming onto the stage will only embarrass the Madame and ruin your already narrow chances of success."

"He can't get away with this—"

"He can, and he has. 'They will steal. They will lie. They will scheme and sabotage, and—'"

"'When they sense the slightest whiff of weakness, they will crush its source with their bare, talented hands.'" Kellan smoothed her skirt and pressed her palm into a pillar, welcoming the heat of Sougare's runes against her skin as Harmon's performance ended. By the time he stepped off the stage and into the crowd, the runes had left their mark in an angry red imprint from wrist to fingertip. The master of ceremony called on Kellan, who stood still in the dark.

"What will you do?" asked Cyn in a panicked whisper.

She didn't know. At the sound of "DuCuivre," the crowd

whispered as well, its drone swelling with each passing second. She couldn't go on as planned, not right after a show so like her own. Not when they already expected the worst.

She'd have to improvise.

The heat in Kellan's palm spread and sparked into a flame, burning Harmon's lingering betrayal into ash. He didn't matter anyway. "Someone here thinks I'm weak." She flexed her fingers at her side, the goldstone of her carver's handle cooling Sougare's mark. "I'll correct them."

Kellan stepped out from behind the curtain before the master of ceremony repeated her name again, her gown's sheer navy train brushing the stage floor in the silence. Each click of her heels echoed against Sougare's steel walls. Mesny'd told her to smile. Kellan didn't. She wouldn't pretend to take Harmon's slight in stride. No. Kellan was furious, and tonight, she'd show them exactly how much.

She began with a doll. She'd carved so many for Pape's Peculiars that even its shell made Harmon's copy look like something he'd made in the dark. This doll didn't dance. From its hand sprung a blade, solid as the gold of the doll's body. Kellan carved zirconium into an illusionary powder that gathered into walls and buttresses, statues and vaults, dulled from metal to blackened rock. A doll, trapped in a prison as beautiful as it was haunting, thick with the lingering ghosts of a fallen empire and a long-lost war.

The floor became Kellan's stage. Another carve, and steps

gathered along the walls. Another carve, and the doll climbed them, blade in hand, off to destroy an enemy neither she nor the audience yet knew.

Soon the doll cleared the step, and Kellan braved Marielo's runes. She'd only seen them once, from a distance. But with them, she created a beast of light and shadow. A storm cloud. A lightning rod. Fog, and fire, and rage made manifest, massive before the tiny golden doll. Her sword was a needle, and the beast was smoke and endless stone.

But the doll grew wings with her courage. And when she slashed the beast, the walls shattered with it. Above, the night sky. Below, the open sea. They met at the horizon, where the doll flew into freedom.

The dust, the sky, and the sea dissipated in an invisible breeze, and Sougare smelled of perfume and alcohol again. She bowed once more, grip tight around her carver's handle, as the room echoed with scattered applause. Soon it swelled so loud Kellan plugged her ears to stop the ringing. She stepped off the stage, slipping past the many people trying to pull her aside, in search of Harmon's mousy face.

Perhaps it was the way of the game. She'd been warned as much. She'd told herself she was ready for it, the schemes and betrayals. After all, she'd endured more for less. But it wasn't just her and a gaggle of troubled children anymore. A threat to her bid was a threat to Edgar's health, and Harmon's trick nearly cost him his life. She found him laughing awkwardly between two old men with glimmering merchant pins, and were it not for the voice that sounded from behind her, Kellan would've broken into a run.

"Are you always so impulsive?"

She stopped. Marielo stood a few feet away with his hands in his pockets. He hadn't changed much since the first trial. His hair, still slick and neat, gleamed under the ball's shimmering light. No slouch to his shoulders or crack in his voice. He was the picture of control, as if this entire event was beneath him. But dark circles lined his sharp eyes, and Kellan knew better.

"Yeah," she said after a train of drunk apprentices cut through the gap between them. "Afraid so."

"Blunt, too?"

"Don't like wasting time."

He watched her for a moment before answering. "Neither do I," he said, then pointed with a purse of his lips toward the patch of hall farthest from the band. Away from Harmon.

Kellan followed Marielo to an animated sculpture away from the audience, which was shadowed under balconies. Had anyone else mentioned his sister? He'd stood alone backstage, and she doubted he remembered much from the Guild archives meeting, if someone had pulled him aside in his state. She never knew what to say when it counted, so she'd kept her mouth shut then, too. Maybe the right words would come to her now.

"Harmon's performance," he said, looking out into the crowd. The party went on without them. From here, everyone blurred into one mass of glitter, the music from the band distorted from distance. "It was yours."

"Good to hear it was obvious."

"It wasn't. From the gallery, it looked like a boy trying his hand at something five steps too complex for him. It might have fooled a few merchants, but the forum could tell."

"And you? How could you tell?"

"Simple." Marielo faced her again, this time so close to her she could finally place the peculiar shade of his eyes: raw axinite, its grays and oiled bronzes brilliant in the light, but swallowed in the dark. Here, Kellan could only see its bottomless blacks. "It was my suggestion."

The music warbled, the world went blurry, and the laughter of the ball's guests dulled in the thickened air. She remembered the first trial, when Izod knocked her to the ground. She'd dropped her carver then. "I almost miscarved that night," she managed. "That was you."

Marielo let the silence answer for him.

"Sabotage, I can almost understand. But murder?"

"Murder implies intent. I never intended for you to die, just to fail." Another step. She could smell his cologne, track the tremor in his tightened jaw. "Now, I'm not so sure."

"Whatever happened to the element of surprise?"

"We're both beyond surprises now."

"We beyond explanations, too?"

"You killed my sister."

Kellan's blood went cold, her breaths jagged and hollow. Through the fog, Marielo's composure began to crack. His cool eyes sparked with a rage so hot it could melt Sougare's steel.

She pretended not to notice how he trembled, how he spoke the words as though it was his first time saying them aloud, equal parts thinnest glass and deadliest venom. Fragile and dangerous.

"I . . ." The bravado she'd found shattered under Marielo's accusation. "I didn't kill her," she said. "We got out. Both of us. Then she went back in, and I—"

"You let her."

"I followed her!"

"One foot. One foot past the threshold, and you stopped. I saw it from the lot." The spark of rage was a smoking flame now. "You watched her die. One less bid in your way."

"No." Kellan had closed her eyes to fog and stone, to sea and stars. That was what she saw that night. She, and no one else. Had it been a nightmare? A memory over a memory, her mind's attempt to block what it knew she couldn't handle? Something more? Whatever it was, she didn't know it'd stopped her from taking another step. A step that could've saved a life. "No, I—I didn't mean to . . . I didn't see—"

"There you are! A marvelous show, simply genius. Maker Villiers warned us you'd be the one to watch!"

A stranger approached from behind. Marielo straightened, the ghost of a smile curving his lips. From farther away, perhaps no one would tell it didn't reach his eyes. He greeted the stranger with a handshake, promising to speak with him after saying goodbye to his friend. Then, he leaned close, pretended to kiss Kellan's cheeks, and when he whispered, the cold edge of his words cut clean through her composure.

"I wanted to humiliate you first," he said in one ear. Then, in the other, "But I'm learning not to waste time."

They were gone before Kellan remembered to breathe. The world went gray again, tilting as she fumbled through the fog. *Protect him,* Maricar said in Kellan's memory, soft over the din of chatter and jazz. *And forgive him.*

She bumped into a pillar. Shook it off. Pressed her palms against her ears when the music, and chatter, and memory flooded her senses. Five things she could see, or hear, or smell, but what could she do when everything blurred together?

"Miss DuCuivre!"

Someone stood in her path, short and hunched with a strong Crestian accent. Then another, taller. Another, slimmer. She tried to focus on their faces, hear something after they'd called her name. To smile, or bow, or see, or *breathe*—

A hand fell to the small of her back. It was warm and firm. She almost didn't recognize the boy beside her now, who stood at his full imposing height, fawnish eyes sharp and dopey smile dazzling.

"One at a time, gentlemin," said Axel, stepping between them. "Another word, and we'll have to form a queue."

Axel shook their hands and led Kellan along the room's outskirts, the rise and fall of his chest just noticeable enough for her to follow its rhythm.

"Did something happen?" he asked when the music was music again. He smiled pleasantly, too pleasantly, and Kellan caught on. The trial hadn't yet ended. The forum was still watching.

"No," she lied. If Axel caught her in it, he didn't let on. "Just overwhelmed."

Kellan watched the crowd from its edges and couldn't find a single friendly face. The last thing she wanted to do was smile and laugh, let alone for people who likely despised the thought of her joining their ranks.

Axel pretended to glance over Kellan's head and spoke just low enough for her to hear. "You'll be fine," he said, mischief in his grin. "We practiced, remember?"

"Shouldn't you be somewhere being impartial?"

"I already made my rounds. And everyone plays favorites tonight."

With Mesny and Cyn lost to the crowd, Axel and Kellan worked it as a pair. When she stumbled, Axel deflected with eerie quickness. It wasn't long before Kellan found her footing. She remembered when to play coy and when to play clever, how to laugh at jokes she didn't find funny and how to parry harsh words with a sharp and subtle tongue.

The evening carried on like that for hours. How many, she couldn't say. She'd stopped remembering names after the inventor behind the rune-powered coffee drip rambled on about beans for so long even Axel just barely covered for her disinterest.

It wasn't so much the talking that bothered her. It was the social chess of it all, the nipping and tucking of everything Kellan was. This was a show. A trial. She knew that as well as she now knew Harmon's betrayal was a slight to be expected, and Marielo's rage would never fade. But the knowledge alone didn't make it any less exhausting.

She must've done a poor job at hiding it. After a drunk alchemist stumbled away with his husband, Axel leaned in before another curious guest could interrupt. "I have an idea."

"You have a lot of those."

"How much time have you spent in Sougare? Excluding tonight, in this room."

"Collectively? Ten minutes. Maybe fifteen."

"Perfect. Follow me."

Kellan's curiosity was piqued. She spared one glance to the crowd before following Axel to the ballroom's outskirts again. When they reached the back wall, he dragged his fingers along the metal, counting so softly Kellan hardly noticed his lips moving at all. He pressed into the runes every few feet.

"Most of Sougare is a series of tunnels. The railways make up most of the largest ones, but there are some the underground used to travel unnoticed during the Liberation. The whole thing is a maze, and almost every place is connected to another in some way. There's always a path, and if you know the lay of the land well enough . . . There we go."

Axel pushed again. A panel slid back and behind, making a way just wide enough for them to file in. She checked over her shoulder to see if anyone noticed. No one had paid them any attention. "Where's it go?"

"And ruin the surprise?" he said with a slight grin. "Never."

"Didn't know you were so adventurous."

"What made you think that?"

"Something about the glasses."

"All right, let's say I'm not. I also just really, *really* don't like this party."

She laughed—genuinely laughed—for the first time all night, but it faded once she looked inside. From under the night sky, the stairwell in the sidewalk didn't look as bottomless. Here, the hole in the wall was the only thing in the room that didn't cast a reflection. She stiffened at the memory of Ol' Matty's carshop, the trial's open door, and the dark Maricar had disappeared into. The dark Kellan thought—Kellan *knew*—she'd followed her through. The dark from which Maricar never returned.

"We can stay, if you want," he said, one foot in and one foot out. His grin softened to something a little gentler, and she cursed the heavy thing that swelled in her chest. "Your choice."

Her choice. So much of the night, of the past three months, of her entire life had been firmly *not* her choice. Two words shouldn't have meant as much as they did, but there they were. There he was. "You go first," she said stubbornly. "If we get lost, I'm blaming you."

And so their journey began. She followed him through the hole in the wall, slipped off her heels when the door closed behind her. The air in Sougare's abandoned tunnels reeked of mold and stale water, its runed walls coated in cobwebs and thick gray dust. Axel led the way with a compass and the peculiar tube of wooden mesh she'd found in his apartment all those weeks ago. It was a gravelight, he'd explained. One of his ancient Aigan tomes told the story of a man who used it to find his way out of death. Long after the sounds of the city faded, after countless dips and bends, Axel stopped beneath a plate in a low roof that still glimmered weakly in his dim light. "Ready?" he asked, his boyish smile returned.

"As I'll ever be," she said. "Especially if it'll get me out of this cave."

Axel pushed at the roof and slid it aside. He climbed up and into the dark, helping Kellan the rest of the way once he found his footing. They'd stepped into a tiny wooden room, its walls crooked and warped from rain and age. Then he found the room's door, and opened it to another world.

Kellan had never seen so many trees, their trunks furry with moss and soaked black with swamp water. They weren't like the manicured trees in the Quarter's centergarden, but ancient and sprawling, their branches eclipsing half the sky. And the sky . . . It was more star than night blue, a thousand twinkling lights washing the bayou in sterling silver. Lightning bugs blinked in the branches and the shadows, little suns come to visit from above.

They'd reached the wetlands outside the city, he told her: the swamps just east of the bayou. He rolled the hems of his pants to the shins, and she tied the trailing fabric of her gown to the knee to follow him farther south. He knew the way well, stepped where his feet wouldn't sink. He held her hand when she nearly slipped into the water and didn't let go.

Soon the trees thinned. Wooden boards on stilts formed a village square over a lazy river. It glistened under the open sky, lantern flame brightening the starlight's dim glow. Slivers of delicate string wove through the surrounding trees' branches in something of a wildly ineffective roof. It was beautiful, though. Intricate. Precise. Like runework, the shape of a spider's web.

"Looks like we just missed it," he said with a heavy sigh, exaggerated to mask his disappointment. "Démansem."

"Is this the part where I pretend to know what that is?"

He chuckled and let her hand go to sit atop a barrel at the edge of the square. "It's an Aigoix festival to bring in the new year. It's the same across the island. The troupe sets up a stage, the vendors sell some food. The Teller chooses a different story every year, but the gist doesn't change. Community and faith and all that." His smile dimmed as he rolled a stray wooden bead under his foot. "I've made it almost every year until now."

Kellan warmed her hands with her breath and sat on the barrel beside his. "That explains the books. The thread, and the mesh in your pocket."

He nodded, smile flickering. In a blink, it was bright again. He told her about festivals past and retold his favorite stories, tried to describe the taste of asaanroux and howled when Kellan pretended to gag at the thought of corn in a dessert drink. He taught her silly dances and serious ones, traced constellations in the stars, and soon the abandoned square became Mesny's ballroom, the two of them moving to the music of the katydids and wind-whistled leaves.

"My mother's a Wanderer," he said into the quiet, the wood creaking lightly under them as they swayed. "She grew up here, hops between the cities sometimes. I was on my way back from visiting her in Il the day you ran into me on the train, actually. She should be in Un now."

The train. It felt so long ago, that stormy day she'd left her ville behind. She should have missed home. She should have missed Cuivreton's red mountains and parched valleys, her workbench in the shop attic and the postmin who remembered her name. Being a stranger in a strange place should have put her on edge. It was an evolutionary precaution, what kept humans from walking off cliffs and into volcanoes since the Storied Age. She should have been frightened of the dark, of the trees and the murky water and the boy she hardly knew. She shouldn't have felt safe here. Or curious. Or happy.

"You heard him, didn't you," she said, staring at the knot of Axel's necktie. "Me and Marielo by the wall."

Axel didn't answer, only tightened his hold on her hand. It made sense now, how thoroughly he helped her navigate the viper's den of party guests. How he arrived at exactly the right time with exactly the right plan. Why he led her out of the city and into the swamps, where his laugh made magic out of the stars and the wind swept her guilt into the trees.

"Did you see it, too? What happened over the threshold?"

"Kellan—"

"I stopped, didn't I? I watched it happen, but I don't—I don't remember."

"Kellan."

She slipped out of his hold, stumbled back as though she'd burn him if she stood too close. No one saw the gray or the water. No one saw the rabbit or the stone. But they did see Kellan stop too soon, watch as Maricar marched to her death. She didn't know which was worse: going mad or turning into a monster. Because if no one else saw the fog or the rabbit, the water and the stone . . . was it ever real at all?

Axel met her step for step. Tilted her chin up. Cradled her cheeks in his hands. *Look at me,* she heard in the brush of his thumb along her cheekbone, in his kind and steady gaze. In his slight smile, soft and sweet as the night breeze. *Five things you can see.*

There were many things to see. The stars overhead. The river through the boards underfoot. The abandoned bead that rolled through its crack, plopping into the water. She'd seen them all. But when Axel's gaze dipped from her eyes to her lips, his breath warming her cheeks in the sudden chill and his touch grounding her here, now, in a place he'd called a secret . . . she couldn't see any of it. Because all she saw was him.

But the moment ended. He stood straight, frowning into the dark. "Did you hear something?"

"Hear something?" she managed once her racing pulse faded. "Hear what?"

"A voice. I don't recognize it, and this far out . . ."

Something plopped into the water again. This time, closer. This time, everywhere. In the reflection of Axel's glasses, Kellan saw three other things. Wild silver hair. A tattered coat, faded sawdust that had once been sienna. And two pit-black eyes, meeting hers in the dark.

FIFTEEN

Kellan peered through the trees, cursing the night she'd loved moments before. Axel's gravelight couldn't cut the dark. The voice echoed from the leaves and the river, the wood and the string. "Stay close," said Axel, his free hand tight around her wrist.

What are you, then, little thing? Maker? Mender? Liar? Thief? Her cackle rang over the running river and the katydids, crackling sparks before a forest fire. *A rat? Or a frightened child.*

"Kellan, don't—"

A streak of sawdust through the trees. Footsteps, quick and nimble, from her left. She'd tried to take off, but Axel's grip held her firm. "Let me go," she said, voice trembling. "Let me go!"

"To what, run blind through the swamp? Now, with a target on your back? At best, you'll get lost. At worst—" Axel swallowed his next words and started again. "The Guild just told every maker of power on this island that a Du is vying for a place. We don't know who or what this is, but if word got out to the wrong people—"

Another plop. Kellan's feet went cold and wet. Water, murky with lime and rust, swelled from the square's center. Beside her, Axel backed away in confusion, his grip around her wrist loosening for a moment. Just a moment. But a moment was all she needed.

Kellan DuCuivre ignored the sound of Axel calling her name from behind. His voice faded with every frantic step she took. Her feet left solid wood for sinking soil, her skirt snagging on thorns and fallen branches. A glimpse of white emerged behind a bend. She spun in its direction, only for a cackle from the other side of a downed willow's trunk to catch her attention. Without hesitating this time, Kellan climbed. She tore through curtains of ancient moss and clouds of gnats until Axel's voice became a memory, and all that surrounded Kellan was a thick and endless black.

Her breaths echoed against the vast empty as she spun, searching for the woman she'd call Foxglove. It was happening again, the change she'd stepped through at Ol' Matty's shop. She knew it in the silence. In the way the ground gave under her feet. It was too level, too consistent. Soil that wasn't soil. Earth that wasn't earth. "I'm sick of these games," she called. "Tell me what this is."

A rat, then. That's what they call you. The voice laughed, the sound so broken Kellan couldn't find its start. *Look at her scurry and squeak. Will you tell us what you're searching for? Did you already forget?*

The black curled like smoke, and the smoke gathered into gray. Cooled and cracked, ancient bricks of harsh granite. Kellan stood at the foot of a spiral staircase she knew well. Too well. So well that when she pressed her foot against the first step, she expected the creak, soft as a cooing newborn. She knew every inch of this shadow of her namehouse. Everything but the golden rabbit glittering at her feet.

Kellan lunged for the rabbit but only caught air. The rabbit dissipated in a cloud of gold. Buzzing filled the silence. Buzzing as the gold fog curled into beads, those beads into bugs, a swarm of bees taking flight so she would make chase.

She swatted at the gathered cloud. If she caught one, maybe Foxglove would give her answers. If she caught one, maybe she could prove it was all real. But they scattered like ripples in the sea, and something pinched under the ear. She hissed, smacked the side of her throat in reflex. Before she pulled her hand back, her nail caught on a snag.

Got a stinger in your neck.

I've been watched for too long.

Kellan stumbled back as the dark closed in like ink on damp paper. The Guild's first trial's password. The gray past the door. The rabbit from the shop, the swamp, the counter in Cuivreton's only train station. The connection she knew existed but didn't want to find.

Answers wouldn't come to her willingly. They never did.

She bled for everything she knew, clawed her way out of her namehouse tower's walls, and took them. Yet her fingers trembled when she gripped the railing, and the sluggish thud of her heartbeat rang in her ears.

Plop. Splash. The bees weren't alone anymore. Something else waited with them.

Light whirled against the rock in soft tides. Plop. Splash. The dark swallowed the stone with each step. Plop. Splash. It swallowed the sound of the creaking stairs, the stink of rust and mildew, the flowers that grew dead in the tower's cracked walls, overwatered and underlit.

She cleared the last step. In a room of dark echoed dripping water in an ornate granite tub.

The plops fell like rain now, filling the tub to its brim until it overflowed, murky and green with lime and copper.

Until the overflow ran black.

It wasn't water. It wasn't ink. It was something strange, like fog or smoke. It gathered like the gold, like the gray. Formed a hand, the tub's edge cracking under the weight of its long-fingered grip, and then a neck, bent and curling up toward her. A head, the black edgeless and vague. But not a face.

No stars tonight.

I see suns in the water.

Cold crawled out from her spine. Seeped into her ribs. Skittered between the bones, and set her lungs aflame. Her dress caught weight, damp from a rain that didn't fall. The bees, gone. In their place hovered lightning bugs, just bigger than the tip of her thumb. There was no sun to play tricks, no high grass to lure them near. Two settled on the gathered dark's empty face where its eyes should have been.

It's time we remember, little thing. The dark opened its maw, but the voice didn't come from its throat. It was something separate, an audience to Kellan's horror as she stood, helpless, facing the end. *A rat always remembers.*

Then the dark was gone. Kellan bolted upright, gasping for air. Beneath her, soaked earth. Above, stars and night sky. Rain pelted the ground in cold, angry streams. There was no sign of the square or the web. She must have traveled far before it began.

"It's not safe here," said Axel, helping Kellan onto her feet. He'd held her up in the water, and when he pulled his arms out from around her, the cold hit her with a vengeance. "We have to go. We'll take the tunnels, find a cab— Would you *stop storming off*? Do you get a kick out of near-death experiences?"

"I need to get to the ball," she said. She wrung as much water out of her skirt as she could, but her shaking hands struggled with the silk. "I need to find Mesny."

The more Kellan worked her skirt, the harder the rain fell to undo it. Every strange thing she'd experienced, from Cuivreton Station to the green-gray stone on the other side of Ol' Matty's threshold, was connected. She didn't know how, and she didn't know why, but she knew there was more to this competition than a potential apprenticeship. She knew danger waited for her. She'd already started walking. Axel caught up with her in a few long-legged strides. "You go into the ball like that, and the Guild—"

"The trial isn't important right now."

"Three months of work, and an hour of malchemy makes the trial unimportant?"

"Malchemy?" She'd heard that word at her first lesson with Mesny but hadn't paid it much mind.

"Minebelt. Right. In the west, I think you call it fleshwork? Taboo? Francom's Fear?"

Kellan stopped, the swamp's mud pinning her feet in place. That was why the word sounded so familiar. If Francom's Theorem was one of makecraft's most fundamental pillars, then Francom's Fear was the shadow it cast in the sun.

It'd taken a great amount of experimentation to discover what sort of matter took to runework and what didn't. Water, he'd found, had no effect. Wood was fickle and unpredictable. The body, however, was more than that. The body was dangerous.

Whatever Francom had seen when he'd first carved into skin was buried with him, lost to history. But there were stories of after, when villages vanished overnight, leaving only runes drawn in dried blood at their heart. Of makers gone mad from carves on their stomachs and backs, or trees of runed bone sprouting from abandoned corpses. For every law, theory, and principle, makecraft always had its mystery, and to many makers, Francom's Fear—malchemy—was the greatest of them all.

She'd never seen it before, of course. Not for herself. But before tonight, she'd also never seen the dark gather into a monster.

Kellan dove through the drunken crowd, mucky feet squishing with every step and Axel trailing close behind. She'd lost her heels somewhere in the marsh. Mesny stood a few yards away from the band and a head taller than the small audience surrounding her, glittering under a chandelier with a glass of sparkling wine in her hand. Maker Jourdain lingered just outside Mesny's circle, whispering with the old man in velvet who'd almost sabotaged her and Edgar's last workshop—Marielo's sponsor, Maker René Villiers.

". . . truly exceptional," Mesny said to a man in a color-changing hat. "There hasn't been a mind like hers in— Ah! Speak of the . . ."

The band stuttered, stumbled over part of the measure, and didn't recover in time to mask the small crowd's murmur. "Disappointing," whispered Maker Jourdain loudly, his yellow hair combed so sleek it almost looked solid, "but not unexpected."

"It's in her nature," said Maker Villiers. "Rats are partial to dirt."

"I need to talk to you," Kellan said to Mesny. "In private."

None of the others noticed the concern that furrowed Mesny's brow; they were too horrified by Kellan's swampy feet and the brown that mucked the bundled hem of her dress. Mesny recovered quickly, though. She laughed and handed someone her drink. "If only we could all be so bold," she said, squeezing through the group. "I, too, would prefer to walk without these torture devices, however flattering they may be. If you'll excuse us."

She led the way to the exit. They had to get aboveground now, out of earshot. With Mesny behind her and Axel at her side, the people parted like a fault in the earth. "Axel, can you find—"

"Cyn, yeah, I'm on it."

The confusion that clouded his fawnish brown eyes hadn't cleared by then, but he nodded anyway. He made to squeeze her arm, but must have thought better of it, and offered an awkward thumbs-up instead. She'd have to thank him. For that, and the jacket she'd tossed over her shoulders in her hurry to leave the bayou. It was a comfortable weight, and the only welcome one when the cold press of judging stares closed in. When they met the night air, she inhaled it until her chest stung, drank in the din of scattered crickets and distant car horns.

"Explain. Now." By then, Mesny's stifled rage showed through the slight flare of her nostrils. "Do you realize who those people were? What that outburst cost you?"

"It doesn't matter."

"Doesn't matter? Doesn't matter!" Mesny guffawed, her anger bubbling to the surface. "The man in the hat? That was Monsieur Jolif. *Master Alchemist* Jolif. Then in you trot, covered in mud and reeking of the outdoors—"

"Did I get their attention? Good! Call them up. Maybe one of them can tell me the truth."

"Don't be ridiculous. I've been perfectly transparent—"

"'There's a stinger in my neck'? 'I see suns in the water'?" Kellan stepped forward, dwarfed by Mesny's height. "I thought the trial passwords were just tradition. Stupid phrases for stupid games. But they mean something, don't they? The Guild knows something, don't they? Something is happening."

Madame Mesny went ghostly still.

"I've seen things, felt things, that I can't explain," said Kellan. "I run through them over and over in my head, trying to find the alchemy, the runework, a trace of logic in what's happening to me and around me, and there's nothing. Just you, these blackouts, and this guild. They're connected. They're connected, and I deserve to know why."

Kellan pointed to the pinch below her ear. A trail of dried blood striped the side of her throat, staining her gown's navy neckline crimson. She hadn't checked, herself, but she knew the thing in her neck did not come from a natural bee. After all, there was nothing natural about what happened in the swamp.

For too long, Mesny stared in unmistakable horror. Then something shifted. Fear and confusion warped into a moment, a split second, of deep thought, until it transformed into the look she wore when Kellan executed a knot she hadn't considered. When, in the middle of dinner, she used hot sauce as ink and her fork as a fountain pen to jot a note on her napkin. When something finally, impossibly, clicked.

"I think," said Mesny, "it's time I introduce you to Pa Maude."

"Everything all right?"

Axel and Cyn stood by the hole in the sidewalk, and Mesny's expression went unreadable once more. "Kellan, Cyn, to the car. Axel, do your best to clean this mess. It's imperative that Kellan doesn't fail. All of this was part of the show. Do you understand?"

"Yes, but . . . And there they go." Mesny and Cyn climbed into the car, leaving Kellan and Axel to the night. "You really made a mess of things in there, you know." He sighed, ducking into the cold.

"It's a talent."

When Kellan pulled an arm out of her borrowed jacket, Axel stopped her with an open palm. "Keep it."

"It's freezing!"

"I run warm." He tried to grin, but unease tugged at the corners of his mouth. "Besides, I've got fires to put out. You should go, before—"

"Kellan!"

"I'm coming, but I . . ."

. . . needed to thank him for spending his night saving her from ravenous gossips. Ask him how he found her by the water in the dark. Tell him how much she enjoyed their time on the barrels, with the stars and the stream, that he smelled like cinnamon and cherrywood, and she wished she could share something as sacred to her as the trees and stories and people from the marsh were to him, but she had so little, and she clung so tightly—

Mesny honked the horn. Kellan waved goodbye, her hand half hidden in his sleeve. As the car pulled out of the lot, she tried to convince herself that that was enough.

The drive was long and silent, aside from the tires clunking over the occasional sewer vent. That silence followed them through the districts, Mesny staring out into the night. Cyn sat so still that Kellan, more than once, stopped to listen for her runes. She didn't recognize this Mesny, either, who sat stiff and turned away, her knees angled toward the door, poised for a quick escape.

When they reached the manor, Mesny sent Cyn to one of the libraries and led the way up the front steps. Kellan followed her down several hallways until they reached the second stairwell. Two lefts. One right. Past the door with the top hat. The framed sculptures on the walls sparkled in the moonlight, but without the sweep and scuttle of the cleaning automi, the hall was deathly quiet.

"My grandfather had this wing built shortly after the Court decided to classify runes." Mesny ran her fingertip along the wire of a golden spiderweb. As the sculpture split and spread, the wall behind it parted with an earthy groan from the floor to the ceiling. One by one, sconces lit the way down, just bright enough to illuminate the steps.

"No one, not even my father, knew about this workshop," she explained on the way down the stairs, "but considering the circumstances . . . yes. Yes, I think it best that I share it with you. At least for a time."

Kellan tried not to mind the stench of mildew and rotted wood. When they cleared the last step, she coughed from the dust and swatted at the cobwebs. Things skittered in the walls, likely mice, although she couldn't imagine how they'd survived so long behind the brick and mortar.

This wasn't a workshop. Not really. A small bench sat in the corner furthest from her with cracked, dust-coated slivers of metal. But that was the only sign of makecraft in the entire space. This was something else.

The maze of bookshelves to the left was more of a labyrinth than a library. Each was covered in sheets of runed glass coated in a layer of dust thick as sheared wool. Kellan stepped farther in and approached one of the displays on the right. It was decorated with oaken figures of many-eyed beasts. Beaded nets woven from straw sat alongside them, large enough to snare an elephant, but bunched into a neat circle and tied with twine. Those peculiar boxes of glass shards stacked into a tower, the wood cracked and warped from age and neglect. A painting of Maudelaire and a scrawny boy with thick hair and a gap-toothed smile hung from the room's only bare wall, their guild pins glittering.

"He was, to me, both a father and a mother. Pa Maude," she said, straightening her grandfather's portrait. "He liked to tell me stories, you see. Told them with such conviction that I could see the rabbits bound across my bedroom, hear the monsters rustle the brush. I couldn't touch them, but they were all around me, every day, separated only by that thin veil Pa Maude lifted at bedtime."

Kellan opened the drawer beneath the painting and coughed at the dust it brought up. Inside were an assortment of handguns, peculiarly runed bullets, and more of the strange shards of dust-coated glass she'd found her first day behind the door with the top hat. She couldn't tell if they were from the same cup, or jar. She shut the drawer back.

"When I asked him why my father never took up the craft, he sat me down, and he told me: 'Minora, Marshall thinks in measurements and puzzle pieces, but you and I know there are rabbits in the kitchen cabinets and monsters in the Quarter trees. We see the parts of this world that don't quite fit. In understanding that, we see making as more than a science. It, like the rabbits and the monsters, is one of those somethings that lie in between.'"

"You're saying you believe me?"

"It's hard not to believe this, isn't it?"

Mesny opened drawers and cabinets as she spoke, shifting frantically through loose papers and abandoned knickknacks until she found a linen-rolled kit of tools. In one swift movement, she plucked a pair of tongs from the kit and extracted the stinger from Kellan's throat. She didn't know what to expect, but it certainly wasn't what Mesny showed her: a sliver of what could have been gold to the naked eye but wasn't. It shimmered like something alive, the air around it warped like heat on concrete. Then, in a tiny plume of dust, the golden stinger vanished like a dream in the dawn.

Their first trial had been to create something from nothing—an impossible task, on its surface. All eight of them knew it. It's why most of them searched for gold, and why Kellan searched for copper. Makecraft was not magic. Makecraft altered what already was. And just as makers could not make something from nothing, they couldn't *un*make something *into* nothing, either. "If it isn't makecraft," asked Kellan, the stinger's last specks of dust winking into the din, "then what is it?"

"The question isn't *what* the stinger is. The question is *why*. Did you ever stop to question the reason behind the Guild of Engineers' secrecy? Why we don't hang banners, or deal in applications and registration forms? Why our bids compete for one spot, every year, from all sides of the Swallow?"

"I assumed it was—"

"You assumed wrong." Mesny opened the most worn of Maudelaire's journals to a page littered with inky script and diagrams, doodles of creatures and places Kellan had never seen before. Massive birds were haloed by lightning. Eels large as whales turned hail to hydrangea petals. Snakes long enough to cut an island in two curled in a dark and endless cave. "It's the theorists. It's always been the theorists. Our guild is the only one with a school dedicated to unlocking the secrets of makecraft—how it works, where it comes from, its limits and potentials. The theorists unlock them, and the Guild keeps those secrets safe. But the Guild is running out of minds, and Nanseau is running out of time."

Then Mesny unfolded the night's copy of the *Report*, paper still warm from the press. Front page. The Fault had suffered another blackout, this one spanning half the city. The Guild had been safe in Sougare's ancient walls, and since Kellan was with Axel in the runeless marsh, she'd have never known.

"It's connected. All of it. Tangled, like knotty string. Left unchecked, these 'blackouts' will spread. Il. Un. Your village in the minebelt. Nanseau will be a husk of what it was, and when the dark is through with us, it will cross seas and borders and won't stop until the map is under its heel."

Kellan had stayed in Riz to save her mentor. She'd never wanted to save the world. But she wasn't a fool. On the off chance Kellan earned a seat in the Guild of Engineers, her victory wouldn't matter if Mesny's warning came true. "So," she said, "what do we do now?"

Mesny ran a hand over her hair, frizzing her fingerwaves. "I'll do my best to limit your involvement—"

"Like you've done so far? Look where it's got you. All these secrets, for what? If you'd told me from the beginning, we could've figured this out by now. Together."

"Kellan, half the Court doesn't even know what I've just told you, and the Guild does not take stolen knowledge lightly. You're brilliant, but you're loud, and getting any more involved than you are already will put you in the sights of two of the most powerful institutions known to man. One girl has died already. If ever there was a time to back out, it's now, before this disaster takes you too."

The mice in the walls scurried behind the brick, leaving Kellan and Mesny in cold silence. Truth rarely outweighed money and power in the hearts of the wealthy, and courtiers were no exception. Kellan knew that. In pursuing this, they risked upending everything the world knew about the craft that earned Nanseau its power. One wayward rumor, and the Court would tear them both apart.

But the Court had tried before. They'd tried for thirteen years, trapping a child in ancient stone. They'd tried, and instead of a broken little girl, they'd created something not so easily shattered. When Mesny gave her warning, Kellan swallowed her fear. She'd do what she could, not for the world that had tried to destroy her, but for the chance to prove she was made of hardier things. For Edgar, who still needed her. For the future they both deserved.

"If they don't like their things taken," she said, rumbling thunder in the quiet, "they shouldn't have let in a thief."

May Bas, of Wrath, aim his ire.

May Craie, of Wisdom, turn her back.

May Ardoise, of Shelter, leave you cold.

May Calcaire, of Death, avenge tenfold.

–Curse of the Pillar First, spoken at the guillotine.
43rd of Granich. 1 Guilded.

SIXTEEN

"Y'all sure you're not hungry?"

Kellan and Cyn stood in Lou's bedroom with Lou at the desk, Cyn at the window, and Ms. Roussel at the door. Chatter and clinking silverware sounded through the floorboards from the restaurant below, just loud enough to mask the crackle of splintering wood.

"We're okay." Kellan stepped in front of Cyn, whose grip on the windowsill would definitely leave a dent. "Thanks again."

Ms. Roussel, with her back-length hair braided into a single plait, stared long enough for even Kellan to shrink back. No wonder Lou had been so hesitant to let them all meet here. "I'm right downstairs if you need anything," she said, as if in warning, then closed the door behind her, leaving the three of them alone. And just in time, too. If she'd stayed for a second longer, Cyn would have ripped the windowsill from the wall.

Before the real work could begin, Mesny insisted they

needed to secure their allies. The Guild had few Master Theorists, and among them, even fewer studied Maudelaire's work, let alone believed in his theories. Mesny sent letters to a few trusted names and tasked Kellan with research. For the next two weeks, Kellan practically lived in Maudelaire's underground workshop. There was little else to do in preparation for the Guild's final trial. Like the Ball, no one knew the date, the time, the stage, or the task. No one would until hours before the final two bids would put carver to metal.

Luckily, Kellan had passed her second trial by a sliver. Unluckily, that meant her final hurdle in the Gauntlet was Elo Bitao.

It didn't take much for Kellan to convince Mesny to give her half of the next day off. She may have been bullheaded, but she wasn't cruel, and Kellan had finished more than enough research to earn a break. She'd needed to get out, away from the textbooks and the quiet. It'd started to feel like the manor grew smaller every day.

A bit of wood split in Cyn's grip. "Is she gone?"

Kellan and Lou shushed her with a finger to their lips. When Ms. Roussel's footsteps were faint enough to blend with the restaurant chatter, they moved again. "Okay, let him up."

Axel, poor Axel, waited below Lou's window in the sliver of space between Ms. Roussel's house and its neighbor. Ms. Roussel didn't allow boys in Lou's room, so the only way for him to join the three of them unseen was to climb up a makeshift rope of Lou's brother's laundry. Thankfully, he'd agreed to play hooky for an hour or two. The comte would survive without his Bonne liaison for one afternoon.

Cyn opened the window, and together, Kellan and Lou let the rope loose. Kellan did what she could to hold it steady, but Cyn was so strong that Kellan and Lou didn't need to pull much weight at all. Soon Axel climbed through, one long leg after the other, and found his footing.

"Hey," he said, straightening his waistcoat. He and Kellan stood toe to toe, so close that she could count the freckles across his nose, measure the curve of his smile. Cinnamon and cherrywood replaced red beans and buttered corn, and creation, she'd forgotten how disarming the sight of him could be.

"Hey," she said in answer.

"I do not like this." Cyn pulled the rest of the rope into the room and bundled it up. "I do not like this at all."

Kellan moved aside to make it easier for Cyn to finish and leaned against Lou's headboard. For someone several classes above them, Axel seemed perfectly comfortable in Lou's modest bedroom. "Nice to see you again, too, Cyn," he said, and made a seat out of the sill. "Ginnel couldn't make it. The comte has her wrapped up in something at the Hall."

"Is she okay?"

"Yeah. Yeah, I think so. She's just . . . overworked."

Overworked. The last time Kellan saw Ginnel at the smithery, before she hailed Kellan a cab in the rain, Ginnel had looked much more than overworked. But this wasn't the time to pry. Ginnel would be fine. She was strong. Stronger than Kellan, anyway.

"You know," Lou said, inspecting the sides of Axel's head. "I didn't see it in the dark, but Kellan's right. Your ears are pretty big."

"I still do not understand why we must meet here." Cyn huffed and stood in the corner. "There are many public places where men and women can congregate freely, and very few of them require acts of subterfuge."

"No place I'd be allowed to go," said Lou, who straddled her desk chair. "Not now."

Kellan had missed quite a bit in her two weeks confined to the Quarter. Since the Makers' Ball, blackouts in the outlying districts occurred almost daily. They were brief, sometimes shorter than five minutes, but frequent enough to spook the entire city. Including Lou's mother, who enforced a curfew even more strict than the Fault's.

The weather had taken a strange turn since the Ball. The skies flashed violet and blush red. Lightning split the clouds with neither thunder nor rain. A willow tree sprouted in the Makers' Strip, growing taller every day. Now its leaves blew against the wind, curling the clouds, sunlight whirling against its bark and branches like tiny dancers. Another unnatural wonder.

So they spoke quietly, in case Ms. Roussel took another trip upstairs, about anything and everything. She couldn't remember the last time she felt as helpless as she had those past weeks, stuck in the manor and buried under a pile of books. The only reason her carver wasn't coated in dust was because she tinkered after the long days. Tiny, useless things like pocket toys and paperweights, but at least in making those, she felt like herself. She could pretend that she was in Edgar's attic, testing prototypes and practicing new runes.

But here, with Lou and Cyn and Axel, above Ms. Roussel's bustling restaurant, she felt more like Kellan than she had in a while. And here she didn't have to pretend.

"I've looked into what I can, it's just not enough," she said when she'd gone quiet for too long. "I'm so close to an answer—*so* close—but I don't think it's in that workshop. All the Mesny engineers are inventors, Maudelaire included. If anyone in the Guild knows more than he did before he died, it's probably the theorists."

"There are other libraries, you know," said Cyn.

"Sure, but I doubt the Guild would keep ancient secrets tucked in the neighborhood nonfiction section."

Cyn stared at Kellan like she was the dumbest creature Cyn had ever seen.

"Are you gonna tell me," she asked, "or are we gonna stare at each other all day?

Cyn sighed, exasperated. "Obviously, I do not speak of common libraries."

"Cyn," Axel warned, "please don't—"

"There are Guild archives littered across the city. Most of them are hidden, of course, but accessible with a guild pin. I only know of one location, as the Madame charges Xo with most tasks requiring discretion."

"I wonder why," mumbled Lou.

"So all we'd need is an address and an engineer's pin?" asked Kellan.

"It's not that simple," said Axel. "Most of them know your face now. They catch you, you're disqualified. If you *take* something?"

He didn't need to finish. She knew where they'd take her. "I won't get caught," she promised. "See this? Common face. It's done me pretty well so far."

"You're a lot of things, Kellan. 'Common' was never one of them."

"The Madame's meeting is tomorrow evening." Cyn stared at her, aghast. "Kellan, you cannot—"

"We'll make it," she said. Mesny couldn't have too much work for her to do the day of her meeting. "I can make it."

They chatted long enough for the sun to sink into the skyline, until Ms. Roussel called for Lou from down the steps. Lou waved for Axel to go through the window as she left, and Cyn tossed the rope over the sill.

"I just want you to know," he said, and stood. "I don't support stealing from theorists. Or, you know, stealing at all."

"Noted."

"It's reckless, dangerous, and I can think of a dozen ways it'll go terribly wrong."

"But you'll give me your pin anyway."

"Not because I believe in it." He unpinned his gold crest from the inside of his jacket and set it in Kellan's waiting palm. "Because I believe in you."

It was only a passing touch, his thumb down the center of her palm, but the trail he left sparked and hummed against her skin like new runework. "As you should," she said in a shaky breath. "Just don't tell the forum. Don't think you're supposed to have favorites."

Axel laughed, and something ballooned in her chest. "I, uh. I got you something— Wait, no, I didn't get it, I had it around and figured, you know, I thought—"

He stopped talking and pulled something out of his jacket pocket: a piece of cracked and yellowed parchment folded into a square and tied with twine. Kellan took it. "What is it?"

"Open it." The tips of his ears went pink. "It's—"

"You two must stop dawdling," said Cyn, trying and failing to whisper again. "The rope will draw attention from Lou's neighbors soon."

Kellan untied the string, carefully unfolded the paper, and realized immediately what she held in her hands. She recognized the shape of the city, could picture exactly where each gate would have been were this a modern map, but it wasn't. Black ink had faded to a warm brown, and their curves and lines snaked in a way that clashed with modern Riz's grid-like streets in rebellion.

The corners were frayed, and the paper was so thin that her fingers shone through it. It wasn't a carver, or a new pair of magnifiers, or a blouse that she would never feel comfortable wearing. In the past three months, she'd worked with platinum and handled diamond, but this . . . It was worn and ancient and so, so very much him.

"It's the tunnels," he told her, and stuffed his hands into his pockets. "A family friend used to tell me the spirits dug them themselves, but I'm not sure I believe all that. I figured, well, in case you wanted to check them out yourself, or if Mesny gives you another day like this. I, you know, I didn't even think you were still in the city. It'd been—"

"Thank you," she said, because she didn't know what else she could say. "Thank you."

He smiled like that was enough. "I'll see you tomorrow?"

"Tomorrow. Right."

A customer laughed beneath them all, their voice muffled from the walls. Cyn said something nagging, something that Kellan didn't pay enough attention to, and Axel climbed down the rope. Into the street. Farther away from her.

Kellan told herself that Mesny's dismissal the next day was a good thing. She told herself that it was for the best, that she wouldn't have been any use anyhow. In fact, it was opportune. Of course, that didn't make it hurt any less.

"It's only for a few hours," Mesny insisted, turning a page in one of her sketchbooks. "Best that we discuss it without distraction. They're all such gossips, every one of them, and so long as you're out of sight . . ."

Kellan plopped the freshly annotated pile of journals on Mesny's desk. They'd spent less and less time in Maudelaire's workshops and more and more in her main office, a massive space like the one above the Parlour, which had gradually become cluttered with research notes. She'd stuck many of Kellan's translations on her windows and walls, blocking so much light that her plants had begun to wilt. "Right."

It made sense. After all, it'd taken a full week for the other engineers to cancel their plans and agree on a date, and after that, they had to stagger their arrivals so they didn't draw too much attention from the press. The final trial was rumored to be only days away, which gave them the perfect excuse for being in Riz at the same time. Anything they could do to make sure the meeting went smoothly, they should do, even if that meant Kellan had to pretend she had nothing to do with it.

That left her a few hours to make arrangements, but because Lou planned to pick her up during her mother's end-of-shift nap, she was forced to wait until after the lunch rush. "Sit tight," Lou told her over the telephone, before her mother hurried her off of it.

So she did sit tight, for the first hour. The next hour, she sat a little looser. By the third, minutes before the courtiers were supposed to arrive, she was still waiting in the foyer, and Mesny had become a pacing mess, practically carving a groove into the marble floor.

"They will come," said Xo from her place by the door. "Monsieur Jolif and Madame Antoinette have their quirks, but neither of them would cancel without notice."

"I can just wait upstairs," Kellan offered from her seat on

the leather chair under the golden tree. "I'll keep an eye on the window and leave through the back."

Had she made the offer half an hour before, perhaps it would have done some good. But when Kellan reached the foot of the steps, the circle's cobbled mudbricks crunched beneath an approaching car. Mesny adjusted her necktie and turned away, assuming Kellan would be a good intern and do as she'd promised, and for the most part, Kellan did. After she finished climbing the stairs, though, she couldn't bring herself to turn the corner. Instead, she sat and hid behind the railing.

She hadn't recognized Jolif at the ball because of his mask, but now that she saw him in the daylight, she wondered how she couldn't make the connection that night. He was shorter in person and completely bald, with a handlebar mustache the color of ash. "Minora, my dear!" He opened his arms for a hug. "It's only been days, but it feels like so much longer."

The change in Mesny was immediate. Suddenly, she was big and bright and kissed the air next to each of Jolif's rosy cheeks. "I know, I know," she said with a dramatic sigh. "And your trip to Turtleback? Tell me when this is all over, hmm?"

"Only over a cold glass of something sparkling."

Next through the door strode Antoinette. She was all steel and grit, dressed ruggedly for her delicate name—denim overalls and a cap, as if she'd just left an auto shop. "This—thank you, honey—better be good," she said as she handed Xo her coat. "I don't think anything's worth this city's . . ."

Maker Jourdain was a no-show. That was what Mesny said.

But all three courtiers peeked out the window when another car rolled down the road and parked behind the other two. The door opened, and she recognized exactly who it was the moment they stepped out.

It wasn't Maker Jourdain.

She'd seen pictures of him. Little portraits in papers and magazines. Handsome, always in suits cut to kill, and too young-looking for his age. But in person, he was as devastating as the rumors claimed: strapping, with skin like amber sap and hair that coiled and shone in the sunlight. She didn't get a bad feeling until he stepped through the door, and the warmth that always lingered in the foyer cooled. His arrogant gait, how he crossed the threshold like Mesny's manor was a thing to be conquered—no, a thing that already belonged to him—gave him the look of a predator. But mostly, it was the eyes. They were capable of joy and adventure. She'd seen it in Crown Hall, and Mesny's ballroom, and the bayou beyond the city's walls. Yet there was something dark, something distant, in Monsieur Bonne. In Axel's father.

He shouldn't have known. He shouldn't have even been in the same hemisphere. Mesny had insisted that he had business across the Swallow, would be too far away to interfere, yet there he stood under her chandelier. "Pardon me," he said, smooth as buttercream. "My invitation must have gotten lost in the post. Not to worry. Delmore told me all I need to know."

Kellan gripped the banister tighter, willed the wild thump of her pulse to soften.

"Bedoier," Mesny said, and patted his shoulder. "Unexpected, but not unwelcome. Remind me to thank Delmore for passing the news along."

Jolif drew himself up and cleared his throat. "You *are* aware of what we intend to discuss, yes?"

"I did say 'all I need to know,' didn't I?" Bonne shook off his coat and blindly handed it to Xo, who hesitated a moment before she draped it over her arm. "After all, what good is a new trainway if the island's most populated city goes dark? No, I have as vested an interest in seeing this blackout business finished as you all do."

"Fine, fine," said Antoinette. "Can we get started? Now that everyone's here—"

"But not everyone's here, are they?" Bonne stepped farther into the foyer, toward the steps, and stopped in front of the tree. He thumbed one of its branches. "Where is your Du? I've heard so much about her."

"*Kellan,*" said Mesny firmly, "is in the library, conducting a bit of last-minute research. You won't meet her today."

"Is she?"

"Yes."

"Then who is that by the railing?"

Mesny, Jolif, and Antoinette all searched the banister at once, but no one quicker than Mesny. Hopefully, it was a trick of the light. Hopefully, it wasn't worry that flashed across Mesny's face.

Kellan stood on weak legs, cheeks hot as she brushed invisible dust off the back of her pants. "I didn't want to interrupt," she lied, but not as well as she'd have liked. "It's all on your desk now."

"Marvelous, thank you." Mesny ushered Jolif and Antoinette further down the hall. "We'll hold it in the dining room. I've had some refreshments prepared—"

"Without a proper introduction?" Bonne said, chuckling. "Nonsense. Come down, come down. Let us take a look at you."

She'd never seen Mesny's jaw so tense, but Mesny nodded to indicate that it was safe to join them. Kellan fought to keep her expression even and walked down the steps, the soles of her shoes thudding too loudly against the marble.

Bonne canted his head, appraising her. Were he anyone else, Kellan would have asked if something was wrong with his face, but he wasn't anyone else. He was one of the most powerful men on the island. And he looked so much like Axel that it hurt. "I imagined you'd be shorter."

Kellan tried to smile. Judging by the way he bared his canines, it was more of a sneer.

"Bedoier, come." Mesny stood with Jolif and Antoinette by the archway. "The food is likely cold by now, and Kellan has quite a bit of unfinished work to do."

Bonne guided Kellan toward the others by the shoulder. His touch was slight, but his hands were cold, and every inch of her went rigid. "Nothing that can't wait until tomorrow, I'm sure. If she's been such a help, I think it's only polite that she join us, don't you think? Enjoy the fruits of her labor?"

Mesny's lip twitched with suppressed rage, but rather

than show him out—a move that Kellan knew would send him straight to the comte's office—she bit her tongue. "Kellan," she directed in answer, "have those journals ready by dessert."

Mesny, Jolif, and Antoinette filed into the dining room, leaving Kellan and Bonne behind.

"I remember my first trials." In the empty foyer, even Bonne's breaths echoed against the walls, booming in the quiet. "It was the same year as Minora's, so you can imagine how that went. She was always strange, that one, but no one could deny her brilliance. They say the same thing about you."

His grip on her shoulder tightened. Slightly. Enough to signal that he was capable of much more.

"I will only say this once." Bonne spoke so lowly that his words crept down her spine like trickling water. "I don't care how brilliant you are. I don't care how many people approve of you. If you distract my son again, I will sever the fingers from your hand myself."

With that, he smiled like a gentleman and strode into the dining room, the echo of his footsteps like distant war drums. She'd been threatened before back home. A few kids even followed through when she was too little to fight back, shoved her into closets and propped chairs in front of the doors to lock her in until nightfall, when the matron checked the beds. But none of them made her so afraid that she couldn't move, or speak, as the cold of their hands settled in her bones.

SEVENTEEN

Kellan, Lou, and Cyn stood outside the entrance to the record shop beside Midton Palace, where the Guild announced Maricar's death weeks ago. She'd run from the manor the moment Bonne left the foyer. Better to wait outside than endure the cold he'd brought with him.

Mesny, true to her word, only told Kellan what she believed she ought to know. Apparently, Mesny didn't believe Kellan needed to know much of anything at all. And so Kellan had no alternative. If Mesny wasn't going to share her information, Kellan would take it on her own.

"Is this a situation in which the hairs on the back of your necks stand up?" asked Cyn excitedly. "I have always wondered what that felt like."

"A bank. A car dealership on the Strip. Pits, a candy shop would've at least been worth it. But if I get caught breaking into a *library*? I'll never see daylight again."

"Or," Kellan offered alternatively, "your ma'll be so grateful you're reading, she might even thank us."

In the distance, the sound of clacking heels from down the street caught their attention. Ginnel waved Kellan down, and Kellan ducked farther into the alleyway, leaving room for her to join them in the shade.

"Sorry it took so long," said Ginnel as she caught her breath. "Just managed to get away. Last-minute meeting with the comte and some highseats."

"The wonders?"

"Something like that."

Ginnel caught a loose missing persons poster ripped by the wind. So many littered Midton's streets, its roads were more paper than brick. For a moment, her shoulders caved, and Kellan felt how exhausted she must have been. Then she folded the page with a tight smile, tucked it into her bag, and all was almost normal again.

"I'm the lookout, right?" Ginnel straightened her bobbed hair in a puddle's reflection. It looked thinner now, her once-brilliant citrine skin now sallow from exhaustion. "Not sure what the Guild has to do with a record shop, but I'll do my best. It's kind of exciting, actually."

"Just like that?" asked Lou. "Not even gonna ask what we're up to?"

Ginnel winked. "Can't give anything away if I don't know the answers."

"Ruthless. I like it. You could learn from her, Cyn."

As Lou and Cyn started bickering again, Kellan pulled Ginnel to the side. "You all right?" she asked, glancing over her shoulder to see if anyone was nosy enough to listen in. "You look—"

"Gorgeous? I know." Ginnel pretended to toss her hair over her shoulder, her smile dim. "Don't worry about me. It's tough work, but at least it's work."

"And that's all it is, right? Work?"

For a moment, Ginnel hesitated, glanced away like Kellan would find the truth in her eyes. Dus like Ginnel, pretty and capable, suffered the most after aging out. And Kellan had long since learned to watch those with the brightest smiles. "Just work. I swear," she said, squeezing Kellan's shoulder. "Thank you, though. For asking."

They smiled again, more in the eyes than the mouth. *I see you,* they said, *and I know.*

After she and Ginnel discussed the details of her role, Kellan used a barrel as a desk and laid out the library's blueprints. She pointed out its security measures, the ones they could avoid and the ones too advanced to trick their way around; traced the quickest path to the floor with the information they'd need; circled the stacks they should check first. "Guild Architects built this place," she reminded them, "so there may be more to the inside than these schematics suggest."

"Just, you know, out of curiosity," chimed Lou, "what would happen if we *did* get caught?"

"Best case?" said Ginnel. "You get a record. I get the boot. Cyn gets reset, and Kellan . . ."

"Gets shipped to mills."

While the weight of the risks settled over them, Kellan handed Lou a counterfeit engineer's assistant pin. Axel had let her borrow his to study its runework. She had no doubt its inner workings were more complex than its exterior, but because she couldn't risk taking it apart, she'd lifted just enough from its exterior to fool the library's older traps.

Kellan held Axel's pin to the record shop's keyhole. The gold shifted into a key that fit perfectly inside. Like the first trial's stage, darkness engulfed everything on the other side of the threshold until Lou closed the door behind them. Then, as though the lock were a light switch, the library shone in all its brilliance. Bookshelves lined walls so tall Kellan had to crane her neck to see where they ended, and even then, squinting hardly helped. A domed stained glass roof washed its spines in brilliant color, fireplaces crackling on every floor. Luckily for them, most of those floors were empty. They only needed to reach the fifth.

"That elevator must be new," she whispered, pointing directly across from them. "It'd be faster than the steps, but I don't know if these dupes will be enough to fool the runework."

"What happens if they don't?" asked Lou.

"Whatever it is," said Cyn in a pathetic attempt at a whisper, "we should not find out."

Lou nudged Kellan's side and cocked her chin toward the

stairwell, where Makers Jourdain and Villiers whispered conspiratorially on their way down.

"No choice," she said. "Elevator it is."

Together, they crossed the first floor and entered the elevator. No alarms yet. They rode it up to the fifth floor, where automi sorted journals and tomes and most of the engineers were too busy researching to notice their arrival.

"Lou, you and Cyn take the theology sections. Stay within my line of sight—"

"How may I be of service?"

An automi hovered over Lou's shoulder. Not Mesny's. This model was at least a decade behind. Still, the way its unblinking eyes bore into Kellan's made her grip the nearest railing to keep from running away.

"You can," said Lou with what she hoped was an authoritative highborn lilt. She motioned for them to go ahead with a signal behind her back. Kellan slipped her Axel's pin. "We're Journeymin Maker Bonne's assistants, School of Architecture. I have his pin, if you'd like to check it?"

With the automi distracted, Kellan and Cyn settled between two bookshelves, leather spines spanning from floor to ceiling. They worked quickly, with Kellan careful to listen out for Lou and her automi shadow, who she'd managed to distract so far. Unfortunately, Cyn and Kellan weren't so lucky. Neither of them could find a single tome on the relationship between unnatural wonders and makecraft. In fact, they couldn't find a book on wonders at all. Just when

Kellan had given up hope, something caught her eye. No, not something. Someone.

"That maker," Kellan whispered. She bounded toward the painting as though it'd disappear. Cyn whispered something urgently behind her, but Kellan only knew the woman on the wall, made immortal in a painting. She was from another time. Her guild pin sparkled with three architects' tiger's eyes, half hidden under wild white hair. Brilliant gray eyes met her own. Unfamiliar, only because Kellan knew them to be black, and had named her Foxglove.

"She's dead." The placard under its frame read *Giséle Gallo, Master Engineer. 172–259 Guilded.* "That doesn't make sense."

"Got you now, you little rat," came the familiar voice of Maker Jourdain. But he wasn't important right now. Not when Foxglove was staring her down through the canvas. Foxglove, who carried herself like a stranger. Foxglove, who'd died almost sixty years ago.

"She can't be dead," said Kellan in a breath. "She can't . . . I saw . . . ."

Jourdain snapped his fingers to summon another automi librarian. "Stop your babbling," he said. "You're caught. With any luck, the ordergarde will have your wrists by—"

"Shut up."

"I *beg* your pardon?"

She needed to think. Just as makecraft couldn't make something from nothing, makecraft also couldn't make life out of death. Yet she knew this face. It haunted her nightmares.

Taunted her in the streets and the swamps. Was Giséle a grandmother, and Foxglove her descendent? That, at least, would make sense. But Foxglove only brought chaos.

Cold metal gripped her forearm, and Kellan dug in her heels. "I must ask you to leave," repeated the automi. "If you refuse, I will detain. I will detain. I will. I."

The automi's grip on her forearm went slack. The sconces flickered with his glowing runes, fading and flashing until nothing remained. The dark erupted then. It took the flames, leaving only the dim light of the moon through stained glass. Jourdain staggered back, in desperate search for shelter that wouldn't come.

It came from the west again. Book after book fell from trembling shelves, inching up from the ground. The elevator wouldn't work. Kellan knew that. She also knew that if they took the stairs, they wouldn't make it out in time, crushed under brick and metal.

The door. They didn't need to make it outside. If they could just reach the threshold, make shelter under its pillars—

Kellan ran, Cyn and Lou close behind. One by one, shelves toppled to the ground like playing cards. Automi crashed around them, falling from the ladders. They bounded down the steps, the dulled remnants of the Guild's secret library whizzing past their ears. Halfway. If they could get halfway down the staircase, they'd make it.

Cyn stopped short, arms wide to keep Lou and Kellan back. "The steps are disintegrating!"

"The next shelf that falls," said Kellan, "we jump."

"If we miss," called Lou, panicked, "we'll die!"

"Then we won't miss."

The step under Cyn's foot crumbled to glittering dust. They scrambled back, Kellan watching the falling shelves for an opening. "Ready?"

A fraction of a second. The nearest shelf leveled with their step, and Kellan, Lou, and Cyn vaulted at once, holding each other for balance. Kellan's stomach flew into her chest, the rumbling world around her a blur of running ink as the bookshelf plunged to the ground floor. No time to talk. She took Lou's hand, and Lou took Cyn's, and if luck would have them one more time, they'd make this last leap—

The entrance. Another leap. Rolling and crashing. Dust and gray.

Kellan pushed up from the broken ground. The Makers' Strip shone faint through a haze of debris, the last remnants of the Guild's library crumbling behind her. She stumbled, caught herself on Cyn's shoulder. Lou'd scratched her cheek. The alabaster facade on Cyn's thigh had cracked. Something, somewhere, everywhere, rang at a high pitch, and no matter how many times Kellan closed and opened her eyes, the world wouldn't come into focus.

"You all right?" came Lou's voice from underwater. "You're bleeding."

Vague figures shone through the ruins, cries and moans echoing in the fading sunlight. In the distance, ordergarde sirens filled the air, their rolling lights washing the dust in gold and lavender. An icy wind swept away the haze. The streets swarmed with those who had been injured from the library's collapse. They lay helplessly as shopkeeps and strangers tended to their wounds.

Then Kellan spotted Foxglove's frayed coattail trailing through the wreckage. Kellan tried to run, but wavered, the constant ringing piercing her skull. A few steps, and dust became fog. A few more, and the brick beneath her feet softened to soil, then hardened to cobblestone. The lazy whorl of gold and lavender faded into glimpses of lush forests, barren wastelands, the darkest depths of the sea. They flashed like deathbed memories, lurking behind curling mist.

Are you always so impulsive?

"Marielo?" Where was she now? She searched for his silhouette through the gray. Nothing. The world beyond it changed again. The northernmost edge of the Strip. She should smell sea salt. Instead, she smelled rotted wood.

We're both beyond surprises now.

"Come out," she called into the gray. No more sea. No more Strip. Twilight darkened to a starless night, all sound buried somewhere in its shade. Her voice, too weak. She tried again. "Come *out*!"

I'm learning not to waste time.

The taunting came from all sides, the world behind the mist shifting with every word. She plugged her ears. Shut her eyes. Still, it came, searing the backs of her eyelids, echoing inside her skull—

Kellan! Maricar's voice whispered, warbled but close. *Behind you—*

Her back met a wall with a force that left her breathless. Two hands around her neck, tightening, cold. She tried to breathe, and couldn't. She tried to pry those hands away, and couldn't. She thrashed and kicked and shoved to no avail, until she had nothing left to do but look.

The figure lifting her from the ground had skin that sagged with age. Its white hair blew in a wind Kellan couldn't feel. It wore a tattered trench coat, the same coattails she'd followed to the Strip's end. But Kellan didn't know this creature. Its toothless mouth curved into something too empty to be a smile, its eyes glimmering with greed. They weren't the bottomless black she'd come to know, but the glow of flesh over sunlight. In them, she found something familiar. A hunger to survive. A fire that burned in the darkest part of her. A pure, wild, endless rage.

Air. Kellan collapsed onto the ground in a wheezing heap, fighting for the breath that left her. The world beyond the fog was familiar again, the Strip's sculptures and shops sparkling under the lamplights. And the creature that wasn't Foxglove disappeared.

"What was that?"

Lou stood at the alley's mouth, wide-eyed with shock. They'd seen everything. The creature. The dancing gray. The world around them, changing in broken pieces. Ginnel, heels abandoned, helped Kellan to her feet. She'd been cut from wrist to shoulder, blouse ripped and dripping red.

"I don't know, and I don't care," said Ginnel, straining under Kellan's weight. "But we're getting out of here. Now."

They climbed into Lou's car before the ordergarde could spot them through the wreckage. But instead of fallen brick and broken glass, rock and green formed from the earth. Glittering dust gathered from the library's ruins, shaping itself into an unnatural wonder carved by the breeze.

No one spoke. Lou pulled over once they'd driven far enough away from the sirens so Ginnel could tend to her and Kellan's wounds, then dropped her off at an apartment complex a few blocks away. On the ride back, Kellan rested her bandaged head against the window. Not even the many glances Lou and Cyn cast her way were enough to get her to talk. She was too tired to reassure them. She was too tired to ask for reassurance herself.

Lou pulled into Mesny's empty circle. All the cars had gone, which meant the meeting was over and the courtiers—Bonne included—had gone home. But none of that mattered when Xo opened the manor's doors.

Because Edgar sat in the leather chair beneath Mesny's glittering chandelier.

EIGHTEEN

"Well, don't just stand there, girl, gimme a hug."

Kellan stood there for so long that Lou had to push her forward. He looked as if they'd only spent a few days apart. From his feathered hat to his tweed suit, which hung a bit looser than it used to, nearly everything about him was warm and familiar. Edgar's smile was so wide, it practically split his face.

In an instant, Kellan broke into a run and squeezed him hard enough for Edgar to grunt. And then she squeezed harder. He smelled like shoeshine and pretzels, but she didn't care. Edgar patted her head, picked a few shards of glass out of her curls, and didn't ask questions. Not yet.

"I didn't say break my ribs," he said with a laugh.

Kellan pulled away and wiped her eyes. "What . . . what are you doing here?"

"The Madame says she's got something for me she can't

send in the post. Bought the tickets and everything. First class! Never rode first anything my whole life."

The prosthesis. It'd been well over three months since the start of Mesny's bargain. And now she was on the cusp of something groundbreaking. The answer to their question was all around her, scattered in bits and pieces she couldn't catch, let alone put together. Not yet. She just needed more time.

He held her at arm's length to take her in, concern swallowing his joy. She didn't need a mirror to know she looked like something dragged in from the road. "What . . . How—"

"They're just scratches," said Kellan. "The alchemists here are so good they'll be gone in an hour. Enough about that, though. When'd you get in?"

If Edgar kept pushing, Kellan couldn't hear him. Perhaps it was the blow to her head that blurred Mesny's foyer, muffled the words of her mentor to a vague murmur when she noticed Axel standing behind the railing. His footsteps pounded down the hall above the stairwell, skidding to a stop when he found her whole.

She couldn't place the look in his eyes, part wild, part livid. He descended the steps two at a time, searching the wound on her temple and the scrapes on her arms and knees. When his gaze lingered on the purpling bruise around Kellan's neck, he reached out to touch her, his wrists trembling with the rest of him. Kellan swore the air between his fingers and her skin crackled with creation. But he stopped short, and Kellan's battered body ached in remembering the beating she'd taken not one hour ago. Strange, how it'd forgotten its hurt for so long.

"Who's this?" asked Edgar when the world went into focus again. "And where'd he come from?"

"I'm sorry, I should—I should introduce myself." After tearing his attention away from her, he offered Edgar his hand. "I'm Axel."

This wasn't the highborn from the Ball. Here his politeness was genuine. Excited, even, like seeing Edgar was seeing a piece of Kellan she'd kept to herself. Watching them together, playing nice and familiar, fed the dream that she could fuse her new life to her old one, pack Pape's Peculiars into a suitcase and set it somewhere in Midton.

"Pleasure's mine." Edgar shook his hand. "I'm Edgar Pape, tinker from Cuivreton. And . . . is that the driver?"

Lou, surprisingly, had kept her distance. She stood by the doorframe and only then approached the rest of them. "Lou Roussel," she said, having lost her usual chipperness in the library's collapse. "Sudton Roussels."

"I see you decided to stick around."

"I guess so, huh?"

After their introductions, Xo and Cyn showed him all the best parts of the manor, from Mesny's smallest dining room, the workshop where they held all their lessons, to Kellan's suite. They even stopped in the halls so he could inspect a few of the smaller cleaning automi as they dusted the windowsills.

Katydids chirped into the silence, and the sea brushed the rocks below. It was so peaceful in the Quarter, so easy to forget that she still had so much to explain. Now she'd enjoy the crickets and the sea, and the sight of his crooked feathered hat.

For an hour or so, everything was normal. Her time in Riz had gone according to plan. Her biggest worry was earning her seat in the Guild's final trial. Edgar would have his prosthesis, and she would be on her way back to Cuivreton, where alchemy started and ended at the neighborhood beauty salon. But nothing was normal anymore.

"Hey."

Kellan nearly jumped out of her shoes at the sound of Axel's voice. She'd been standing in the same spot, staring into nothing while Cyn gave Edgar and Lou a more-than-thorough historical explanation behind the paintings on the walls.

"Hey."

He'd straightened his waistcoat, his wrinkled sleeves rolled up to the elbow. They walked like that for a while, in silence, far from Lou and Cyn and Edgar. Far from the world outside the manor, falling apart at its seams.

"Lou has your pin." She tugged at the string around her wrist, desperate to do something with her hands. "Jourdain recognized me, but the Guild'll be so busy cleaning up the mess they won't think about what let me in."

"Right." He huffed a humorless laugh, staring straight ahead. "The pin."

"Can they trace their owners? I could've stolen it, easy, if you're—"

"Pits, Kellan, I don't care about the rusting pin."

"But the Guild—"

"The Guild could dissolve tomorrow, and I wouldn't care. But this?" When he looked at her again, that wild something in his eyes returned. His clenched jaw and steady breaths—it was as if he were fighting for the control that always came so easily for him.

It frightened her, how she hung on to the silence, waiting for him to fill it. *But this?* "This" could have meant many things. Their breaking world. The mass confusion. The growing thing hovering between them, like the tension between lightning and thunder. "I didn't ask for this," he said in a trembling sigh, fingers curling at his sides. "The name, the seat . . . I never wanted any of it."

"You're a Bonne. What else could you possibly want?"

"The bayou. The barrels. A place where none of this had to happen, and you . . . You could just . . . ."

He spoke soft as a memory. There was so much she could say. She could say that she wanted nothing more than to share stories in the night and cast shadows in the grass. That he was beautiful and kind and more than Kellan could ever deserve. That the sound of her name on his lips was an alchemist's masterwork, that it touched a wound she didn't know she had, and all she wanted was for him to say it again.

"They're probably in the next wing by now," he said

when the quiet became too heavy. "We should catch up with them."

In the end, she said nothing. She'd stolen enough already.

"Kellan tells me you're quite the fashion connoisseur," Mesny said, "so we were careful to give you many choices in finish. See the knobs there, very subtle. Unless your customers kiss your hand, they wouldn't know them from a wristwatch."

It wasn't until Edgar turned one of the knobs and the metal plates shifted from a glossy black ceramic to a matte gray tungsten that she swelled with pride. He turned another knob and settled for the bronze-leafed titanium. She'd had a feeling he'd like that best. "I . . . I don't know what to say."

"There's nothing to say, Mr. Pape, at least not to me. I've left a card for a prosthesiologist. I'm sure there's one in Cuivreton, but Dr. Boucher is the best in the business, and between you and me, he owes me a favor. He can be in Cuivreton by the week's end. Now, I do apologize, but Xo, Mr. Bonne, and I have business to attend to."

"I'm sorry, Bonne?" Edgar looked from Mesny to Axel and took a small step back. "As in . . . Ah, well, I didn't know you from a—"

Axel managed a small, polite smile. "There wasn't a reason to, ser. We'd only just met."

"Of course, of course. I'm just . . . just might need a sit-down, that's all."

"We'll be back in . . . Actually, I'm not too sure when we'll return. Before sunrise, preferably. If not, have Cyn call an automirun, and they'll escort you to the Fault to visit your brother. The Mesny seal should be enough."

Kellan had almost forgotten about Edgar's brother. Tonight would be too dangerous for him to visit on his own, but if they avoided the northtowns, it should be safe by the morning. She still didn't like the idea of him behind that ugly wall, sunlight or no, but she supposed family was family.

"You must be exhausted. As much as I'd like to stay for dinner, this is a bit of an emergency. Please, make yourself at home. Axel, with me. And, Kellan?"

"Yeah?"

"The Guild has sent its official notice. Your final trial begins at sunrise."

Kellan tried to catch Mesny before she left, but Mesny was already halfway up the steps by the time Kellan opened her mouth. Axel said nothing, only waved a vague, half-hearted goodbye and followed Mesny out. Cyn and Lou whispered in one of the workshop's many nooks, leaving Kellan and Edgar alone. She couldn't see them, but it sounded like an argument.

"So." Edgar cleared his throat, still cradling the prosthesis. He'd made a chair out of one of Maudelaire's trunks. "I don't think we ever had that talk."

"Talk? What talk?"

"You know what talk."

"If I knew what talk, I wouldn't be asking you about 'what talk.'"

"I didn't come all the way across this island for no sass, now." He patted the patch of trunk beside him. "Figured a little distance would at least get me a little kindness, too. Still as mean as a snakebite."

She sat, picked at the curling leather at the trunk's corner, and answered every single one of his questions about the odd contraptions she'd shown him around the house, the nature of the Quarter gate, and then about the chaos still unfolding downtown. She didn't tell him about how badly she wanted to join Cyn and Lou, who'd started laughing somewhere in the labyrinth, or that she couldn't get the sight of Axel's frustration out of her head. That if she were to go home, she wouldn't be able to smell cinnamon, or look at a willow tree, or open an old book without being reminded of him.

"You know, girl." By then, the radio played the blues. Edgar tapped his toe to the back beat. "I didn't get to tell you how proud I am of you."

"Don't count your stones. Still got one trial left."

"Not about that. This here's nice, real nice, but no. I'm proud about them." He pointed to the labyrinth. "Lou and Cyn, they talked about you like you hung the moon. Ms. Mesny's a tough one, I know, but she cares about you like kin. And that Bonne, Axel? The way that boy looks at you could lead a ship to shore."

"I don't understand."

"You made friends, girl. Good ones, too, from what I can tell. You get to my age, and you see things in people, between people, keeping them together. The four of you . . ." He smoothed the feather in his hat, smile fading. "You had a hard life. Harder than most. The world is cruel and unfair, but I like to think there's hope in what connects people to each other. I'm just glad you found it. Hope."

So that's what they were. "Friends." It seemed so small a word for what she felt for Lou, for Cyn, for Mesny. For Axel. She could spend hours trying to find a phrase that fit, but it wouldn't change that Pape's Peculiars was still waiting for her across the island. It wouldn't change that Kellan's time was quickly running out.

Edgar and the shop needed her much more than they did. She couldn't leave him to recover from surgery on his own and trust that the shop would keep while he healed. If she left, the others would survive. They'd solve this mystery on their own. And Kellan . . . she'd make herself too busy to miss them.

Maybe they sat for minutes. Maybe hours. However long it was, it wasn't long enough. She'd missed him terribly, and it wasn't until he stood and stretched that she realized how much.

"I think I'm gonna check the Fault gate again," he said, setting the prosthesis back in the box and taking the pair of cards Mesny taped to the lid. One of them had a wax seal with an *M* in triplicate. "See if this pass is any good."

"Tonight?" She stood, almost snatching the cards out of his hand. "You can't. It's—"

"This city's always been dangerous. Still not gonna keep

me from seeing my brother. I've spent half my life here, and I know you think you know it, but I got twenty-five—"

"Thirty-six."

"—years on your three and a half months. I've lived through worse, guarantee it."

They only had a few more hours, enough for some sleep and a quick breakfast the next day. Who knew how long it would take for them to save up enough bill for him to visit, if they could find the time? Even if Mesny paid his way, it'd take at least a month or two for him to heal from the surgery and adjust to the new prosthesis. And this was his city. His brother. "At least let Lou drive you." Kellan was already on her way to the door. "Or I can go with you. Or—"

"Nah. Y'all had a long day. I'll just catch a car in Nordton. Probably missed the chance to ride with Mesny and that Bonne, but it'd have probably been bad form. They got 'business' and all. I leave you for a few weeks, girl, and you're already tangled with half the Court."

It sounded like such a feat when he said it, but she didn't feel any different. She was just as small, just as lost. She tried to grin. "Guess that's what happens when you don't tell me to stay outta trouble."

He laughed again, but this time, he hugged her, too. "Well, I'm telling you again. Get your rest. Stay outta trouble."

"I'll do my best."

And then he was off. Up the steps, through the wall. She didn't move again until the sound of his footsteps disappeared, which was precisely when she noticed the whispering stopped.

Cyn peeked out from behind a bookshelf. "Has he gone?"

"Yeah. Yeah, he's gone."

"Good. Come here. I have made a discovery, and I must ask you a question."

As much as she wanted to sit and close her eyes for a few minutes, Kellan did as Cyn asked. Cyn had covered a desk with so many books that Kellan couldn't make out the wood under it all. This wasn't a discovery. This was a mess. Lou, who curled a piece of gold foil around her finger, looked equally unimpressed.

"The Madame keeps no books like this in the libraries she sends me to," Cyn turned a page in one of them. "Those have no pictures. In these, there are so few words that I hesitate to call them books. *These* are what you have been 'reading'?"

Lou ironed the foil between her finger and thumb and curled it again. "Me and Cyn browsed a little so we didn't feel so weird listening in on you and your grandboss."

"Lou speaks for herself," said Cyn, who turned another page. "*I* listened."

Lou whacked Cyn on her arm, and to her credit, only winced slightly as she rubbed her sore palm against her thigh.

"It was only a conversation. If they wanted it to be private, they could have spoken upstairs."

"I could've driven him, you know. Wouldn't have put me out none, and it could've gotten my mind off . . . all that."

“He’ll be fine,” Kellan said. He had to be. “He doesn’t have to pass through Midton to get to the Fault, anyhow, right? He can go through Sudton.”

“Technically, yes,” said Cyn, “if we assume that whatever anomaly occurred in Midton stays within its walls, but without the data to—”

“Hey, Cyn!” Lou gestured toward the cobwebs that hung from the corners. “Wanna tell me why you don’t put the books down and dust that stuff up, instead? I know you don’t have lungs, but the rest of us could breathe one of them in. And choke. And *die*.”

While Cyn and Lou bickered, again, Kellan flipped through the pages of the books they hadn’t yet put back. They’d taken them from the shelves Mesny warned her weren’t worth investigating, the ones in languages neither of them knew. Lidonch, Kellan could pick out. Ital and the Crescent dialects, Mesny spoke fluently. Then there were the scrolls and tomes from North and South Vast, and cords of knotted string Mesny suspected came from southern Turtleback, none of which they could translate on their own. Maudelaire kept those in a far, far corner, its doors thick and fuzzy with dust.

The pages of this tome were coarse and gray, the faded characters drawn in thick, aggressive lines. It looked like something from ancient South Vast but pulled at something inside her just as the Quarter’s gate had her second night in the city. Just as Cyn had warned, there wasn’t much to read even if Kellan could have understood it. She flipped through page after page of paintings with thick lines and flat colors that had faded to sepia long ago. On one page, the artist had illustrated a spiked bear who traipsed over a snow bed with a dark-eyed winter hare at his heels. The next, they'd painted that same hare . . . stealing honey from a hive.

Kellan wanted more time for many reasons. To think. To finish the work she and Mesny had started. To find the answers that burned so close they warmed the tips of her fingers. The others . . . she wouldn't think about the others. Now she'd take what little time she had left by the scruff.

She turned another page. Little men toppled castles made of ice, or crystal. On the next, a bird, or a whale, or a snake dove from the sky into the sea. And then, a tiny, twelve-legged and twelve-eyed spider stood before a great, looming cloud of dark.

"Cyn, you understand these languages?"

The bickering stopped. In Cyn's brief pause, the radio's music traveled to their dim corner, warped by the distance. "I can recognize them, but I cannot translate them."

"Were there any on the shelf that you didn't recognize?"

"Yes."

"Can you bring me some?"

As Cyn took off, Kellan flipped past pages of creatures and landscapes and stopped at the one that made her go cold. Where the other pages were more paper than ink, this one was almost completely etched over in faded brown, once black, with the faintest traces of foliage except for a single point of parchment gray.

"What's that?" Lou creeped over Kellan's shoulder. "Looks like a—"

"Lightning bug." Kellan knew it the moment she'd turned the page. She could almost see the single speck of light pulse in and out, in and out, like they had in the bayou, at Cuivreton's only train station. "It looks like a lightning bug."

These stories, these . . . things. The hare that wasn't a hare, the lightning bug that wasn't a lightning bug. They'd crossed seas and spanned continents. They were older than Nanseau. Older than Lidon. Older than Riz and runetheory and the books in Axel's cabinet.

Cyn placed another stack of books beside it, all of them in the lost languages of Aigo. "I do not see the point in this exercise," she said as Kellan flipped through them, one by one, until she found one full of pictures. "These languages are dead. There is no translating them. And the illustrations are unimpressive at best."

Page after page, Kellan matched creatures in the book from Aigo to creatures in the tome from South Vast, then the scrolls from North Vast, a few from Old Crescent and Ital before the Lidonch. The stories were different. The places were different. But always, there was the black-eyed hare. Always, there was the little spider, first with twelve legs, then with eight. And always, always, there was the lightning bug.

Kellan, Lou, and Cyn took in the open pages, the painted creatures staring back at them. Lou traced one of the spider's legs like it'd come to life. "What's it mean?"

The question, Mesny had told her after the Makers' Ball, *isn't* what *the stinger is. The question is* why.

It was entirely possible that this was all a coincidence. Spiders and rabbits and flying bugs were common animals, and where there was an ocean, a shore, and a boat, there was a way for a story to travel from one place to another. It was also entirely possible that Kellan was overworked and underfed, and after a nap and a sandwich, she'd come to her senses and recognize her suspicion for what it was. Ridiculous.

But maybe, maybe, Mesny had been right in a different way. Maybe there were more immeasurable parts of the world than they thought. Parts Maudelaire had come close to discovering. Parts hidden from their human eyes.

Maybe the veil he had lifted for Mesny at bedtime wasn't wholly symbolic, and Foxglove's illusions were bigger than malchemy.

And maybe, in the time of Aigo, before Lidon and Riz and runetheory, there were rabbits in the kitchen cabinets. Monsters, waiting in the trees.

Kellan stepped back, nearly toppling one of the bookshelves. If this was what Maudelaire Mesny had come close to discovering, that spirits once lived among them all in an age long past, then this didn't just threaten Nanseau's authority. It meant the force behind Riz's blackouts and the destruction that followed them had a face and a strategy Nanseau knew nothing about. It meant their power spanned borders and ages and eons, and confronting it would make for the biggest fight their island had seen since the Swallow.

Behind them, the music stopped. In its place chimed a three-note bell. Kellan, Cyn, and Lou all looked to each other before approaching the radio.

". . . interrupt this broadcast," came the voice from the radio, "for a message from our comte."

The comte cleared his throat. She could practically see him pulling his jacket over his belly as he approached the microphone.

"All citizens are urged to return to their homes," he said. "The City of Riz is hereby under lockdown."

NINETEEN

Edgar.

Cyn, Lou, the workshop. Kellan saw, or didn't see, everything through a milky fog. The radio host put the comte's message on a loop. She shut a drawer, grabbed something heavy, shook off a hand on her shoulder, then another.

". . . stupid and thoughtless . . ."

". . . let her go . . ."

". . . will come back . . ."

"Kellan."

She checked to see what it was she had taken. Cold metal casing, a wooden handle polished to a high gloss. The revolver she'd found in the drawer the day Mesny first showed her the workshop. A thing Kellan hadn't fired once in her life.

Cyn blocked the exit. If it wasn't for how heavy she was, Kellan would have pushed her out of the way. "Kellan, stop and breathe. You will need a clear head if you intend to—"

"To what? To what, Cyn?" Lou raised her voice for the first time since she and Kellan met. "I've lived here all my life—*all my life*—and there ain't never been a lockdown. Never. And I don't wanna see what's out there that done inspired the comte to call one now."

"But Edgar—"

"He's a grown man! More important, he's a smart man, and as soon as he gets wind that something's going on, I'm sure he'll duck into the nearest shop until the comte lifts the ban."

"But you cannot be sure—"

"Kinda like we can't be sure we'll find him out there if we go wandering. Y'all need to *think*. It's a big city, and luck only goes so far. We got lucky at Ol' Matty's, and we got lucky tonight, but this is too far."

"What if it was your mother?" Kellan's voice felt far away. She spoke anyhow. "If it was Agathe. Would you hole yourself up and cross your fingers?"

Some of the fog cleared. She could hear Cyn's runes again, make out Lou's face, spot the mess she'd made of the workshop's only workbench. The foil sat crumpled on the floor, and she'd only half closed the drawer.

"If you had a car, and the gas was full up, and she told you just about where she'd be, would you leave it up to chance?"

Lou sucked in her cheeks. She didn't respond.

"Edgar might not be my blood," Kellan said, gaining strength, "but he's the closest thing to family I have." She adjusted the gun in the back of her pants. It was heavier than it looked, but her suspenders did their job well. "So you can stay if you want, maybe wait and see if he shows up. But I'm going."

The comte's message repeated one last time, and the host said something about tuning in within the next hour for more information. Lou was right. Mostly. Kellan didn't know what awaited her outside the Quarter gates. She didn't know how she'd find him, or how she'd get past the Fault on her own. But another blackout was only one reason why the comte would lock down the city the night of the Gauntlet's final trial, and with Edgar searching for his brother in the Fault, she wouldn't risk him coming to harm. She'd figure it out. She had no other choice.

Lou took a long, deep breath and scowled, looking so unlike herself that even Cyn inched away. Just when Kellan was convinced Lou had nothing else to say, Lou pinched her hands like crab claws. "Gimme."

"Give you what?"

"The revolver. Can't have you breaking your hands from the recoil. You wouldn't know the first thing to do with it anyhow. I could tell the second you picked it up that you never held one before."

"And you have?" Despite her reservations, Kellan handed her the gun and the bullets from her pocket.

Lou answered by loading it with nimble fingers. "My dad taught me and my brother when we was little. He used to try his hand at making them, you know. Wanted to go to school to be a weaponist, but the military is cheaper. No tuition. And it pays."

"A weaponist? Your dad or your brother?"

She clicked the cylinder into place. "Both."

"Do we need it?" Cyn stood aside and watched as Lou pulled a leather holster from the drawer Kellan left open. "Would you fire it?"

"Probably not." Lou attached the holster to her belt. "But if it's bad out there, there's no harm in a warning shot. And I got good aim."

Kellan didn't need to ask how Cyn intended to protect herself. She was two hundred pounds of chrome and steel, and if Lou knew her way around a gun as well as she knew her way around a steering wheel, she'd be fine, too. The only one in real danger, aside from Edgar, was her.

All those days spent in this murky room, and she couldn't make sense of anything in it. Not the knickknacks in the drawers, the statues in display cases. Apparently, until a few minutes ago, not even the books on the shelves. She knew the workbench in the corner, though. She knew the carver she'd let clatter to the floor, the dust-coated metal scraps scattered around. So she took some of that. She stuffed a few sheets of foil, a few copper tubes, and her carver into her pocket and left with Lou and Cyn close behind. What she'd do with them, she didn't know. How much use they'd be, she didn't know either. But she knew she felt safer with them than without.

The pond in the center of Mesny's circle reflected the moon; the golden lily pads glittered under its light. The only sound for miles was Kellan's, Lou's, and Cyn's footsteps as they ran.

When they reached the car, they shot onto the roads with the sputtering roar of Lou's engine trailing behind them. Tires streaked against mudbrick. The massive gate shut behind them.

They rode under a shifting sky for what felt like an eternity. The city had locked and guarded every gate to the Fault from Midton to Sudton and the alleys between. She searched for Edgar in the streets, peered through purples and blues and violent reds and loosed papers of missing people. No sign of a gangly old man in a feathered cap. But she wouldn't give up.

She strained to read Axel's map in the dim light and just made out the faded lines of the tunnels under the city and the dots that marked entrances aboveground. There were no gates on that map. But Kellan knew where those were on her own. And now she knew how to get past them.

"Lou, can you pull over? I know a way through."

"What? How?"

"I'll tell you when we stop, I promise. There's an alley near Ol' Matty's. You can park the car there, nobody'll find it."

"If something happens to my car," she grumbled, "I swear on everything I own, I'll never forgive you."

"This may be my first citywide emergency," said Cyn, "but I suspect that this vehicle is among the last anyone would think to steal."

By the time Lou pulled into the space between the wild-garden and Sudton's border, Kellan could have redrawn Axel's map with her eyes closed. She took in the layout of her surroundings, the orientation of the buildings, the way the streets curved and turned. This would be the last time she would have enough light to comfortably read the map. The strength of her memory would be all that kept her between getting to the Fault and becoming hopelessly lost.

Kellan stepped out, old rainwater splashing the hems of her pants. She tapped the ground with her toe and pressed her hands against the alley's dead end until, like the map showed her, something gave: a secret way, hidden behind a stack of crates.

Those were easy to move. She kicked the crates away, pressed all her weight against the brick wall until part of it gave, then pushed the hidden door aside. The hole it left, black as spilled ink, seemed to go on forever, but she knew it'd lead them to where they needed to go.

"Nope." Lou stepped back and waved her hands in refusal. "Nope, nope, nopenopenope. I'm not going in there. There's no way. I don't know what you did with that wall, and you don't know your way out."

"I do! Now I do." Kellan held up the map as evidence. "I studied it the whole drive here."

"For what, three minutes? Three whole minutes?"

"Closer to ten, to be fair. I was under duress."

Lou went on and on about why else they had no business going down that hole, but Kellan tuned her out. Instead, she made a table out of the crate, took her carver and a few sheets of foil out of her pocket and, with a few knots and a steady hand, made something that would help light the way. It wasn't pretty—a little sphere that glowed in the center, the lightning bug from the Exposition without the bug—but it would keep them from stumbling over rocks and walking into walls.

"I know it." Kellan pocketed the rest of her supplies. "I know it well enough to get us to the Fault. You're just going to have to . . ."

For a second, Kellan worried Cyn had malfunctioned. She stood perfectly still, transfixed by the tunnel entrance. But her eyes were still lit, and the hum of her runes bounced off the alley walls.

"Cyn?" Lou noticed, too. She waved her hand in front of the automi, and the motion was enough to bring her back in a startled jump.

Cyn tried her best to look unbothered, even lifted her chin to give herself an extra inch of height, but it trembled slightly. Of course Cyn would have feared the dark after the first trial. In her rush to save Edgar, Kellan had forgotten to consider the two people right next to her, risking their lives to help her.

Kellan set her hands on Cyn's shoulders. "If you want to stay, that's fine. I won't blame either of you. I promise, I won't get lost."

They'd followed her this far. That was enough, more than she could have ever asked for. It didn't matter that, now that Kellan saw the city for herself and the hard edge of her determination had dulled, fear had taken hold of all her senses, made gales out of every brush of wind and bombs out of every bump and crash. She'd do this, and if she had to, she'd do it by herself. Not because she didn't want them with her, but because she wanted to keep them safe, too.

Cyn took a breath. If Kellan hadn't known any better, she'd have thought there were lungs in her metal chest.

"I would appreciate it if you, or Lou, were to talk along the way. So long as it does not interfere with your concentration."

Before Kellan could answer, Lou closed her car door and strode toward the entrance. "Happily," she said, like she hadn't spent half their stop listing reasons why she wouldn't go. "You're way too easy to annoy."

"I am not!"

"Oh, yeah, because that's *so* convincing."

Kellan took one final look into Sudton's street, the soft alice blue dancing over the flower bed, and the wind felt like wind again. While she would have braved the tunnels alone, it did a wonder for her courage to know that she didn't have to. Kellan led the way, and Lou took the back—closing the hole in the wall behind them—until they were swallowed by the dark.

She didn't expect the tunnels to feel any different. They still reeked of mildew, and even with her tiny light, she couldn't avoid tripping over the occasional rock or mound of dirt. But the walk was longer this time. Colder. Cars sped above their heads, and occasionally, someone would shout. Someone would cry out a name.

Every turn, she counted. Every dip, she counted. When the tunnel split, she double-checked the map, but never for too long because Cyn grew anxious in the dark. She would not get lost. She would not lead her friends astray. Most importantly, though, she would find Edgar, and she would get him safely to the manor.

"We're here," Kellan announced. Her voice was hoarse from neglect, so she cleared her throat and spoke again. "We're here."

Lou cracked her back. "Good, almost ran out of arguments. You can only add so many zeros to a fraction without losing count."

She stopped in front of another break in the wall and pressed hard enough for her feet to slip against the metal-plated ground. The alley it opened into was as dark and murky as the one in Midton, but here there were no racing footsteps. No panicked cries or squealing tires. Just silence. The chaos in Midton had become a distant echo. The wail of a faraway ghost.

It took a while for her eyes to adjust to the new light. From the alley, which sat on a small hill, the winding roads and sidewalks of the Fault appeared very nearly abandoned. It was as though they'd stepped into a different place, a different time. There wasn't a trace of Riz's world-renowned architecture. No metal, no filigree, only moss and parched ivy and harsh Lidonch stone, the sharp points of its once ornate spires dulled and rounded with time.

"Why does it look so . . ." Kellan unfolded the map again, compared its curves to the shapes of the roads. "Different?"

"I dunno. I think they just . . . just ran out of funds in the tear-down back in the day? Never did well in history." Lou scratched her head and pursed her lips in thought. "It's always been that way. Saved this coast for last, I think, but once the nation got back on its feet, they . . ."

"Forgot about it."

"Yeah. Guess so. Little sad, I guess, but I mean, the district gets on fine. Lots of nice little shops. But it does look kinda creepy at night, huh?"

In the distance, a tower pierced the night sky, cut the horizon in two. Rotted vines snaked along the cracks in the stone as though trying to suffocate it, to drag it back into the ground. The silhouettes of Lidon's gods held vigil over the tower and the district both, weather-warped into unrecognizable grotesques. At least Cuivreton's namehouse didn't have those beasts at the windows, ever watching from a time long past, but watching still. As if the matrons weren't enough. As if the walls, and the Dus, and the ever-looming threat of destruction weren't enough.

"Yeah," she said. "Kinda creepy."

Kellan led the way down the hill and into the district. Edgar's brother's shop wasn't too far away, but she kept the map out in case. It was easier to read under the streetlights. They kept to the walls, ducked into the shadows when they thought they heard footsteps or an approaching car, but there wasn't really a need. There were very few people on the streets, and none of them were guards. Instead, they hurried past old men under blankets in the dank hollows between buildings, young women who made beds out of benches and moth-chewed sheets, and wandering strangers plucking coins and cigar foil from the ground and shifting through garbage bins for cans and bottles. Once, she swore she saw a toothless old woman, tattered coat like a withered foxglove, watching her through milky eyes. Kellan looked again, and the woman was gone.

Soon they crossed into the neighborhood she knew Bastien's shop to be in—a twisty path of stone cottages with hardly any room between them. Little brown liquor bottles rolled along a sidewalk plastered in yellowed paper, tinkling like bells over the faces of Riz's missing. Edgar was a brisk walk away. "This is it," she said. "We're close."

Something flashed nearby. A long, gangly shape. It was hard to see in the dark, even with the streetlights, but she recognized his silhouette from the photographs of him on Edgar's refrigerator. Tall, lanky, as though a younger Edgar had been stretched on a taffy roll. He hummed, plucking liquor bottles from the ground. Then he looked over his shoulder, and Kellan saw it—the angle of his nose, the deep bronze of his skin, his brother's bushy eyebrows.

"Bastien."

"What?" Cyn chimed in from behind.

"Bastien. That's Edgar's brother. He's probably off to his shop. We should— Excuse me? Bastien?"

Maybe he hadn't heard her. He kept walking, so Kellan called again. Nothing. He turned the corner, so they followed the clinks of his gathered bottles and the warm bass of his work song.

He skipped over the rises and cracks in the sidewalk, swung low to pluck other bottles as he went. Not once did Bastien turn around to greet her, but he didn't have a reason to do that either. Even in the off chance Edgar had written to him about her, it was probably too hard for him to see her in the dark. Kellan, Lou, and Cyn followed him anyway, despite the chill in the air and the bottles that had stopped rolling. Despite the streetlights above, which had begun to flicker.

By the time they reached the corner Bastien turned, he was half behind another corner. They chased and chased, careful not to break into a run, but he was always a strip of stone ahead, always around the next bend. The walls warped the melody of his strange song, carrying its dissonant echo on the breeze.

"This don't feel right." Lou walked with a hand on her hip, too close to her borrowed pistol. "This don't feel right at all. Kellan, we should . . . You sure that's him?"

She was. At least at first. But when they finally reached his shop at the bottom of the hill, Bastien's back to them in the silence, she found some doubt. The window to her left had a sign that read Bassy's Bakes, and the lights were on inside, so he hadn't led them astray. Yet something was very, very wrong.

He buried his bottles under patches of brittle yellow grass that dotted the thin strip of lawn in front of his door, what little of it she could see through the layers of wax paper and soda cans. He dug up the dirt with his bare hands, as if the litter were wildflowers and not soggy piles of trash.

"Bastien?" She spoke tentatively, worried she'd spook him. Cold nipped at her neck and ankles. Her jacket wasn't enough to withstand the chill. "Bastien, you don't know me, but I'm Kellan. I'm Edgar's assistant. Have you seen him . . . around . . ."

Silence. Silence and darkness, until he hummed again. *"Run, run, run."* He dug another hole. Planted the bottle in the soil like a seed. *"Run, run, run."*

Kellan took a small step back. Everything in her body wanted to take Lou and Cyn by the wrists and tear for the closest tunnel entrance. Everything, anything, to get as far away from him as she could.

"Kellan?"

The bell at the top of Bastien's front door jingled. Edgar opened the door from inside. A chill unlike anything she'd ever felt swept from her toes to the crown of her head.

"Ed," she said, voice low, steady. "Go back insidc. It's not—"

But she was too loud, and it was too late. Bastien rose to his feet, a broken bottle dangling from his hand, and opened his eyes. They shone brighter than the buds of lightning bugs, than the lamplights above, than two little suns. And then, he sped straight for Edgar in a blur of body and gold.

TWENTY

Bang.

The jagged teeth of Bastien's bottle cut into Edgar's middle. She'd never forget the squelch. Edgar gasped as he staggered back against the door. Kellan caught him before he collapsed, before he could dent his best hat, and pulled her jacket off to sop the blood. Blood. There was so much of it. So much. Iron and copper and something else dripped hot and sticky against her fingers, seeping into her skin, into the soil and the stone.

Bang.

Lou fired her gun. The bullet casings clattering on the ground. Something crunched, then clanged, then grunted and rolled. Maybe. The clearest sound was of Edgar's breathing, which was far too shallow. Kellan pressed harder against his wound.

"Edgar, Edgar," she said over his rasps. "Eyes open. Gotta . . . eyes open, keep—"

Bang.

She couldn't move, couldn't breathe, couldn't feel the tips of her fingers in the cold that settled around them all. But she could sop the blood. She'd done it before, the day of his mis-carve. If she pressed hard enough, he'd stop bleeding. Harder, and she'd have carved a prosthesis that didn't rot him from within all those years ago. Harder still, and she'd never have mentioned the Exposition at all. They'd be closing the shop for the night, and in the morning, she'd have found some other way to save it. She'd have found some other way.

Screeching tires. Burning rubber. A car sped toward them, stopped a few yards away and kicked up the neighbor's dirt. Not an ordergarde's. No sirens. She wouldn't have cared if it was, wouldn't have left Edgar's side. They'd have to drag her away, and even then, she'd keep one arm around him and one hand in the cracks between the road's cobbles—

"Kellan?" The voice, Kellan realized, belonged to Axel. He squeezed her shoulders, a slight tremor in his voice. "You need to get up, and you need to get up now."

"I can't."

"You can. The gate, it'll close soon, so you've got to move. If you don't, he'll die." He crouched beside her and cradled her face in his hands, angled it up so she could meet the smoky quartz of his eyes. "Get Edgar in the car and get someplace safe. Agathe's, not a hospital. Xo's in the back seat; she'll make sure he makes it, and Mesny and I, we'll take care of this."

Behind him, Cyn wrestled with Bastien on the ground,

struggling under his unnatural speed and strength. When he pulled himself out of her grip, he tore for Lou, trailing streaks of brilliant light. Lou fired again, and again, but it only slowed him down enough for Cyn to grab another limb and pull him down in an endless, bloody cycle of hisses and clamors and bangs. When Lou fired the last bullet in the chamber, she reloaded, and it'd start again, and still, he wouldn't stop. He wouldn't stop.

No. She had to stop calling it "he." That wasn't Edgar's brother. That was a monster. A monster in human skin. A monster with eyes like the sun—

"Kellan," Axel said. He brushed something off her cheeks with his thumbs.

"Will you be okay?" She shouldn't have wasted the time it took to ask, with Edgar's blood pooling between her fingers, but the thought of him and that *thing* . . . He wouldn't survive it. How could he, when he was so gentle, so good, and not even bullets or Cyn's iron grip could keep the creature down?

He couldn't hide the fear in his eyes on his best day. Tonight, he didn't try.

"Hold him, Cyn." Mesny stood a few feet ahead, an empty glass jar in her hand, her fingerwaves frizzed in the humid air. "Don't let go until I say, and when I do, run straight for the car."

"Ready?" He said it like goodbye. Although her cheeks had dried, he brushed them with his thumbs as if to commit the feel of her skin to memory. In answer, she held the back of one of his hands, so much bigger and warmer than hers, and found the strength to stand.

Bastien thrashed in Cyn's arms, but she held steady, a few of her bolts popping at her shoulders and elbows. Axel rose and pulled something out of his pocket. A small glass jar. "Lou—"

"I got it." Lou was at her side then, and she made immediately for Edgar's ankles. "Get his shoulders, Kel."

Kellan left her jacket on top of him and followed Lou's lead. She tried to ignore the tortured sound of Edgar's ragged breath, the drip, drip, drip of his blood that swelled from the wrinkles of her ruined jacket, the trail it left in the Lidonch stone.

Xo opened the door from inside. "Lay him on his back," she instructed, full of command as she flipped on Mesny's overhead light.

They laid Edgar across the seat, his legs across Xo's lap and his head cushioned by Kellan's soaked jacket, then Lou climbed into the driver's seat. Already Xo was picking shards out of his wound with a pair of tweezers.

"Okay. Okay." Lou, sweating and panicked, looked over the dashboard of Mesny's Chromeroller for a keyhole to the ignition that wasn't there. "We gotta go, and I don't know how to work this thing, and *where is Cyn*, that petty hunk of bolts, we're not leaving her here—"

Outside, Mesny carved gold into walls and shields, blades and flame, the sparks of a master at work lighting the night in colors Kellan had never seen before. Axel stood with his empty glass jar, searching for an opening. And when Mesny carved her gold into a chain that coiled around the monster's ragged limbs, he found it.

"Run!" she called to Cyn.

Bastien, trapped, roared in fury. The chains wouldn't hold for long. Axel pressed the lip of the jar against the beast's open mouth, and the little suns of his eyes dimmed. He fell slack, clinging to the glass as though it was all that separated him from life and death.

Out of Bastien's mouth came the smallest of lights. In the dark, it pulsed like a lost lightning bug, only as big as the tip of her thumb. And for a moment, all was still.

Until Axel capped the jar. And the jar cracked.

"Go!" Axel set the jar down and stumbled back. "Go, now! Drive!"

The engine hummed to life the second Cyn climbed into the passenger's seat. Xo worked with an unnatural quickness, even when Lou sped off so suddenly that Kellan's head crashed against the window. The screech of tires against the stone road wasn't nearly as sharp as the creature's. Kellan could only just make out its form in the rearview mirror. It wisped at the edges, bled like ink into frigid air. It formed a hand, a neck, a head, its limbs gangly as it grew from its shattered cage. Before Lou cleared the corner, two lights shone where its eyes should have been, and they left Axel and Mesny with a thing that was all darkness, like the night had decided to play at being human.

◆ ◆ ◆

"The city of Riz is hereby under lockdown. Citizens are urged to return to their homes. Tune in at midnight for more, live from our comte."

The radio station had stopped playing music an hour ago. Maybe more. Kellan didn't know for sure, since Lou hadn't turned it on in the car ride to her mother's house. She only knew that for as long as she sat in Ms. Roussel's living room, the fireplace sputtering the last sparks of its flame, there'd been no music.

Ms. Roussel had twenty-three photographs on her mantel. Twenty-three. Kellan knew because she counted them all a dozen times. It was all she could do not to think of what Ms. Roussel and Xo were busy doing in the next room over, with Edgar splayed across one of the tables. The blood on her shirt and skin and fingernails had dried from red to muddy brown and flaked onto Ms. Roussel's carpet. She didn't know where they kept the broom. If she had, she'd have swept it up. Better to be busy, to be useful, than this torture of sitting still and waiting for . . . no. No, she wouldn't think like that. Couldn't think that far.

Instead, she watched the clock.

Another hour passed. Then another. She counted each tick of the small hand, then each tick of the longer one, each beat like shattering glass in the silence until another guardcar sped by, sirens blaring. Cyn and Lou sat on either side of her, each stunned in their own way. Still no Mesny. No Axel.

If she closed her eyes, she could imagine that the ticks belonged to Cuivreton's clock tower. She could imagine Ms. Roussel's sofa was her train station's single bench, and that the crackling flame was rainwater against a rusted rooftop. Maybe. There was no mistaking the fire for rainfall, the down-stuffed linen for iron slats. But those ticks. Those ticks could be clock tower bells. She didn't even need to try too hard to block out the murmurs on the other end of the door as Xo and Agathe scrambled to keep Edgar alive.

She should sleep, they'd said. Rest away the iron and copper stench of Edgar's blood, the memory of Mesny and Axel disappearing around the corner. The dark reminded her too much of the monster—the *thing*—they left behind in the Fault. So she counted the ticks again. She counted and counted until another hour passed, the glow of the flames blurred and spread, the fireplace's embers became all she could see—

The front door opened, then closed. Someone new spoke with Xo and Agathe in hushed tones before stepping into the living room. Mesny. Alone.

"Edgar is stable for now. Xo recommends rest, and Agathe agreed to keep a watchful eye," she said softly, carefully, as though speaking too loudly would make Kellan crack. "When we returned to an empty manor, we assumed you'd accompanied Edgar to the Fault before Pierpont issued the lockdown. I tracked Cyn's location, and the rest . . ."

A guardcar sped past the window. Kellan nodded into the silence. It was all she could do.

"Kellan, my dear? How did you find Bastien?"

"Brother. Edgar's brother."

Mesny nodded slowly, calculating in silence. "He's a forum member," she said. "Missing for months, but I hadn't seen him in ages. He was my grandfather's first apprentice, you know. A brilliant theorist, in his own right. Eccentric. Practically family."

The forum's perpetually missing seat had belonged to Edgar's little brother. Did he know how far his sibling had climbed to meet so tragic an end? That he'd stood beside one of history's most brilliant makers, a child immortalized in color and canvas?

"Axel is in the car, trying to get ahold of his father and the comte. No response from either of them. Perhaps tomorrow, after the lockdown is lifted . . ."

Kellan let out a tiny breath, gripped the edge of the sofa cushion until the tips of her fingers went numb. Mesny wasn't alone. Axel had survived. They both had, and the thing that was once Bastien had died. There couldn't have been an alternative: if they'd tried to outrun it, they'd have failed. Whatever it was, it was fast and strong and very much not human. But how did they stop it? And how many were there left?

"I think I figured it out." Kellan looked over Mesny's shoulder and into the flames, her voice brittle. "The blackouts."

The truth hung heavy in the air between them. Mesny's lips pursed in a rigid line. "Kellan, you don't have to—"

She pulled Axel's map, her carver, and two sheets of gold

foil out of her pocket and set them on the coffee table. "You said when you were little, you thought your grandpa's stories were all around you."

"I was a child. Children are renowned for believing ridiculous things."

"Cyn found books in the labyrinth from other continents with the same stories. Rabbits. Bears. Spiders. I thought it was stupid at first, but after tonight—"

"You're exhausted." Mesny finally approached the table, but not to watch Kellan work. "Please, go upstairs and rest. You too, Lou. I'll attend to Cyn's injuries."

Kellan didn't listen. Just as Mesny had done in their first lesson together, Kellan carved the Push rune in the center of one sheet and the Pull rune in the center of the other. But she didn't stop there. On one, she outlined the map of Riz and separated it into its districts, carved little knots of Spark and Dim until the sheet resembled a bird's-eye view of the city at night, each of the runes glowing like a building's light in the distance, all surrounding Kellan's tiny rune for Pull. "We're looking in the wrong direction. Forward instead of behind. Maybe we weren't looking far back enough. Or we were looking instead of seeing."

The rest, she did quickly. If she didn't, the foil would catch fire. There was no glass bulb to contain the heat, but she had a feeling she wouldn't need one. She had a feeling this would work, even though she didn't want it to.

Her hands weren't as steady as Mesny's, and she didn't

have time to find a pair of tongs, but she held the Push above the one with glittering lights and Pull at its center and lowered it until they both hummed and trembled. When they did, so did the knots below. "I thought for a second that maybe once, a long time ago, those stories weren't just stories. They were here, all around us, or maybe they still are, separated by something, like a—"

"Veil," Mesny finished, with a breath. "Like a veil."

Like the city lights from the blackout downtown, the knots flickered and swelled, burning bright enough to warm her fingertips. "I don't know what made them, or how long ago and why, but I think the things in the stories are trying to push through. Each time, they get a little further. Each time, they leave something here. The garden, the willow, the stream, those aren't wonders. They're pieces from the other side."

The closer she hovered the top sheet, the longer the lights dimmed. They rippled out from the center, snuffed one district, then another, and another.

The lights went out the moment the map cracked.

Mesny sank into a lounge chair, fingers steepled over her mouth. Another guardcar sped past the window, washing the living room in purple and gold.

"What do we do about it?"

Axel. He leaned against the doorframe like it was the only thing keeping him upright. A thin streak of red cut a line from his ear to his lip, the mark of a stray glass shard. But he wasn't broken or bruised.

"The garden at Ol' Matty's, the willow in the Makers' Strip, the stream at the Guild's library . . . It's too much to be coincidental. If anyone can figure this out and stop it from spreading, it's the theorists. Whatever's on the other side knows that, so they're taking them out where they know the theorists will gather en masse: the trials. The Ball's details were secret, so they struck on a rumor. But this time, the whole map knows."

Kellan stood. Through her exhaustion, the sudden and overwhelming ache in her muscles felt like she'd been hit by a train at full speed. But as she spoke, she caught traces of realization dawning in each of them. Mesny. Axel. Cyn and Lou. They believed her. More, they saw it for themselves.

"It's the last trial. I'm sure of it. If we can't stop it there, we can at least hold it off."

"And if you're wrong?" asked Mesny.

"Then I'll think on my feet."

At least they had a plan. A flimsy one, with enough room for error to park a car in. But with Edgar in the next room over, and the night that harbored monsters in its shadows waiting for them outside, Kellan would take any chance she could get.

I dove into the dark and found our undoing.

–The Journals of Jaquet Francom. Final entry before his death. 37th of Calcaire. 57 Guilded.

TWENTY-ONE

Kellan and Axel sat in the front seats as Mesny's automirun escorted them to Nordton at an infuriatingly slow pace. They moved like molasses through Riz's misted streets, but it was the only way they could stay safe when the world shifted around them.

"There is traffic ahead," it would say when shops and brick roads became endless deserts and abandoned temples, forests of trees that watched with wizened faces in the bark and boughs that curled like living ribbon. "Would you like to take a different route?"

Kellan and Axel never answered. Edgar's blood had caked under her nails and stained her blouse so thoroughly that, if she hadn't known any better, she'd have had trouble believing her blouse was ever white. She couldn't escape the metallic stink of it, trapped in Mesny's overly cautious car. Unfortunately for them both, opening the window wasn't an option either.

The only constants were the glass shards that peppered the streets, reflecting the shifting skies. The sight of it all chilled the tips of her fingers with dread.

"A few more blocks," Axel said. "Won't be long now."

Silence. Heavy, thick-enough-to-swim-in silence. Enough that she couldn't ignore the cut on his lip that had opened sometime between the Fault and Nordton's gate or the way he picked at the automirun's leather wheel, determined to pull the thread from its seam. Determined not to look at her.

She should have said something. Anything. Thanked him, at the very least, for saving their lives. Axel had pulled Kellan out of her panic when her world lay bleeding into the stone. But even more, she wanted to thank him for surviving. Because she didn't know what she'd have done if the dark had taken him, too.

The words settled somewhere in her throat. By the time the automirun spoke again, Axel had snapped the thread. Kellan had swallowed those words.

"There is traffic ahead," said the automirun.

No, there wasn't. All that surrounded Kellan and Axel were wisps of smoke and ash, ghosting through abandoned streets. Then she listened. A faint, broken melody sounded above the warped echoes of the riots they'd left behind. One voice hummed a crooked rhyme. Then another.

"Go." Kellan could hardly hear herself over her heartbeat. Beside her, Axel fumbled through the dashboard's many knobs in search of an override. "Drive."

"There is traffic ahead."

Another voice, another song, this time clearer. Closer. So close, Kellan could almost make out the words. So close, she could have mistaken the curling smoke for warm breath, whiting in the cold.

"Nothing's working." Axel opened Mesny's coffee dispenser, then a compartment of earrings and tie clips. "I can't get it to—"

"There is traffic ahead."

Two lights flickered in the dark. She knew them well now. Breath curdled, dense as the wisping smoke as the little suns' victims slunk nearer. And Kellan went stone-still.

"Drive," she said again.

"There is traffic—"

Four lights. Eight. Another song, metal scraping against the brick road top. Then they took shape. An old woman. A girl, around Kellan's age. A boy, not yet tall enough to reach their knees—

"DRIVE!"

Axel broke one of its levers. The automirun tore down the street at full speed, just missing the shadowed figures whose eyes shone like bright streaks through the window.

The monsters had slipped through the Fault's gates.

"Can this thing go any faster?" Kellan called over the screech of metal on asphalt.

"I don't even know how I got it this way," said Axel, peeling around a corner. "Let's just take what we can get."

As they sped through Nordton's streets, streams of Rizans raced past them, stumbling over each other to escape whatever waited by the docks. The air chilled the condensation on the windows, but through the frost and fog, Kellan just made out the shape of Axel's apartment. The lot and the pier were almost completely abandoned. Even the gulls had flown away from the cold and the danger that lurked on its docks. Yet while most of Nordton had fled, Kellan and Axel weren't completely alone.

Axel squinted. "Is that . . ."

"Faustin?"

The slip of a boy carved titanium into a makeshift shield, as someone—some*thing*—rammed into it hard enough to dent the metal. Another carve, and the metal repaired itself. Another ram, and Faustin's work was undone. A *bang!* split the night as Izod fired a round from a handgun, shielding Orana behind him. The creature whirled, and Faustin tossed a rock at its head, stealing its attention again.

"They won't last long like that." Axel unbuckled his seat belt and scrambled for another glass jar.

Kellan forced herself not to flinch when Izod fired another round.

"Neither will we if we catch it like that again," she said. The shot was Izod's last, it seemed. He set the pistol in its holster and pulled out a tiny knife. "There has to be another way."

"And until then? We just let them die?"

"I didn't say that! I just—"

Axel didn't wait for her to finish. He climbed out of the car, motioning for her to stay put, and raced in the direction of the havoc. Kellan, who was never much good at following instructions, took off after him.

The air reeked of fish and runed metal. The gulls had long since abandoned the harbor, as had most of its ships. Kellan almost tripped on a stray heel, which seemed to have been lost from someone escaping the scene unfolding before her—a bloody game of survival. The creature's roars pierced the coming night sky.

"Funny meeting you here," Faustin shouted over the creature's frustrated growls. "You wouldn't happen to be expert monster catchers, would you?"

"Less talking." Another of Izod's knives landed in the back of the something's thigh. "More bashing."

"How long have you all been at this?" Axel asked in search of an opening.

"Too long," said Orana. "It isn't tiring out."

"It won't. They're—" Axel stalled in horror when he spotted Kellan. "Why aren't you in the car?"

"Because someone has to stop you from being stupid."

"And how do you expect to do that? Wait, no, that's not what I—"

"Not the time for a lovers' quarrel." Izod tossed Axel a hooked blade. "Make yourselves useful or get out of the way."

"We tried civil conversation first." The creature rammed into Faustin's shield again, sending him staggering back. "He never was much of a talker, was he?"

Kellan recognized the creature's face before she could ask who. Harmon Barbier, the mousy boy Marielo had convinced to steal her second trial performance.

She and Axel exchanged a glance. Then they dove into the fray. Axel helped Izod, wielding his borrowed knife as best he could, and Kellan took Orana by the wrist in search of someplace to hide.

"I left my carver on the ship," Orana told Kellan as they crouched behind a barrel. "Do you have a spare?"

"Afraid not."

"That's unfortunate. With Axel's help, I'd hope they'd gain a brain cell to split between them. But evidently—"

The creature that was once Harmon yanked the tiny knife out of his thigh and hurled it at Izod. Fortunately, it missed. But it whizzed by Kellan and Orana's barrel, nicking Kellan's ear. The pain was hollow, but sharp. She hissed at the blood that dotted her fingertip. "Not," she finished.

Orana peeked out from behind the barrel, watching the boys edge Harmon closer to the water. "Do you know why we carve into metal?"

"What? Why?"

"Francom's Theorem. Carving metals are True Solids. Consistent and reliable. It isn't like wood or skin. Or glass."

Kellan followed Orana's line of sight, which led her to the jar Axel kept in his left hand.

"Funny thing, glass," said Orana. "You'd think it's solid, but it's not. It's not liquid either. It's—"

"Something in between." Glass, Kellan knew, was a viscous substance in constant movement, its flow so slow when it cooled it retained shape. But that made it brittle. If she could give a durable metal those same qualities for a moment—just a moment—perhaps that would lure out the lightning bug. Then, when the metal stopped shifting and was made True once more . . . "We could trap it."

"Theoretically," Orana said. "What are we trapping, exactly?"

Steel. She needed steel. Kellan snatched the tiny blade from the ground and carved onto the flat end, stretched and molded it into a lidded bowl. A knot of Melt and Harden at the base—not quite opposites, but close enough to risk a miscarve. If something went wrong, she'd toss it over the docks. Let the sea have the chaos.

"Are you sure that'll work?" asked Orana from over Kellan's shoulder.

"Not even slightly."

"Good luck, then. Try not to die."

Not-Harmon knocked Faustin to the ground, his shield clattering beside him with a tinny thud. Izod helped him onto his feet, and Axel lodged his hooked blade into the creature's shoulder. But he couldn't get it out. The glass jar shattered at his feet as he pulled with both hands. Not-Harmon whirled on him with blackened teeth and blinding eyes—

Kellan took the opening. She tore her way through the stink of blood and death to Axel's side and pressed the mouth of the bowl she'd carved to Not-Harmon's face. He went slack, his eyes less blinding, as the metal heated under her palm, past her wrist, her shoulder, her chest. A horrible pain beat against the inside of her skull, and the abandoned dock morphed into a cobwebbed temple of gold and ancient stone . . .

"We got it," came Axel's voice. "Kellan, let go. We got it."

The metalglass jar cooled, its lid melding with the bowl. A screech echoed from within, so violent the steel bucked wildly in Kellan's arms. But it didn't crack. Soon, the screeching stopped, as did the pain. Harmon lay battered at her feet.

"He's still breathing," Izod said. "Tenacious little twig."

"I never liked him," Faustin said, catching his breath.

"There should be a physician's kit on the ship," said Orana. "I'll get it."

"It'll probably be locked away," Axel said. "If you can't find the key, we should—"

"Pick it," Kellan, Orana, and Izod said, speaking in unison.

"—call an ambulance," Axel finished, exhausted. "Exactly."

Faustin went on to explain that the four of them were on their way out of Nanseau when the creatures attacked. Lightning bugs too big to be lightning bugs had burrowed up noses and down ear canals, transforming strangers into strange beasts. While Orana searched the abandoned ship, Kellan and Axel explained what they knew: a veil between their world and another had cracked and would likely shatter completely. The final trial could be their only chance to stop it.

Faustin sneered in disbelief. "You're asking us to run headlong into danger?" he said. "Is there a punch line?"

"How much does it pay?" Izod said, wiping blood off his last knife.

Kellan answered before Axel could ruin everything with talk of morals and mortal peril. "Mesny's got bill," she said. "Bonne does, too. Not to mention the Crown's favor, if you trade in that instead."

On the ground, Harmon whimpered painfully.

"I'd like to help," Orana said. She'd cleaned a knife wound with something smoking. "There's nothing to do on that ship anymore."

"Izod might be a pirate, and Elo might be a psychopath," Faustin mumbled, taking a cautious step away from Orana, "but the kid always scared me the most."

After some convincing, they agreed to join. Izod rigged Mesny's automirun. Faustin helped Axel haul a protesting Harmon into his apartment, and Kellan and Orana searched for tools among his collection. "I've heard of a lamp like this," she marveled when she found one of his gravelights. "It once led a man out of death."

Izod drove them downtown, where the chaos in the outer districts could have been a distant nightmare.

No shattered windows. No shifting skies. The street in front of Crown Hall had been swept clean, the cog and crown at the top just as imposing as it had been her first night in the city. That night, jazz had filled the air, and the district had hummed with life. Now, as the sun crested over the district's skyscrapers, the air crackled with tension.

Faustin, Izod, and Orana waited for Lou by the stairs while Kellan and Axel started their trek to an alley near the Guild's entrance, where they'd planned to meet the others. They walked in silence, hugging the walls. At the faintest sound of footsteps, they froze, ducking into the nearest patch of shadow they could find before venturing on. The gaps between the buildings they passed were just wide enough for a crate or two. Axel wouldn't look at her. He'd tug at Kellan's sleeve in warning when he'd hear or see something she'd missed, or hold out an arm between her and another passing fleet of ordergarde who patrolled too close to their hiding spot, but he'd always look away. To make it easier, she wouldn't look either.

Five blocks later, and the elevator was in sight. Beside Kellan, Axel had taken off his waistcoat and offered it to her in a neatly folded pile. "You should put this on."

"No time." She kept walking, glanced sidelong at the innocent bundle of fabric in his hand. For a moment, as they crossed the road to the alley, it was like she was in the bayou again. Just a girl in a pretty dress, beside a boy who wanted to protect her from the cold. "Still got fires to put out."

He stopped. Right there, in the open road. He didn't stay long enough to draw attention, or even enough to slow them down, but it was long enough for Kellan to turn. He looked at her, and all at once, the words she'd swallowed at the manor came to life again, pushed against the cage of her teeth. Say it, she told herself. If it'd rekindle the warmth behind his eyes, if there was a chance he'd smile again, just once, just for a second—

"You're covered in blood," he said.

. . . Oh.

Axel caught up with her in two of his long-legged strides and unfolded the waistcoat. "It's no jacket, but it should cover most of the stains. Roll your sleeves up to the elbows, and you'll look like another overworked reporter who got clumsy with their lunch."

They'd crossed the street. The alley near the elevator was wide enough for them to stand comfortably apart. He held open the waistcoat as if waiting for her to step into it, but then handed it to her by the collar and inspected the toes of his shoes.

Kellan slipped it on. The warm scent of cinnamon and cherrywood snuffed out the stink of alleyway piss and faraway smoke. Old rainwater dripped from a gutter overhead, rippling the puddle near her feet and filling the half silence between them. Axel stuffed his hands into his pockets and toed at a bottle cap the sweepers must have missed. It was such a quiet, simple moment that Kellan nearly forgot about the shifting skies. The coming dark. The loss and the chaos and the many things that kept them from being anything but quiet and simple.

The familiar rhythm of Mesny's clicking heels cut him off, and soon after, Kellan and Axel weren't alone anymore. Mesny and Cyn joined them in the alleyway. Kellan and Axel took another step apart.

"We've little time to waste," said Mesny. "Are you ready, Kellan?"

No, Kellan thought. Who could be ready for the world's end? But she kept the truth to herself as Mesny took her place by the Guild's secret way.

"There's a spider in the dark," said Mesny.

Kellan took in the open air. The peace before the storm. "Keep its secrets and its spark."

TWENTY-TWO

The Guild's entrance led Kellan, Mesny, and Cyn to a small round room built somewhere in Sougare. Kellan stared at her reflection in the mirror. She'd changed out of her bloodied clothes and into something Mesny thought suitable for the occasion. It fit well, the suit and waistcoat. The tie, though, felt more like a silk noose.

"I've heard a rumor that the president of the Crescent Isles is in attendance," said Mesny, "although there's no way to be sure. Axel should keep an eye out, I suspect. Half the globe is in those stands, making shelter out of our ruins. A box of praline, and it'll be dinner and a show. . . ."

The hum of the audience grew louder overhead.

In minutes, Kellan would step on a platform that'd bring her onto her final trial's stage. She'd have to pretend her world hadn't shattered, that she hadn't lost people she'd grown to care for, and that those waiting in the stands weren't in mortal danger.

"We should get everyone out now," said Kellan, "before things get bad."

"We can't stop a moving train."

"But they have no idea—"

"Precisely. They have *no* idea." Mesny lowered her voice to an urgent hush and adjusted the gold pins in Kellan's braided hair. "And they won't until it's too late. We don't know why. We don't even know if it will strike here, do we? No. Because we are in the dark, just as they are, just as the thousands of people in the Greater City who haven't yet made it home."

Her words hung heavy in the silence. Cyn, who had been fussing with Kellan's clothes, dropped the train of Kellan's jacket. There was still so much they didn't understand. Choosing to make their stand here was a risk on its own, a guess based on a vague pattern and a thimble's worth of evidence. They could still be wrong. And even if they weren't, they could still fail.

"All we know for certain is now. This moment." Mesny loosened the tie at Kellan's neck until Kellan could breathe again. "And in this moment, you are safe. The next . . . I suppose we leave it to the stone."

She squeezed Kellan's shoulder, reminded her where to find the rest of them in the stands, and left her with Cyn to join the audience above. "That was encouraging," Kellan grumbled.

"The Madame is nothing if not practical," said Cyn, tone hitched with worry. "I will be by your side either way, and Lou and Axel will not be far from—"

Before Cyn could finish speaking, a dull, mechanical voice sounded from across the way.

"Wait," Kellan whispered. She pressed her ear to the door. "That's an automi."

Harmon, they'd left to heal in Axel's apartment. But Faustin? Izod? Orana? The rest of the bids still on the island knew as much about the coming chaos as Kellan did. All but Marielo, who prepared for the final trial in a room within earshot.

"He hates you," said Cyn.

"I know."

"Then focus on the task at hand. Nothing you say will convince him not to crush you tonight. If not physically, then certainly professionally."

"I should at least warn him." It was the right thing to do. What Edgar would have her do, were he there to guide her. She'd never known the pain of losing family, but she'd seen what it did to the occasional Du who remembered. The ones who knew exactly who to blame.

Marielo blamed her. Perhaps he was right to. She couldn't go back and save Maricar's life, but she could give Marielo a chance to fight or flee.

It took no small amount of convincing to get Cyn to distract Marielo's automi long enough to give them time alone. "Five minutes remaining," came a cool voice from overhead, marking the time left for the last two bids to take their places below stage. Five minutes to convince Marielo of a truth Kellan still didn't know how to explain. Five minutes and all the charm of a wet rag.

A soft knock on a nearby wall. Cyn had finished her part. Kellan slipped out of her room, shoes in hand to tread softly across the circle to Marielo's side. His automi had left the door cracked. It creaked when she opened it. Inside, Marielo stared at his reflection, hair slicked and gaze hollow. He only noticed his new company when Kellan shut the door behind her. "If you're here to slit my throat, get on with it," he said, adjusting his cuff links. "At least then I can claim self-defense."

"We don't have long."

"Get out."

"The world, it's cracking. Breaking down," she tried to explain, but the words came in jumbles of nonsense. "I wanted to warn you."

"Get *out*."

"There are these things, these monsters, and when the cities black out, they latch themselves on to—"

"I don't think you understand how much I despise the sound of your voice."

Marielo whirled on her, each word like tumbling gravel. His rage wasn't ice. Ice cracked and melted, and its cold left its mark in burns and decay. Marielo's rage was a void, empty and endlessly dense all at once.

"Every second you spend breathing is a second that belongs to her." His words didn't cut, like shattered ice would have.

They took. Robbed the room of what little life lingered. "I never want to hear it again."

"Two minutes remaining."

He opened the door and pushed past her. She felt it then, the mark Maricar had left on her brother. Perhaps not the full force of it, but faint enough a trace to finally understand.

"You hear her, too," she called. "Don't you?"

Marielo stopped, one foot on the platform.

"It's not your grief. It might be that, too, but it's more. She's . . . she's *there*. You can feel her voice in the air, like she's right beside you. Like she never left."

Three steps was all it took to clear the distance between them, the light's dim glow eclipsed by his looming form. There it was. The rage in him was so like the rage she'd spent thirteen years hiding from in the shadow of her namehouse, it frightened her. It showed in all its jagged horror, Marielo's dark eyes alight with fury and pain—

"Mr. Bitao," came a pleasant voice from nearby. "There you are."

Marielo stopped short. Ginnel stood by the gallery entrance, cool and collected despite the scene before her. It couldn't look good. Kellan hadn't moved. Not because she was frozen, but because one hand wielded her heeled shoe like a small blade. The other had found its way around her carver's handle the moment Marielo's gaze went wild, its point ready to cut. Instinct, she'd call it. Maybe one day she'd believe it.

"The comte sent me down to make sure all's well," Ginnel

continued, heels clicking as she approached. "It is, isn't it? Well?"

This wasn't the first time Kellan had underestimated Ginnel. Looking at her, Kellan had almost forgotten they'd both endured the stone towers. They shared the same quick feet, thick hide, and silver tongue because namehouse Dus needed them like they needed water and air. There was no surviving its ivy-veined walls without them.

"One minute remaining," said the voice from overhead.

Marielo's chest and shoulders heaved with a deep breath. He stepped back. Stood down. Spared Ginnel a second's glance. Then he left for his platform on the other side of the room as though nothing had happened.

"The comte didn't send you down here, did he," said Kellan.

"Of course he didn't." Ginnel winked and guided Kellan to her place with linked arms. "I wanted to wish you luck. Phenomenal timing on my part, though, if I do say so myself."

Even in the dark, Ginnel couldn't hide the toll working beside the comte had taken on her. It showed in the faint purple circles under her eyes, just visible from beneath a thin layer of concealer. Her pleated skirt was wrinkled, her stockings slightly frayed, and she'd stained the palm of her left glove with sauce from her lunch. Time and circumstance had changed Ginnel just as it had Marielo, who'd stormed toward her with madness in his eyes. Like Marielo, this Ginnel was similar but hardened. Changed.

"He didn't hurt you, did he?" asked Ginnel in a soft voice.

"No. I don't think he would have. Not really."

"Good."

"Thirty seconds remaining," said the voice from overhead.

The audience above went stone-still in anticipation, and Ginnel dropped her act. "Kellan," she said, squeezing Kellan's shoulder. When she spoke, it was in a quick, determined breath. "Beat this. You have to."

"I will," she said. "I promise."

Then the platform underneath Kellan rose. She held her arms out to keep her balance.

Below, Ginnel waved goodbye, and Kellan looked ahead, deafened by echoed applause and blinded by smoking bulbs and camera lights from every curve of the gallery. It made it impossible for Kellan to tell one shadow from another. When the cameras eased, she spotted the panel directly below. Monsieur Bonne was seated calmly in the center.

A master of ceremony introduced them with flair to amused applause. Kellan heard none of it. She peered through the light and the smoke, searching for Mesny or Lou or Cyn. Nothing. The audience had blended into a mass of glitter and flesh.

Gold dust gathered into shapes downstage. Strengthen. Weaken. Fold. Cut. Close. Above them shone a massive glittering clock. Five runes, and an hour to make them something nice.

A workbench piled high with materials faded into view. It was filled with every metal or tool Kellan could ever want or need for the final challenge. In another life, she could win this.

She could earn her seat, prove herself, change the future of countless Dus in countless namehouses who dared to dream of more than gray walls and high towers. But not in this one.

The heat of the auditorium didn't reach her. There was only Riz's namehouse, looming over the Fault from the district's second highest hill. The crunch and scrape of broken glass. Edgar's blood on her blouse, under her fingernails, pooling over cold Lidonch stone. Two eyes, piercing the dark like little suns.

The music faded. The crowd hushed. "Your hour begins . . ." started the master of ceremony in a dramatic whisper while the audience hung to the silence, and Kellan let go of her chance. " . . . Now."

Sparks filled the stage. Beside her, Marielo carved into platinum, rhodium, gold, silver. His metal twisted and whirred, dithered and split, washed the audience in its glow. Kellan took in the theater. Counted the exits. Measured how long it would take to reach the closest one and how many people could fit through at one time. The crowd was restless, their confused murmurs bouncing off Sougare's ancient walls. She couldn't carve metalglass onstage, else they'd take her out of the game and away from what she knew would be the site of certain disaster. Instead, she held her carver at the ready, its point a hair over sheets of steel.

Kellan . . .

Marielo's carver clattered to the floor, and Maricar's voice sounded from everywhere. Gold dust fell in a fading curtain, and the clock stopped fourteen minutes in. Marielo watched Kellan with horror and confusion, his rage changing shape. Stage lights blinked in and out, and the metal became stone, then sand, then forest, then sea. Then nothing at all.

Darkness fell, thick and all-consuming. A dark that swallowed sound. A dark that yielded for nothing. Nothing but eyes, above, before, and below, shining like little suns.

TWENTY-THREE

Screams. The screams were everywhere. Chair legs grated against steel and clattered to the floor as the audience raced from their seats in horror. All around, their footsteps thumped, their heels clicking against shattered lenses and debris. Chaos echoed in the ink-black dark. The sudden chill swept through Sougare's halls. Tiny flames from pocket lighters streaked left and right, nearer and farther, summoning flashes of Bastien in the Fault. And beneath the war-drum thump of her heartbeat in her ears, beneath the screaming, was the earthshaking growl of monsters in the shade.

"Over your head!" shouted Cyn from backstage. "Get down!"

Kellan fell to her stomach. What was once steel softened to parched earth and knotted roots. In the audience above, the bloodcurdling wail of a man tore through screams all around. It was so clear that Kellan could make out his prayers. Then he was gone, and the steel ground was steel again.

Cyn pulled Kellan to her feet, shielding Kellan as best she could from the chaos erupting around them. Aside from the soft glow of her runes, the little suns' eyes were the only lights in the darkness. They tore through the dim in streaks, shadows carrying unsuspecting victims into the unknown. Kellan searched for Marielo on the stage and found only metal scraps.

"What do we do?" Cyn asked.

"Contain them," Kellan answered. She bundled as many sheets of metal under her arms as she could carry. "Hard to do in the dark, though, so we'll need—"

"Kellan!"

A soft violet glow shone from the north. A guiding star. Axel held his gravelight aloft, searching through the dark until he found her.

Gunshots. The sparks of new runework. Lou and Izod had gone to work with metalglass bullets that only slowed the beasts down long enough for Faustin to keep a few away. Mesny carved from upstage with expert fury, cutting beasts down in waves of brilliant gold. But it wasn't enough. Already the dark outnumbered them, closing in like fingers at their necks.

"Are you all right?" asked Axel at her side.

"Wouldn't it be strange if she was?" said Orana. "We're being attacked by . . . What do we call these? We should give them a name. After we defeat them, of course."

"Fighting won't work," she said. "We need a jar that won't crack. A big one."

"Your trick on the docks? It nearly killed you!"

"Don't know if you noticed, but the stone has a nasty habit of keeping me alive."

They worked together. Cyn covered their backs as Kellan and Axel carved, stretched metal to cut off half the stage. Mesny, who caught on quickly, led Lou, Izod, and Faustin in fending off the beasts and herding the survivors through the shrinking opening. It was only metal, denting and ringing as the beasts fought to push through. But it wouldn't be metal for long.

"You trapped us here," said Izod. "Can't tell if you're brilliant or deranged."

"The interior design leaves a lot to be desired," huffed Faustin, "but I can work with it if it means one of our new friends doesn't rip me in two."

The beasts rammed into the metal, thunder ringing throughout Kellan and Axel's makeshift cage. The people huddled, cried, cowered against the wall, waiting for their deaths to come.

"Let me be blunt," called Mesny from beside her with all the power of a hurricane, fingerwaves wild from the onslaught. At once, the crowd fell silent. "This is not a time for panic. This is a time for action. The sooner you calm yourselves, the sooner we will get you out."

"Where is the comte?" one reporter called. "Where is Monsieur Bonne?"

Kellan scanned the stage and the crowd, but neither Cesaire nor Monsieur Bonne were in sight. They must have escaped already, leaving everyone else to fend for themselves.

She'd save her anger for another time. Besides. In searching for them, she'd found something familiar.

A golden dwarf rabbit.

It sat patiently by one of Sougare's walls, its black pearl eyes unblinking. All-knowing. She felt its call in the pit of her stomach, in the marrow of her bones. Whatever instructions Mesny gave wouldn't matter anyway, because in that moment, Kellan made a decision.

"Maker, take the lead. They'll follow you anywhere," Kellan told Mesny. "Axel will lead you through the tunnels. Cyn, Orana, keep them calm. Izod and Lou will guard the rear, and Faustin will take the center."

"And you?" Mesny asked as though she already knew the answer.

"I'm staying."

Kellan didn't know how long they spent on the stage, the air around them heavy with goodbyes they refused to speak. She couldn't leave with them. Not when everything in her knew to follow that rabbit, and knew that the answer to everything lay on the other side, at its destination.

"You don't need me to get them topside, but if someone doesn't stay behind, it'll never end. I need to figure this out. I need to fix this, and to do that, I need to stay."

"You're sixteen." In the flickering light, Kellan couldn't read Mesny's expression. It was soft, though. Softer than Kellan had ever seen her. Soft as the crack in her hurricane voice. "You're just a child."

Had she ever been? The world had never treated her like one. No one but Edgar, who'd taken her in. Mesny, who'd helped her rise. Who looked at the braids she'd woven in Kellan's hair, with fingers that carved miracles, like they were her finest work. Like Kellan was her greatest pride.

Mesny stood straight and cleared her throat. "Be quick, will you? No dallying. The rest of you, with me."

As Mesny walked into the dark, Lou and Cyn pulled Kellan into a tight hug. "Don't do anything stupid," said Lou.

"Can't promise that."

Cyn squeezed so hard she'd left a bruise. "Then you will come back."

They left after Izod, Faustin, and Orana's farewells, leaving Kellan alone with Axel in the middle of the stage.

She looked at him, gravelight washing him in lavender, then shadow, then lavender again, and wished the distance between them away. There was too much to do, too much at stake, too many things keeping them apart. Despite it all, despite the dark that only gave her glimpses of his beautiful face, she read the question he'd written on it, clear as the morning sky.

Is this what you want?

She should have lied. She should have said that because this was the right thing to do, the brave thing to do, she knew with certainty that she'd turn everything back to the way it was. She should have said that she wasn't terrified. But she couldn't. Axel then cleared the space between them in three quick strides, pulled something out of his pocket, and placed it gently in her palm.

A peculiar spool of fine, shimmering thread.

There it was again. That strange feeling of the world around her fading, leaving only her and him, making seats out of barrels as the stars winked through a roof woven from glittering string. They weren't those people anymore, finding magic in tree trunks and the night between stars, desperate for shelter from life's cruel edge. But if spirits were real, if there was a veil to be torn, then surely there was magic in this. This moment. This feeling.

So when she kissed him, she didn't kiss the Guild's youngest architect or House Bonne's eldest son. She kissed the warmth of their laughter in the woods. The dancing dust in Mesny's ballroom. The lines they drew to connect the universe's endless suns in tales of endless possibility. Her lips parted for safety and freedom and love, and he answered with sureness in his arm round her waist, desperation in his fingertips along her cheek, a wish in how his mouth trembled against hers, yearning for the same.

Her fist closed around the spool. He kissed her temple, her nose, the crown of her head, and lingered long enough for her to remember the sound of their stream. They stayed that way long enough for them to say what they couldn't against his gravelight's ebbing glow and the voices around them that rushed like water. Long enough to say, *Keep it. Be safe. Come home.* Then he was gone. And Kellan was left in the dark.

The rabbit led her to a hidden door in the wall, which led to an abandoned trainway. She followed its glittering light down cobwebbed tracks. Soon the only sounds around her were the occasional plop of leaking water and the click of her footsteps along the tunnel's metal walkway. She followed through every turn, down every fork, the air growing colder every passing moment.

Then, there came a set of whispers from somewhere close ahead.

"—shut the girl up," came the sound of Bonne's voice.

Kellan ducked behind a pillar, careful to stay perfectly still. The rabbit had left her behind, its glow fading in the distance.

"Come now, Bedoier," came the comte's voice. "I hardly think it's worth—"

"Were you not in the audience minutes ago?" He shouted loud enough for his voice to bounce off the walls. "Do you truly believe the forum will deny her a seat after she's saved their hides?"

"Jourdain will take care of it."

"Jourdain is *dead*, you idiot. It's anyone's game now. Villiers's boy needs to win, else I'll—"

"You'll what, Bonne?"

Bonne took a steady breath and smoothed the front of his jacket, looking too much like his oldest son in the flickering light, and bent so close to the comte that his spittle freckled the comte's cheeks. He grinned when Cesaire stumbled back a step.

"Go on," Bonne crooned. "Say it."

"Y-your house is nearly bankrupt. Your eldest hasn't a claim, and your heir hasn't an engineering bone in his body. You don't have the pull to—"

"Wait."

Kellan pressed so close to the pillar that her ribs ached, her eyes shut tight. Danger lurked in the bass of Bonne's voice, that one word heavy enough to crush her where she stood.

"Someone else is here."

She dug her fingers into the pillar's concaves. What had it been? A breath too deep? Her reflection in the steel? His steps grew louder with every click of his loafers, his nearness prickling the hairs at the back of her neck.

"It's a rat," said Cesaire. "No one followed us. I made sure of it."

The clicks stopped. "Perhaps you're right," he said. "A rat."

Kellan waited until their footsteps faded to open her eyes. Her lungs stung from holding her breath, but had she been discovered, she would have suffered much worse. She didn't have time to think about the conspiracy against her. Not when the answer to the city's madness waited at the other end of this tunnel.

She stepped out from behind the pillar and into the blinking dark and nearly lost her breath all over again. Her body reacted on its own, thrashing what she could of her arms and legs against whoever's chest pressed against her back. Then she stilled.

Because against her neck, thin as copper foil, pressed the blade of a pocketknife.

"A rat, indeed." Bonne's hot breath reeked of cigar smoke. When she kicked, he only pressed the knife closer to her. She stopped when it pinched her skin.

She caught his eyes. Warm in color, but cold and faraway as he looked into the distance. His grin, just as hollow. "I can't recall the last time I dirtied my hands like this."

"It can't have been too long ago, old friend," said Maker Villiers, his cane clicking like a time bomb as he stepped out of the dark. "Then again, we do what we must to survive."

"Survival." Kellan willed her heart to stop pounding, her breaths to calm and tone to level. But fear and anger shook every syllable. "You dusty crats wouldn't know the first thing about—"

Bonne pressed the knife closer to Kellan's throat. Something warm trailed down her neck, pooled at her collarbone. "Lineage," he said into her ear. "Order. Tradition. They're what secures this nation's power. What would happen, Maker Villiers, should a rat slip into its foundation?"

"You don't understand," Kellan said, straining, careful not to speak so loudly as to stress the muscles in her neck. "I need to—"

"An infestation, I'd imagine." Villiers stood so close Kellan could count the clouds in his cataracts, a brewing storm of steely gray. "It's never one rat, is it. No. One paves the way for another, and before long, they're all chewing at the wood. The nation crumbles. Centuries of blood and loss, wasted. An age of sacrifice made meaningless because of one greedy girl who refuses to stay in her place."

A shadow lingered by the pillar behind him. The gold octagonal pin of an engineer's assistant glinted in the tunnel's dim light. Marielo had come to watch. From the distance, Kellan couldn't tell what he was thinking. Then again, she rarely could.

"Then it was always them." She spoke loud enough for Marielo to hear. To help. See reason in her not being his enemy. "The game was always rigged."

"She understands!" Villiers laughed, and Kellan barely kept herself from heaving in disgust. "They did say you were smart."

The Bitaos. Two refugees from the Bones, come to Nanseau in search of asylum. Bonne and Villiers didn't want them to win because of their talent. They wanted them to win because their desperation made them easy to control. But they'd miscalculated.

"Did it even matter which one?" she asked, apology in her eyes. She hoped Marielo saw it. She hoped he understood. Because when Villiers next spoke, even her flesh crawled in the cruelty of his answer.

"Does it ever?"

"Enough with the dramatics," said Bonne. "Move, so I can finish this. Can't have blood on your jacket, now, can we?"

Yes. They'd certainly miscalculated. Desperation may have made some easy to control, like Harmon, desperate to belong, or Jourdain, desperate to ascend. But the Bitaos were desperate to survive. And that, Kellan knew, made them dangerous.

Villiers wailed. His cane had split in two, cut by a flash of paper-thin metal. Bonne pulled his knife a hair's length away from her neck from the shock, which was just the amount of give she needed.

Kellan stabbed him in his thigh with all her strength, and when he howled, she wriggled out of his grasp.

"Go!" called Marielo mid-carve. "Now!"

Kellan hesitated under Bonne's venomous gaze, under the blood that darkened his pantleg and the pathetic remnants of her carver, but she took off nonetheless. She tore through the dark until she left the sound of Bonne's struggling behind her, leaving only the thud of her boots against the ground.

Eventually, she couldn't run anymore. Her lungs were on fire. Kellan kept close to the wall and walked, leaning against it as though it was all that kept her upright. After a time, she gave up on searching for a trace of the golden rabbit, pulled forward by hope alone.

She didn't know how long she'd walked for. Minutes. Hours. But soon the smell and feel of the air around her changed.

Sunlight rolled the darkness away. Color thinned the black like water in an inkwell. There came the distinct smell of sweet potato pie. Of fresh-cut grass. Of sulfur and chicken dung.

It wasn't just any sunlight she'd stepped into. It was Cuivreton's.

TWENTY-FOUR

Patches of too-green grass peeked out from beneath Cuivreton Station's familiar tracks, swaying in a breeze that Kellan couldn't feel. Crates and barrels stood stacked in odd shapes around the ticket counter. Up ahead, she caught sight of a namehouse. Like the village itself, Cuivreton's namehouse wasn't particularly large. In fact, it was known to be the second smallest namehouse in the minebelt. That wasn't to say it didn't loom over them all, a constant reminder of an age long past, left erect to ensure the island Nanseau reclaimed never fell again. But this tower was different. Massive in a way Kellan's had never been, its spire piercing Cuivreton's watercolor sky like a dagger through paper.

No, this wasn't Cuivreton. This wasn't even Nanseau. The rabbit had led her down a crack in the veil, and somewhere in Sougare's tunnel, she'd slipped through it like she had at Ol' Matty's car shop and the dark of the bayou. This time, whatever summoned her here was trying awfully hard to make her feel at home.

But she wasn't home. It was a pin in her chest, the way she realized that Cuivreton had become as much her home as the tracks under her feet were tracks at all. Home was Mesny's smallest kitchen, the front seat of Lou's car, Edgar's feeble attempts at bear hugs, Cyn's awkward smiles. Axel's hand in her own.

She moved slowly at first. Carefully, since she still didn't quite know how to cage the fear that threatened to rip her open from the inside. No matter how many steps she took, the ticket cabin loomed on her left like a shadow in the sun.

Eventually, something approached from the other end of the tracks. Foxglove's silhouette shone hazy through the distance. A blink, and it was a swarm of golden bees. Another, a golden rabbit, so large it towered over her, its eyes as reflective as still water.

Its voice shook the distant trees. *What brings you here, little thing?*

Kellan tried not to tremble. She struggled to remember that she'd once chased this same creature down train tracks and through swamp water. Now she could hardly will her quivering knees to hold her up long enough to speak.

"My home's in danger," she said. "I need to fix it, and—"

Why must you "fix" it? It bent until its whiskers grazed Kellan's cheeks, its smile wider than the width of her splayed arms. *Is your world broken, little thing?*

Breathe. Breathe. She'd forgotten how to breathe.

The creature stood again and stretched its front legs. The grass continued to sway. Cuivreton's red dirt swirled in tiny whirlwinds. No breeze. No heat. No chill. *I have a bargain for you,* it said. *I'll show you the way through, and you'll find the way you need to go.*

Its smile darkened into a smirk, revealing the stains on its teeth. It wasn't the rusted color of blood that frightened her, but the shapes. The largest two curved out and over its bottom jaw like pincers. *In return,* it said, *I want a story.*

She'd never told a story before. She didn't know where to begin, whether this creature wanted something from the tellers or something from a history book.

Quickly, it said, and Kellan nearly jumped out of her skin. The beast sighed and shook its mane. Behind the fur, she could have sworn it had at least one other set of eyes. *You haven't very long.*

"What? Wait—"

Five.

Oh no. "I can't just—"

Four.

"I don't know what you—"

Three.

"I need to think!"

The rabbit smiled, each of its massive teeth as long as one of her hands. It blinked, and its eyes flashed from gold to bottomless black. *Two.*

Something clicked in Kellan when it lowered to the ground and the tracks beneath her rumbled to the pitch of its growl. No use in wasting her last second on trying to recite a story she didn't know would work. She needed to survive. She needed to do the one thing she'd tried desperately not to do the entire time she'd spent in that terrifying reflection of her train station.

She needed to run.

The rabbit pounced, and Kellan darted to the right. She knocked down a pile of crates behind her, but she didn't look back. Only forward, only ahead, even though the train station followed her every step, every turn.

She couldn't outrun anything on her best day, but her legs carried her around pillars and behind stacked barrels. The echo of the world around her, however, wasn't so faithful. The grass, the dirt, the platform's wooden planks shifted, and she nearly slipped and fell onto her back. She found her balance by gripping another of the station's pillars. Something warm and wet coated her ankles and calves. Blood? No, not blood. There was too much of it, pulling her into the ground until she could hardly move.

Mud. The ground had slicked and turned into mud.

The cabin. She could practically feel the rabbit-shade's breath on her back as she made another sharp turn, hurrying for the door, hoping against hope that it wasn't locked. When it gave, she ran inside and slammed it shut.

The rabbit rammed into the door hard enough for Kellan's

ears to ring, and she pressed her back against the door to keep it from opening. Now she couldn't see. Angry tears, terrified tears, blinded her. This must be a game it liked to play with its prey, and she had been doomed from the start. Doomed, as Riz was always doomed, and Kellan was a fool to think she could save it. A fool to think that all she needed to do was follow some lights and tell a . . .

"Tell a true story." Her voice shook harder than the cabin's walls. "Tell a true—a true—"

Something cracked above her. An iron slat clanked to the ground at her feet, exposing a sliver of watercolor sky.

"Once," Kellan called, hopefully loud enough for the rabbit to hear through the door. The creature rammed against it again, and splinters fell onto her head. She spoke louder, but that wasn't enough to overcome the tremor in her voice. "Once, there was a girl, and there was a rabbit."

The rabbit stopped. It growled between the cracks in the door and the roof, its breath scorching the back of her neck. "A girl and a rabbit, and the rabbit asked the girl for a story. The girl, the girl, she found the rabbit on her way to save her friends."

Kellan's voice broke, and she'd become too aware of the tears that slicked her cheeks. She couldn't wipe them, not with the rabbit so close to her back, so she closed her eyes and settled for the dark. The rabbit stopped growling.

This was all she could do—realize that she knew nothing, that she could bare her soul to this spirit beast, and if the beast didn't find it bare enough, it'd eat her, or whatever it was that spirits did to souls and bodies, and that would be that. Still, she pressed on. "The rabbit, it stood in her way, and asked for a story. But the girl, the girl, she was so scared she couldn't think, so the rabbit tried to eat the girl, and she ran, and she hid, because that's what the girl does. She, she hides."

The thump of her heart. The pit-pat of falling debris. The squish of Cuivreton mud beneath her, seeping through the cracks in the cabin door. Kellan pressed against that door, against the death that awaited her on its other side. That was all she did, wasn't it? She hid behind pillars, behind railings, in toy-shop attics. She wanted to hide with Edgar forever, where she knew she had a friend, and no number of months spent in the city would change that.

How does the story end, little thing?

She could say anything. She could say that it ended with the rabbit swallowing her whole, which was most likely. That, by some miracle, she managed to outrun it. That it ended with her in the cabin, hiding in the same place she'd hid for so long. But the truest thing, the thing that frightened her the most . . .

"I don't know," she said. "I don't. I don't know how it ends. I just, I just know that I have to do something. I have to get past you, and I have to save my friends. I have to."

And she couldn't do it by hiding.

She patted the ground for something—anything—and found a piece of iron the size of her forearm with a pointed edge. It was no knife, or carver and sheet of gold, but she would make do. She squeezed her eyes tighter and breathed deep, deep, deep enough for her ribs to burn as hot as her tears, her grip on the splinter so tight it shredded her skin.

That was the truth. Even if she could sit against the crate forever, could push into the door until her spine cracked, she wouldn't. She had friends to save. She had work to do.

So Kellan, oversized splinter in hand, climbed to her feet. She stepped out from behind the crates and barrels, she squeezed her hand around the splinter, and she dug her heels into that cursed Cuivreton mud. Or so she had thought. There was no mud. Where her feet once sank into the ground, they stood instead atop solid Lidonch stone.

Kellan knew her namehouse well.

This wasn't her namehouse. Cuivreton's steps were made of wood, not stone. Its walls were granite, not slate. Lidon's gods didn't watch from atop its pointed arches, their hands covering their hooded faces as though even they didn't care what happened inside because the tower was never meant to be a shelter, but a cage.

"Hello?" Kellan cleared the tower's last step, morning light shining like fog between the window's tracery. "Is someone . . ."

A girl stared out the window. She was slighter than Kellan remembered. The light washed the rose out of her taupe-brown skin. "Hey, Kellan," came the voice of Ginnel DuRiz, a tired relief in her words. "Took you long enough."

This had to be another illusion, another trick. There was

no other reason for Ginnel to be here. She was in Sougare, lost in the crowd, on her way topside with Axel at the head of the line. Yet there Ginnel stood, her face shadowed by the light that surrounded her from all sides but above.

Maybe this was okay. Maybe this was a good thing. Ginnel could be like her—curious and concerned, trying to find a way to fix things. Maybe she already had an answer. "It's a mess out there, in Sougare," she said. "It's been a mess in the city for months, so I figured—"

"You figured that by coming here," Ginnel said, "you'd find some way to fix it."

Is your world breaking, little thing?

Something tiny crept up the side of Kellan's neck, freezing the blood in her veins. The rabbit's words echoed against the walls of her skull, more a breath than a whisper. But she'd left the rabbit in Not-Cuivreton, and there was no sign of the massive beast in Ginnel's tower. Still, the creeping thing on her neck reached her ear, and dread made its every step feel like a blade's cold tip. She glanced at her reflection in the glass, where a glint of gold sparkled just above her earlobe.

Kellan kept perfectly, perfectly still. That wasn't a lightning bug. That was something else. Something she didn't know whether to fear less or to fear more.

"Did I ever tell you about my folks?" Ginnel said.

"You remember them?"

"Kind of." She looked to her gloved hands, folded gracefully in her lap. "I remember a humid sandhut. Dried plum orchids.

So, so many trees. I think we lived up north, near the Wailwood, because it rains in every dream I have of home."

Was it envy or pity, the fluttering ache in her chest? Another thing Kellan couldn't decide. Kellan's first memory was of the namehouse bathtub. Rust-brown water, filling her ears and her nose and her mouth and her lungs. Withered ivy eclipsing the window, swallowing the moonlight as the water swallowed her.

"They came early in the morning. Guards, probably from Zarisburg, if I'm right about the Wailwood. I know, because the sky was colored like the clouds are here—like pink, but not? Blue, but not?" Ginnel tried to smooth the wrinkles in her skirt, her voice distant and frail. "They dragged my folks out. Burned the sandhut. Took me south. I don't remember my folks' faces, but I remember that night."

Kellan couldn't remember anything about her parents. In truth, she'd never tried. After all, there was a reason stories like Ginnel's were rarely told. The namehouse forbade many things, and talk of family, real or imagined, meant being shipped someplace far, far worse. The matrons never explained why. The Dus, in turn, never questioned.

"I know you must be confused. Let me help." She took one look at Kellan's wound and tore off a piece of her sleeve, took Kellan's hand, and wrapped it in voile. "You're here because something led you here."

"The city." Kellan winced when Ginnel tied the last knot. "It's—"

"Falling apart. I know."

"You haven't seen them. The, the *things* the lightning bugs turn into."

"I have."

"Then we should do something!"

"Should we?"

The creature on Kellan's neck skittered further, making a canopy of the nook between her earlobe and her canal. She'd swat it away if she could, but the hard lines of Ginnel's resolute expression frightened her into stillness. Kellan had always thought of Ginnel as three rungs above: wiser, sharper, kinder. Better in every way that counted. Now, as they faced each other in the marshy earth and the lightning bugs' ever-blinking glow, Ginnel looked every bit the namehouse girl she must have been not long enough ago.

Always the fixer, whispered the glittering thing. *Always the mender. Always the maker.*

"I saw what you did. What you said to Villiers and Bonne." Ginnel took Kellan gently by the shoulders. "You were brave. More, you were right. But what do you think will happen to you on the other side? How do you think the Crown will repay that bravery?"

The fingers on Kellan's shredded hand twitched in knowing. She hadn't just stood up to a courtier. She'd confronted the head of one of Nanseau's—one of the world's—most influential families. Then she'd stabbed him in the leg and left him to bleed.

"So, what?" Kellan spoke so softly that she could hardly hear herself over the passing flutter of lightning bug wings. "We just . . . stay here? While the city burns?"

"Of course not." Ginnel laughed. She bent the two inches it took for her to be eye level with Kellan. They sparkled with joy and hope, each passing glow flecking spots of soil brown to honey gold. "Burning the city isn't enough."

Kellan stumbled back, nearly tripping over a loose stone. The distance cast Ginnel in shadow, a graceful silhouette under the light of a false day, which curled into tiny bulbs. Lightning bugs, blinking like dry and tired eyes in the dark. "What did you do?"

The creature crawled out of her ear, down her neck, her arm, its many legs leaving a trail of prickling, metallic cold. But *it* was the least of her worries.

Because the stain on Ginnel's glove Kellan once thought was blood had deepened to vermillion, darkest in the center, where it jagged in the shape of an unfamiliar rune.

Where Kellan once pictured mindless monsters crossing the veil for greed's sake, she pictured Ginnel performing malchemy instead. Ginnel, overworked and disrespected, who'd noticed a tear in the veil from her desk on Crown Hall's highest floor as the city blacked out in ripples below her.

Ginnel, with all her hidden namehouse bruises, escaping to a place where namehouses didn't exist.

Ginnel, visited by a lightning bug slightly larger than the tip of her thumb. Ginnel, who chose to follow it.

Fingernails. Tufts of hair. How Ginnel seemed to shrink a bit every time Kellan saw her. Hair always just a bit shorter. Skin always just a bit more covered. Gloves under an island sun. Dark circles and sunken eyes. Her complexion, once so bright and tawny, dulled from whatever else she'd given the spirit in the shadows to summon them here. To shatter the veil.

"This place you want to save isn't a home," Ginnel pleaded. "It's a leech. It takes. It takes our parents, it takes our bodies, our memories, our names, just to keep its strength."

"Stop it."

"What do you do with a leech? Do you let it feed? Do you set it free?"

"Stop it!"

"No. You rip it off, you crush it under your heel, and you survive."

Ginnel took Kellan's shoulders again and looked her in the eye. None of Villiers's quiet greed. None of Bonne's cold detachment. This Ginnel was the same girl who'd let her explore the Exposition, who'd wished her luck her first day at the manor. Wise. Sharp. Kind.

"Do you know what they want? These spirits?" Ginnel gestured around her in awe. "They want what we want. A new world. A fresh start. All we have to do is let them through."

To fix or to change? whispered the creature. *To mend or to shatter? To make or to destroy?*

Something shifted against her hip. *It* had burrowed into the pocket with Axel's spool of thread, but its voice rang as near as it always had. From everywhere. From nowhere. It turned the spool like an hourglass, and although Kellan couldn't see it anymore, she knew this was its way of offering to help. Of offering her a choice.

Quickly, whispered the creature. *You haven't very long.*

"One of 'them' almost killed my friend." What shook Kellan's voice? Anger? Confusion? Betrayal? Whatever it was softened Ginnel's grip as Kellan's fingers twitched at her side, inching closer to her pocket. "'They' turn innocent people into monsters."

All at once, the lightning bugs froze. They hovered around them, stars torn from the night sky. Ginnel didn't notice. Slowly, her smile returned, and she stood straighter, patted Kellan's shoulder while the creature in her pocket climbed up and out, down her leg, Axel's spool of thread unwinding all the while. Kellan didn't know what it planned to do. She didn't know what would happen next.

But she knew she had to save her friends. And she couldn't do that without stopping Ginnel.

"I know it sounds scary," Ginnel said. "I'm scared, too."

The creature in her pocket couldn't have been larger than a pen nib. It certainly wasn't as large as a hare. Nevertheless, a golden hare sprinted along the walls, Axel's thread taut in its teeth.

"Then why do it?" Kellan's voice broke. She didn't bother to wipe her face dry, but Ginnel did it for her, pulling out a handkerchief to dab at her lashes and cheeks. "Why put everything you know at risk?"

"This place wasn't made for us, Kellan." Ginnel folded her handkerchief into a neat square and pocketed it, fingers trembling slightly. "If it's a choice between this and a chance at something new, I'd rather be afraid for a little while than . . . than trapped in this pit that takes, and takes, and takes, until there's nothing left but the monikers they give us and the few roles we're allowed to play. You and I, we're the lucky ones. The fighters. As much as the namehouse tried to beat it out of you, you're still fighting. You climbed your way into the Quarter, of all places. Would you have done that if you were afraid?"

"I *was* afraid."

From a hare to a bird. It clutched the thread in its beak, soared through the tower's vaults in an eerie silence. Soon the thread would run out. It was closer now, it and the other end of Axel's string, her spool growing barer by the second.

What was its plan? To trap Ginnel here? Wrap her in a cocoon of thread. And then what? Leave her to starve? To rot in a strange land? Alone again?

"Imagine a world where you didn't have to be afraid, Kellan." Ginnel stepped back and spoke to the sky, smile wide and arms outstretched. "A world with no walls. No guards. No namehouses. You can study. You can make. We can do anything we want to do, and no one will stop us, because that's the kind of world we deserve."

Kellan braced for Foxglove's next transformation, but it didn't come. For a moment, Kellan wondered if it had abandoned her, and tried her hardest to ignore the relief that buckled her knees.

Then, slow as a bead of trickling sweat, a tiny spark descended from the tower's vaulted rib. The same spark Kellan caught in her murky reflection. The creature in her ear, her pocket, her thoughts. The thread and the creature glittered in the moonlight. It paused beside Ginnel's cheek, and in a breathtaking rush, Kellan realized what it was.

A spider.

Would you like to save your friends, little thing?

The golden spider disappeared behind Ginnel's shoulder, leaving only the thread that hung from the tower's ceiling and wove between its ribs in an open web.

Would you like to fix your world, little thing?

Kellan's heartbeat thrashed in her ears. What was she doing? What had she done? Ginnel wasn't her enemy. She was tired, like Kellan. Scarred, like Kellan. Lost and frustrated and scared, and while the world Ginnel imagined felt like an impossible dream, Kellan was no stranger to dreams of the same sort.

More, Ginnel was Kellan's friend, too.

"With a little help, we can change *everything*." Ginnel laced her fingers behind her neck, her torn sleeve drooping at the elbow. She sighed into the still air. "Everything."

A low growl shook the tower's walls. The golden beast rose from the ground, its pincers large as elephant tusks, but sharper, its points aimed at both sides of Ginnel's neck. Its fur ruffled in a breeze Kellan couldn't feel, parting to reveal another set of round, black eyes. Then another. Then another.

Very well. Fix your breaking world.

It opened its mouth wide, wide, wide enough to swallow Ginnel whole, and the fear that held Kellan still shifted as the spider did. Before her mind could catch up with her body, Kellan released the spool and tore through hovering lightning bugs, hurrying toward the little bit of space between Ginnel and the monstrous golden spirit. Hurrying to protect her friend.

She and Ginnel fell to the hard ground, the golden spirit's shadow cold over their bruised bodies. "What's this?" asked Ginnel, scrambling back, eyes wide with fear and confusion. "What's that?"

The rabbit spider grinned, pincers gleaming. Then, in a burst of glittering gold, it dissipated into the air. . . . *Fascinating*, it said in parting, leaving Kellan and Ginnel alone with the lightning bugs and the consequences of Kellan's decision.

"What was that?" Ginnel asked again firmly. She tried to stand but winced and gripped her elbow, skin torn by the stone.

"I can explain—"

"It tried to kill me."

"I stopped it!"

"*You* . . . tried to kill me."

"I—I didn't. I wouldn't. I just—"

Ginnel rose to her feet, her once-perfect hair wild from the impact. Rage rolled off her like heat on asphalt, and the lightning bugs pulsed again. "I thought you'd understand. Of all people, you would understand."

Her rage. The lightning bugs took to it like bees to blooms. They clung to her skin, her hair, her bleeding wound, until there was nothing left but a massive monster of pulsing light. Beautiful. Terrible. And all Kellan's fault.

"You," said the creature that was once Ginnel in an inhuman growl, "will never understand."

Ginnel swung her fist. Had Kellan not rolled away in time, Ginnel would have crushed her like she had the ground, leaving a pile of smoking rubble in its wake. Kellan stood, ducked when Ginnel swung again, trying her best to think and breathe . . .

. . . when she remembered the window. And her splinter of iron.

The creature that was once Ginnel howled and leaped to crush Kellan in her blazing grip, but Kellan slid under her, singeing her shoulder to grab her dropped splinter. Strengthen. Weaken. Fold. Cut. Close. She carved over glass and rock and wood faster than she'd ever carved anything in her life, desperate to turn this tower into a jar large enough to contain the beast that had overtaken her friend's body. She didn't know if it would work. She didn't know if it would kill her. But she had to try.

Kellan's carve burned to the point of blinding, the heat of Ginnel's beast hot on her back. The namehouse shattered like a fallen mirror, and the ground, the ceiling, the window, and the arches faded into memory, leaving Kellan and Ginnel drifting in a place the color of the night sky. Light danced against the navy, whirled as though warped by the skin of the ocean. A place of endless sea and stars.

. . . *Keep it.*

A train's whistle blew from somewhere beyond. The web Foxglove tangled over their heads glittered in slivers of silver, then floated gently into Kellan's shredded palms. She tugged and found its other end taut. Liferope, come to pull her from the veil's depths.

"Ginnel?" Kellan called into the vast empty. Tentatively, she waded through the sea and the night in search of her friend.

. . . *Be safe.*

Kellan found her staring into the distance. Stunning. Tired. Ginnel stared where the echo of her namehouse's window used to be like it had never left. Like she had never left. "I can't go back," she said, cracking under the weight of her tower's ancient stone. She'd carried it so quietly that Kellan had called it grace. Now Kellan didn't know if she'd ever seen someone who looked so alone.

"You can." Kellan set the thread in Ginnel's hands, who refused to grip. Slowly, the stars faded around them. "You have to. We'll find a way. We'll make it better."

"Maybe you can. There's nothing for me there."

"There is. There's me. I'm there."

Ginnel smiled, the smallest, saddest thing Kellan had ever seen. It was more in the eyes than the mouth. *I see you,* she said in her trembling chin. Her rounded shoulders. The shine in her vacant gaze, once sharp and brilliant. *I know.*

"Make it better, Kellan." Ginnel smoothed Kellan's hair, her touch gentle as a passing breeze. "For all of us."

The stars and the whirling glow blinked out of the sky. Ginnel faded into the night, there one minute and gone the next.

. . . *Come home.*

TWENTY-FIVE

"There is no correlation between the intensity with which you stare and the rate at which she will recover."

"I ain't *staring*. I'm, you know, trying to make sure she's breathing and all."

"You have not blinked in eleven seconds."

"Not true!"

"Well. Now it is not. Now you have not blinked in eighteen."

Kellan groaned. Everything ached. Understandable, considering the last thing she remembered was throwing herself in front of certain death. Only, nothing should ache. She should be gone, not on her back in the feather-down softness of her bed in Mesny's manor, and certainly not with Cyn and Lou on either side of it.

"She's awake." Lou took Kellan by the shoulders and shook. "She's awake. You're awake!"

"Thanks for letting me know."

It was her room, all right, which Kellan determined after her eyes adjusted to the sunlight. Her friends hadn't drawn the curtains, so all of midafternoon's glow flooded through the windows, along with a soft breeze and the salty smell of the sea. It was nice to breathe fresh air. She'd thought she'd never get to breathe it again. Even though she couldn't sit up without the world going blurry, she took in the relief on her friends' faces, and every worry about how or why she'd made it back drifted out the open window.

"Well, forgive me for getting excited," Lou said, obviously affronted. "It's not like you almost died or nothing."

"I will find the doctor," said Cyn with an awkward pat on Kellan's foot.

"And something to eat!" called Lou, but Cyn had already walked out the door. "You're probably starving."

"I'm fine. Just stay for a while?"

"Bet you twenty curones she brings back something stupid, like crackers or something." Lou stood and stretched on her way out. "Mama sent some stuff over yesterday. I think there are some leftovers in the cooler."

"I'm *fine*. Just stay!"

Kellan was too slow. Lou left before Kellan could finish repeating herself, leaving her alone again in a room too big for her. But at least she had the breeze. The warmth of an actual sun. Cyn and Lou bickering down the hall.

Footsteps thudded lightly outside her door. She recognized their rhythm. Although Lou had left the door open,

Axel knocked against its frame before he peeked in. He looked . . . well, tired. More tired than she felt. Dull hair, dark circles, glasses crooked from wearing them through a bad night's sleep. He smiled anyway.

"Hey."

"Hey." Kellan tried to sit up again, only to collapse, the many tubes and needles connecting her to plastic bags and whirring machines—none of which she'd noticed earlier—tugging her down. "You should have seen Cyn and Lou. It was like I came back from the dead."

Axel hurried to her bedside before she could finish. "Can you blame them?" he said stiffly, straightening the tubes and wires. He even fluffed her pillows and, by pressing a button on her headboard she swore wasn't there before, adjusted her mattress so she could finally sit up straight—a kindness Kellan was too exhausted to refuse.

"They're a little dramatic, yeah, but I mean—"

"How long do you think you were out for?"

"I dunno, a few hours?"

"Three days. You were out for three days."

The sun lost its warmth. A chill swept through the window and rustled the magnolias in the vase on her nightstand. Their purple petals had already brittled and browned at the edges. Three days. Three days since the trial, the monsters, the loss. Had Edgar recovered? Was the city still intact? And Ginnel, did she make it back, too?

"Edgar's fine. Ginnel's complicated." Axel loosened his necktie out from under his collar. "He's at Ms. Roussel's, stabilized the day after they found you unconscious on the train tracks. Minora wanted to treat him here, but Ms. Roussel says transferring him so soon is too risky. He likes the food, anyway, and no one told him about . . . We figured it was best to wait until his wound healed, at least."

Kellan pictured Edgar at one of Agathe's dining tables. No doubt, he'd be stuffed on blackened fairy mullet and red cabbage soup, blissfully unaware of how close the world had come to ending in his sleep. Unaware that his younger brother had died, a victim of something no one quite understood yet. Later, she'd tell him herself. For now, she'd let him eat and rest. "And Ginnel?"

"The comte found a written confession on his desk the same day. No one's seen her since, and the ordergarde haven't found a . . . you know."

Kellan worried her bottom lip, unable to meet his gaze.

"I'd tell you what happened," she said, "but you wouldn't believe—"

They were interrupted when the physician who'd healed her after the first trial stepped in without knocking. "Ah. Miss DuCuivre, alive and well." She went on to inspect the tubes and machines with expert speed. Lou and Cyn returned sometime after with armfuls of food, and before long, they'd fallen into their old routine: banter, bicker, and laugh. Like nothing had changed. Like Kellan really did just collapse on the train tracks, and all it'd take to heal was a week's rest, some medicine, and three square meals a day.

But Kellan didn't collapse on the train tracks. And everything, *everything*, had changed.

As Lou told the tragic tale behind her car's untimely death—they'd found it half a block away from the alley she'd hid it in, upside-down and on fire—Kellan swiped her shoulder and neck, wishing away the ghost trail of spider legs skittering across her skin. When evening gave way to dusk, coloring the suite in a wash of peach and periwinkle, Kellan watched the window, jumped at the blinking stars. And when the conversation died, she counted the machine's ticks and whirs and searched for rhythm in the crickets' song. Anything, anything, to drown out the whisper that shook her bones. The whisper that came from everywhere and nowhere:

You haven't very long, little thing.

"Why?" It was hardly a breath, the question she asked the lingering spider spirit while Cyn and Lou laughed at a joke she'd missed. She gripped her blanket between sweaty palms, and the sound that once filled the room—the breeze, the rustling curtains, the laughter—deadened by something she couldn't see. "Why help me? Why stay?"

A chuckle, low and dark, then tickled the shell of her ear.

Patience, said the spider.

Eventually, it came time for Lou to return home and for Cyn to continue reorganizing Maudelaire's underground study. After they said their goodbyes, Axel still sat in the corner, his warm fawn eyes now dark with concern. Even if he couldn't believe, he would listen.

"Try me," he said.

So she did. It took a while, long enough for the sun to sink in the sky and the shadows in her room to creep closer to the walls, but she told him about the half world she left behind. The spider. The mud. The tower. He listened to every babbled sentence, every part of the story she stumbled clumsily through. Everything but the parts about Ginnel, which Kellan kept to herself.

Kellan never mentioned Ginnel's plan, or Kellan's role in saving her life after putting it in danger, or the spider spirit's voice that lingered still. She didn't know how. She didn't fully understand it herself. And whenever she tried to make sense of it, the world around her shifted and crumbled, and the crickets below became the tower's crumbling stone, and she had never left, and this was all another trick, another nightmare—

At some point in her story, Axel had abandoned his seat in the corner for a spot at her bedside. "Breathe," he said. "Breathe. It's okay. You're okay."

"You believe me? You believe me, right?"

"Yeah. I believe you."

The whistling wind lightened to a whisper, a breath too soft to billow the curtains at the still-open window. He took his hands off her shoulders like they'd catch fire if he kept them there any longer, leaving her cold again. He hadn't shaved in a few days. Stubble shaded his chin and cheeks. She hadn't noticed that before, either. It suited him. "We, um. We couldn't do much about him," he said, staring at something just above the place his hand had once been. "My father."

Her scar. The cut on her neck must have healed sometime during those three days. She trailed the mark with her thumb, the skin there slightly raised but fully mended. That explained his exhaustion. It couldn't be easy to accept that his father was capable of murder.

"Courtiers are practically exempt from the law, and his house . . ." He clenched his jaw so tightly that Kellan worried one of his teeth would crack. "Mesny and I, we believe Marielo too."

"I know."

"He won't get away with it. He won't. I won't let him."

"Axel."

"What?"

"Did I ever tell you about the time I drowned?"

The words left her lips and hung in the quiet. By then, it had become a tangible thing. Thick. Heavy. Axel's smile faded, but he didn't turn away. He didn't fiddle or flinch. He looked at her with soft eyes and parted lips, like she was a once-faded page whose words he could finally, finally make out. She'd have to thank him for waiting. For wanting to read it. For holding on to the book.

"I must have been five, maybe six," she said, tugging at the thread around her wrist. "When I try to think any further back, my memory goes fuzzy, but I remember two things clearly. Waiting on the namehouse steps and drowning in the namehouse tub."

The tip of her finger yellowed, so she loosened the thread

and started again. Gentler this time. Careful. Each way round, a breath.

"The tub wasn't even that big. We had rusty, old-world pipes, though, so I couldn't see through the brown. I don't know if someone forced me down, or if I fell asleep, or what, but somehow, I went under and couldn't fight my way out. It was like something pulled me, pinned me to the bottom of the basin, and this tiny little tub became this vast, hungry . . ."

She cleared her throat, shut her eyes when the world went blurry again, and the ticking machines echoed the drip, drip, drip of rust and water in the dark.

"Anyway. I blacked out. I thought I did. I spent years convinced that I did, because what happened next didn't make sense."

Each way round, a breath. Each way round, hawthorn leaves rustled outside her window. Each way round, the sea kissed the shore.

"I remember thread. Fine, gold thread, like rope down a well. So I grabbed it. I grabbed it, and I came to. It pulled me up. I could breathe again."

Kellan took Axel's spool out of her pajama shirt pocket. It shimmered the same gold as it had in the water. As it had the night of Démansem, when she and Axel used barrels for chairs and danced to the music of the bayou. She shouldn't have known exactly where to find it, should have questioned how it got there in the first place, but stranger things had happened, and she was far too tired to fight this little oddity. Besides. It wouldn't be the last.

"There's so much more to this world than I thought. More than I wanted to believe for a long, long time. And I can't say for sure," she said, offering him the spool, "but this might be the second time the 'more' saved my life. I don't know how, and I don't know why, but—"

"Seigneur Bonne."

Xo stood at the doorway, and Kellan's heart leaped into her throat. Immediately, she searched for some sign of Axel's father, listening for the clip of Italish loafers against Mesny's marble floors, waited for the cold he carried with him wherever he went. It never came.

Because Xo was asking for Axel.

Strange. Traditionally, the Court didn't allow bastards to have honorifics. More, Axel had never seemed to want one. Yet Xo referred to him as anyone would the recognized son of a courtier.

Axel must not have heard. If he had, he'd have taken the spool and left, maybe with a polite goodbye, maybe in a hurry to get away from Kellan and her impossible stories. But he stayed, and the way he looked at her, the wonder that lit his gemstone eyes . . . This was more than a scholar and a faded page. This was a boy and a universe.

"Seigneur Bonne," Xo said again, "you have a telephone call in the Madame's primary study."

"You got a title now?" Kellan tried to grin, but her soft tone betrayed her exhaustion. "Fancy."

It took a few moments for Axel to straighten. "It's a formality," he explained gently. "The family is under fire, and its advisers suggested featuring me for a time would make the House appear less . . ." He sighed, stood, and adjusted his cuffs. "Either way, I should answer."

"I'm never calling you that. Just so you know."

His shoulders shook with a soft laugh. "I'm counting on it," he said, retying his tie and straightening his glasses. Then, after one last glance, he closed her hand around the spool and set it in her lap. *Thank you,* he said in his lingering touch. *For coming home.*

He was gone before the breeze could cool the warmth of his palms, which had somehow traveled to her cheeks and her chest.

"Kellan."

"Huh? Yeah?"

Xo still stood by the doorway, although now she faced the other side of the frame. Probably to hide her smirk, which she'd miserably failed to do.

"The Madame would like to see you."

With that, Xo helped Kellan into a wheelchair—after, of course, roughly five minutes of Kellan insisting she could do without it. Soon they left Kellan's bedroom behind her, then the stairwell to the foyer, until Xo rolled Kellan down the hall that led to Mesny's smallest dining room. The smell of leftover gumbo lingered by the doorway, dishes clanged behind the door to the kitchen, and Mesny sat at the table by the window, holding a telephone against her ear and a copy of the *Report* in her free hand.

"Oh, I've received every trifling letter and every trifling basket," she said to whoever was unfortunate enough to be on the other end of the line. "I do hope they made the trip back intact. I hate to waste food, you see, however lazily arranged it may be."

Instead of waving, she slid the paper across the table and gestured for Kellan to join her. After Xo rolled her to the table, Kellan smoothed the copy of the *Report* on the tabletop. This issue was at least two days old. That wasn't the most peculiar detail, though. The most peculiar was the photograph beneath the date. The photograph of her standing vigil at the Guild's final trial.

Even in the dark, through the crowd and the gray-scaled smoke, her profile shone sharp as a carvepoint's edge, the stage lights haloing her wild hair. She only read one line, and really, that was all she needed to know this paper marked the start of something big:

. . . Master Engineer Madame Mesny's first apprentice, Kellan DuCuivre . . .

Kellan brushed the words with tingling fingers. There may as well have been magic in the ink.

"Send Cesaire my condolences for his wasted efforts, if you

will." Mesny drew the switch hook closer to her. "If he would like to try again, encourage him to pad his bribery budget. Honey wheat muffins? Disgraceful."

She hung up. Kellan smoothed the page again, pushed it away. "They called me your apprentice."

"Of course they did, my dear. What else would they call you?"

Mesny looked tired, too, but she masked it better than Axel had. She crossed her legs at the ankle and laced her fingers on top of the table, waiting for Kellan to say something, but nothing would come. The sight of her name in ink on the front page of the nation's biggest paper, her face in profile taking up half its space, rendered her speechless . . . and ashamed.

She'd won her seat in the Guild of Engineers. Kellan, the apprentice. Kellan, the hero. Kellan, the namehouse girl who climbed over its stone walls and into a place of gilded gates and endless opportunity. Kellan, who left her friend behind.

When the kitchen automi finished washing their dishes, and the setting sun gave way to the moon, Mesny spoke up again. Her voice lost its clipped edge. "I suppose," she said softly, "we have much to discuss."

EPILOGUE

It'd been a good few months since the chaos the papers dubbed the Blackout Below. "If only there was a fine for lacking originality," Mesny had sighed upon first hearing the title on the radio between sips of her too-sweet coffee. "Honestly, of all the possible combinations of words within the Nansi lexicon. Lazy."

The biggest catastrophe in Riz's modern history wasn't enough to slow the city down. Not that Mesny gave Kellan many opportunities to enjoy it. The Eighty-Fifth Annual Makers' Exposition was a few weeks away, and by now, Kellan was ready to pass out from all the preparation.

"'Ordinary' will not do," Mesny had told her from the other side of a pile of papers so high, it may as well have been a partition. "In this house, *extraordinary* is standard. Perhaps we should invite Maker Odil for a reading."

When Kellan first took up her apprenticeship, which was

all but official thanks to the comte and his need to make things right with the most influential house in the nation, she hadn't done much paperwork. Studying, yes, under Mesny's advice and many books, but never telephone calls and order forms. Much more went into the Makers' Exposition than she thought—reviewing lesson plans, preparing materials, contacting guest speakers. . . .

That day, though, Mesny gave her a break. At least what Mesny believed counted as a break, which wasn't a break at all, since Mesny "gifted" Kellan the "opportunity" to practice A-level runes on an automi's script-plate. A tiny model, one that belonged to something toy-sized, but still one of the most difficult carves she'd done thus far.

They sat on one of Mesny's many decks, this one facing the front yard. Kellan huffed as she traced over the knot again, deepening the carve the few fractions of a millimeter Mesny demanded. "Don't you have someplace to be?"

"As it so happens, I do not. But you do, so I advise that you hurry."

It was true. All the practice, preparations, and demands in the world couldn't distract her from what waited at the Quarter's golden gate. Kellan finished quickly, tucked her carver in her pocket, and met Lou and Cyn in the foyer.

"Go, go, go," she urged them, ushering them toward the door. "Before she changes her mind."

"I'm going, I'm going," Lou said on her way to the driver's seat. Her new driver's seat, rather. With Mesny's pay, she'd bought a new car: saddle-brown and cream with a satin-smooth ride. "Train probably hasn't gotten here yet, anyhow. Reconstruction and all."

"We sent three pairs of tickets for three different times, all three hours apart, and padded the itinerary," Kellan said as she opened the passenger door. "They'll be there."

Cyn slid in first. Again. "Have you considered coffee without caffeine? Clearly, the standard variety overwhelms your fragile nervous system."

Kellan ignored that, and Lou drove off with the top down, leaving Mesny's manor in the rear view.

Mesny hadn't allowed Kellan outside the Quarter lately. Reporters hovered like vultures by the gate for the first few weeks, but after some time, their numbers dwindled. She couldn't have snuck out if she'd tried; Mesny kept her schedule full to the point of bursting. Still, Mesny's attempts at protecting her from Riz's masses couldn't keep Kellan from hearing about the goings-on beyond the Quarter.

"Try not to worry," said Mesny whenever Kellan asked. "The Court is handling it."

That was as far as she'd ever get. Even if Kellan was her apprentice, Mesny was a courtier. There would always be secrets Kellan wouldn't be allowed to know. However, the fact that there was a secret to keep at all did little to quell her unease. The Court alone couldn't possibly be so powerful as to keep a truth that earthshattering to themselves forever. Spirits were real, and they couldn't comprehend the scope of what that meant for the craft and the map. Everything they thought they knew about runetheory was forfeit.

When Lou drove past the fork in the road that led to the Bonne estate, Kellan couldn't help the slight hollowing in her chest. The manor, the city, even Lou's back seat felt emptier without Axel in them. She couldn't imagine how busy he must be, navigating his new life as the eldest son in a household he'd been denied since birth. More than once, she'd drafted him a letter. More than once, she'd walked to the fork by herself and waited, hoping he'd spot her from a window and meet her halfway. In the end, she never finished the letters, and she always left for the manor. Because he was busy, of course. And she was, too.

Busy was good for her.

Lou stopped close enough to the gate that the rooftops of Nordton's many mansions shone through the pickets.

"Stay here." Kellan climbed over Cyn to get out on the sidewalk. "I'll be back soon."

"You better," Lou called, although Kellan barely heard it over her own curse. She'd hit her knee on Cyn's thigh, which would certainly leave a bruise. "I'm starving. You rushed me out before I could eat."

Edgar stepped out, leaning too heavily on the car door. Even with half his weight on his cane, he stood tall as he could, and she swore the feather in his favorite hat had lengthened by at least two inches.

Soon the gate peeled open. When it did, Kellan approached

its entrance. She ignored the sense of déjà vu when she neared the ancient gate, and the thump of her restless heart at the cab engine's hum from the other side. He was there, and he was alive, and his new prosthesis glimmered in the Quarter's lantern glow, and he was okay. It was okay. Everything would be okay. Wouldn't it?

"How're you feeling, girl?" asked Edgar, his smile dim with grief.

Kellan slowed. She hadn't heard those words in a long while. When her mind wandered between lessons, Mesny gently cleared her throat. When Lou and Cyn noticed her staring off into nothing, they'd laugh a bit too loudly, touch her arm or shoulder to bring her back. No one ever asked, though. That was fine, because Kellan hadn't quite known how to answer.

She wiped her cheek and tensed when gold beaded her fingertips instead of salt water. The aches of loss and exhaustion sent her swaying on her feet, blurring her vision into a mass of spilled ink. Then, over Edgar's shoulder, the fading sunlight caught the glint of a rabbit waiting in the road.

Very well, little thing, came its voice, whisper-soft and everywhere. *Fix your breaking world.*

When Kellan lived in the namehouse, she took things apart. Its ancient stone may have been three years behind her, but it lived in Riz's metal walls and polished filigree. It lived in the shadows Lidon's towers still cast in the sun, in the clocks whose clangs still rang through the night, in the world that couldn't find her friend, and in the nation where Kellan's victory was an exception. Foxglove's black pearl eyes sparkled with mischief and knowing, curiosity and delight. When she smiled, her pincers shone like carvepoints over her maw.

Kellan DuCuivre was not a fixer. She was a maker.

She would not put her world back together in the way it was before. Instead, she would shape it into something beautiful.

After all, what was the world but another piece of metal?

ACKNOWLEDGMENTS

Thank you to my amazing agent, Rebecca Strauss, for believing in my work and working so hard to find Kellan's story a home. I'm incredibly lucky to have you on my side, along with everyone else at DeFiore and Company.

I couldn't have asked for a stronger support than my brilliant editor, Elizabeth Agyemang, whose vision helped make this story into what it is today. Thank you, as well, to the incredible team at HarperTeen and HarperCollins: Erika West, Ana Deboo, Catherine Lee, Ajebowale Roberts and Vicky Leeks across the pond, Jeryce Dianingana for the US cover art, Marcela Bolívar for the UK cover art, Audrey Diestelkamp in marketing, and Anna Ravenelle in publicity. It takes a village, and I truly appreciate everything you've done to help Kellan's story reach the readers who need it.

This book wouldn't exist without the many readers who cheered me toward the finish line. Briana Smith, Storm

Navarro, Jean Thomas, Juliette Martin, Emily Yorty, and SO many others, I can't thank you enough for your support.

Thank you to my mentors, Kathryn Miller Haines and Timons Esaias, for your patience and kicks-in-the-butt.

Thank you to the beautiful city of New Orleans, Louisiana, for inspiring the city of Riz.

Thank you to my found family, Corwin Petersen-Snyder, Kali DeDominicis, and Amber Ferguson. "Friends" is too small a word.

And thank you, Papa, for everything. I hope you like it.